Robin Hood

An

By

Nick Collins

For Donna

Acknowledgements

Cover Artwork – Paul Ashby

Cover Model – Michael Mackinnley

Table of Contents

BOOK ONE

A finder of trails

KIRKLEES – THE END

Kirklees Nunnery, England
The Feast of Adam and Eve
24th December 1211.

She hurried through the cloister. The echoing slap of bare feet on cold stone, a solitary figure in the frosty gloom, her billowing white habit stained red with blood. Elizabeth de Stainton, 45 years old, Prioress of Kirklees, giddy with success.

By my own hand she thought, and she fingered the skraeling[1] necklace she wore hidden beneath her wimple. The large bear tooth was yellow with age now but it still felt as thrillingly sharp as ever.

"By my own hand." She murmured it aloud this time, tasting the words in her mouth. I have changed the world, she told herself. I have changed it forever. Now, whenever they tell his story they will have to tell mine too.

In the nearby chapel the other sisters were already singing the new day's praises. Eyes aglow with candlelight, they entered in single file, their lengthening shadows stretching up towards the high alabaster ceiling which folded over them like two hands clasped in prayer.

Elizabeth stopped to listen, pressing lightly on a thick wooden door and causing it to groan open a fraction so a little of the joy could escape. *Veni, Veni*

---

[1] ***Norse word meaning 'indigenous people', and used by Viking explorers to describe North American Indians.***

Emmanuel. Mournful and harmonious, their voices drifted out with the smoky incense, filling the draughty corridors and empty quadrangle beyond with a sweet and holy melancholy.

He could hear them too as he approached on horse. He sighed heavily, his breath steaming in the cold dawn air. Not even light and already singing. *From the malice of religious women O' Lord deliver us.* Despite the early hour, he rode alone. A risky thing to do in these parts but he knew an escort would only arouse suspicion.

It was a desolate place to be sure. Dense gorse thickets and stubbly meadows, all watched over by arthritic trees that hunched together bleakly on the horizon like uninvited mourners at a funeral. He picked his way carefully along the trail. A light snow had fallen in the night, filling the deep cartwheel channels and obscuring the thick muddy ridges that rose like frozen vertebrae on either side.

He paused in the saddle as Kirklees came into view, a mouldering collection of monastic buildings, crenulated in part with thick stone walls and narrow windows, clustered on the edge of a sleepy black lake, and graced only by the surrounding wilderness.

The small finger on his left hand was starting to irritate him again, as it always did when he was apprehensive. He tried to ignore it. Fifty one years old he thought and still travelling down the same roads. Fifty one years, the damp settling in his bones, his neatly trimmed beard greying at the edges, and still no end in sight.

He closed his eyes for a moment and found it was all still there, waiting for him. The flash of war paint, the thundering green seas, those strange black tears on Rosamond's cheek, the skraeling fire arrows, Tomakin's rasping voice *"this land is death to thee!"* And of course Marian. Always Marian…

He opened his eyes and drew a fresh breath. Only a fool fears the past, he told himself. Aye, and only a fool with a past that won't yield fancies himself plagued by a finger torn free at the bone some twenty eight years before!

Unaware of the approaching rider, Elizabeth continued to linger outside the chapel. A few moments ago she'd been hurrying through the building in a state of near jubilation. Now all of a sudden she wasn't so sure.

Her eyes travelled up to the guilty little sprigs of holly and mistletoe that despite her strict instructions continued to blossom over every arch and doorway in the building. She thought of the young pilgrim they'd taken in nine winters ago. Robbed and left for dead on the trail outside, she'd helped carry him to the infirmary, sat at his bedside as they tended his wounds, prayed for his swift recovery.

Where was he now, she wondered, that young man whose life she'd helped to save? And why hadn't she gone with him when he'd left, as he had begged her to? *By my own hand* she thought. And she pictured herself at the main gate, still waving goodbye long after he'd disappeared from view.

A chill wind drove through the nunnery, extinguishing the last of the night candles, and bringing with it the first real shivers of doubt. She glanced down at the blood on her habit. What if she was wrong? She stared out at the trembling dawn, past the high stone wall to the misty trees beyond. What if she was remembered badly for this? Worse still, what if she wasn't remembered at all?

"By my own hand," she mumbled, but this time with no delight or wonder. This time it sounded like an accusation. *Veni, Veni Emmanuel*. What had she done? She felt the first tremor of panic take hold. In desperation she reached for her rosary and started to pray. *O Lady of the patriarchs, O day star brighter than the sun, present me at this dread hour, most gentle lady, most certain hope, remember my prayers…*

She stopped abruptly and opened her eyes. She had an answer. Not by *'my hand'* she told herself, by *His hand*. Yes, that was it, by *His hand*. It all made perfect sense now. She was nothing but an honest servant going about her master's work. Loyal and devout, a humble instrument of *His* will. And all at once she was pious again.

Now she had a divine sponsor anything was possible. After all, the saints were celebrated every single day of the week and look at how some of them had behaved. The secret was not in the tale, but in the way it was told. Inscribe it in ink and everyone believes you. After all, who goes to the trouble of recording something if it isn't true? Hadn't Robin himself been a beneficiary of this process? He'd proved beyond all doubt it was possible for a person to be celebrated in his own lifetime. Why should it be any different for her? The first thing to do was get it written down, and in order to do that she needed to find Sister Marjorie.

She stiffened resolutely against the cold, straightening up again as she imagined the glowing tribute Sister Marjorie would record for her in the convent necrology. *A woman of grace and beauty, blessed with a pureness of heart. For love of her a sick man can be brought back to health, and a healthy one rendered sick.* And she continued to write it in her head as she hurried off towards the library.

She could see it all clearly now. Once it was done she would spend the rest of her days in mournful repose. The penitent Sister, praying for the sorrows of the world. They would flock to Kirklees from all over just to get a glimpse of her. *By reason of her excessive goodness she must remain at a distance,* the crowds would be told. *Elizabeth, pray for us,* they would cry. *Love God and put your children to learning,* she would call back to them. A hush would descend at the sound of her voice. *She can heal* someone would whisper. Perhaps there would even be a miracle.

No doubt Elizabeth de Stainton told herself these things in all sincerity. She had never been happy at Kirklees and had survived the last twenty eight years thanks largely to an imaginary world which ran parallel to her own and into which she could nimbly step whenever daily life became too difficult. Thus when she wasn't scrubbing floors or bruising her knees in prayer, she was running wild with forest outlaws or fighting off red-skinned savages who nightly scaled the convent walls to ravish her. Indeed, so easily did she slip between these two worlds, it was small wonder she occasionally became confused as to which was which.

And that was why he had come in person this time, the rider with the missing finger, who even as she hurried towards the library was already there, waiting for her. He needed to look her in the eye when he asked the question. He needed to know for sure that she was telling him the truth, and not one of her fanciful tales.

The library lay on the far side of the nunnery. Galleried and well stocked, it had been fashioned from so many adjacent rooms; it felt almost labyrinthine. It had a strong odour of decay, even though the windows had been boarded up to protect the parchment, which included rare Gnostic and Arabic texts, so exquisitely detailed none bar the visiting priest was allowed to view them, though Elizabeth still came secretly at night, to peruse and wonder.

At first she didn't see him as she burst through the doors to find Sister Marjorie sat alone at her sloping desk, a quill-less hand poised at her inkhorn, a fretful expression on her face. A wilful oblate of nineteen years, Sister Marjorie had taken well to the arts of calligraphy and illumination. But she'd rebelled against celibacy the moment she'd reached adolescence, and now the fruits of that 'rebellion' were growing plain for all to see, as each month passed and her habit strained to conceal the truth. But that wasn't the reason for the look of consternation on her face this morning. Something else was wrong and Elizabeth sensed it the moment she entered the room.

"Marjorie?"

Marjorie shook her head, too frightened to speak, but her eyes travelled up past Elizabeth to the dark gallery immediately above her. Elizabeth turned quickly and peered up into the darkness. Someone was stood there amidst the stacked rows of books, but she couldn't make out whom. She cleared her throat high-handedly and addressed the mysterious figure.

"Who comes this day to the house of the Lord?"

He descended the rickety stairs slowly, boots first, then the hem of his thick grey coat and finally the man himself, stepping forward into the flickering light. "A humble Officer of the Crown," he assured her, "with pure intentions and a worthy heart." He paused and handed Marjorie back her quill, together with the small knife he'd used to sharpen it.

Elizabeth knew him now of course, knew him well. Philip Mark; High Sheriff of Nottingham, Derbyshire and the Royal Forests.

He inclined his head courteously. "A peaceful day," he said in greeting.

"By the grace of God," she answered, and waved him towards a chair. "Take breath and relax. Sister, fetch a jack of ale for our guest."

With some difficulty Sister Marjorie started to rise but he held up a hand to stop her. Experience had taught him to be extremely cautious of any food or drink offered in places such as these, and Marjorie's 'condition' only confirmed his worst suspicions. "In this Holy Season I would not add to your troubles," he proffered graciously. “Simply tell me what I wish to know and I will be on my way.”

Elizabeth looked at him. It was true what they said. A king’s posting had indeed been his ruin. Yet despite the passing years and the crinkled weariness around his eyes he still retained something of his original good looks.

For his part, Philip found himself making the same appraisal of her. Yes, time had taken its toll, but she was still a graceful beauty, even in the coarse white habit of a Cistercian nun. For a brief moment he wondered what it would be like to bed her, and almost immediately hated himself for wondering.

Elizabeth noted his interest and smiled knowingly. *By His hand* she thought feverishly *and by my own hand too*, working together, like husband and wife, in complete harmony. She remembered the ship, and how she used to watch the two of them sat together. For hours and hours she would watch them, with the sea swelling up like Marjorie’s belly, and the wind straining in the sail. She’d look on as they sat in a corner, huddled together, deep in conversation, Philip and Robin, Robin and Philip, always the two of them, always huddled together, always inseparable.

Many years had passed since then, but sometimes it felt as though none of them had ever really left that ship. He hadn’t paid her much attention back then of course. Neither of them had. But that would all change now. Now the whole world would pay attention. She felt herself bathed in a holy glow, a glow that made her both radiant *and* desirable. She pulled on a cord and gently lowered a wooden chandelier.

"If not a jack of ale, perhaps I may tempt you with something else?" she asked coyly as she picked up a piece of pumice and chipped away the calcified wax on the chandelier, replacing each spent candle with a new one.

Philip shook his head. He'd already noted with some disquiet the blood stains on her habit, and now there was something untoward in her expression too, something that instinctively put him on guard. Could it be true what everyone had told him? Was Elizabeth de Stainton, Prioress of Kirklees, really going insane?

"A man was here, no more than eight days ago. I have it on good authority he spoke with you."

She feigned innocence. "I speak to many travellers, my lord. Perhaps if you gave me his name…?"

Although he had become notoriously short-tempered, Philip retained his composure. "This man is special. You would know him by sight."

There was a glint of devilment in her eye. "All men are *special* in the eyes of the Father. And alas my sight is not what it once was."

With a sense of dismay he realised she was trying to make him say it, almost as though it were a dare. He sighed wearily, not insane then just cantankerous, with a healthy pinch of spite thrown in for good measure. Well, two could play at that game.

"You were given a sum of money," he began, with patience his eyes did not reflect, "and in return you were to ask him but one simple question." He fixed her with a look before adding, hopefully with enough steel in his voice to leave her in no doubt, "if you have his answer, tell me now. Or I shall have little option but to return with a force of men and ask some questions of my own!"

Normally that would have done the trick, but she just beamed at him as though he'd paid her a compliment. He was tempted to cast aside all protocol and simply cuff her sharply across the cheek, but the distant singing and saintly shadows reminded him he was still in a holy place, and in holy places it was always better to travel with the Magi rather than Herod's assassins.

"Robert," he growled through gritted teeth. "The man is called Robert, though others may know him by a different name."

A thin smile played over her lips. Clearly he wanted to draw this to a quick conclusion but she had no intention of allowing him to do that. She was having far too much fun. And anyway, she'd seen the passion flare once in his eyes and was keen to see if she could rouse it again. She carefully levered the swaying chandelier back into place and then slowly pulled the skraeling necklace from beneath her wimple. He took in a sudden breath at the sight of it.

"You could have kissed me," she reminded him, with an unexpected softness that briefly sapped all his anger, "that night on the ship. You could have done anything. I would have let you."

Veni, Veni Emmanuel. He stared at her in astonishment. How on earth had she remembered that, and after all these years?

She seemed to read his mind. "It was the only occasion you ever really looked at me," she told him, and her eyes dipped demurely in recognition of the fact, "*properly* looked at me. The way a man should look at a woman". She nodded at the wooden cross on the wall, a thrilling hint of sacrilege in her voice. "The way *He* looks at me."

Philip felt his inner shadow stir, that part of himself he kept hidden from the world, shaped by jealousy and regret. Maybe it was just the memory of that night on the ship, or maybe it was the feast day itself, Adam and Eve; the two innocents, coupling together in everlasting sin, but he suddenly felt himself impelled by the woman stood in front of him. "I'm looking at you now," he told her quietly.

Sister Marjorie blushed deeply. Despite her present condition she wasn't quite as wanton or reckless as Elizabeth would have everyone believe and all this talk of 'kissing' and 'looking', together with the strange atmosphere that seemed to have settled on the room was making her feel distinctly uncomfortable. She shifted in her seat and gave a little cough to remind them she was still there. It did the trick and Philip quickly blinked free of his reverie.

"Elizabeth," he said awkwardly, his tone almost imploring, "I know he was here. My spies saw him. Please, just tell me what I need to know and we can both be finished with this for good."

Her eyes shone triumphantly. "Your spies are too late my lord. And you are too late as well." She raised her arms in supplication and victory, and his attention was inexorably drawn back to those blood stains on her white habit, and the sense of foreboding he'd felt when he first saw them.

"What have you done?" he asked, though in truth he already knew the answer.

Choose your words carefully she told herself. Be mindful of their echo down the years. But she could not keep the delight from her voice. "I have done what you and no other man alive could do," she told him. And she held out her hand and showed him a small silver coin. "I have killed Robin Hood!"

ONE

Twenty Nine Years Earlier…

Church of St Mary Magdalene, Barnsdale Forest, England
Holy Rood Day
14th September 1182.

He rode in on horseback with his arms outstretched, hands open, palms forward, like a man crucified. Kneeing his mount slowly on through the gauzy staves of sunlight that fell at slanting intervals between the trees, past the two teenage monks hammering in the last of the 'sanctuary posts'.

Philip Mark, twenty two years old, his beard trimmed neatly to a point, riding into Barnsdale Forest to meet the man who would change his life forever.

The young monks looked up at him as he rode by but neither offered a challenge. Perhaps it was the disarmingly wide spread of his arms. Or perhaps it was the day itself. The long summer had grown weary these past few weeks, and a balmy fatigue had set in. Apart from the rider and the incessant shimmer of midges, there was a drowsy stillness in the air. Even the forest, so bright and fresh in June, was beginning to look a little yellow and haggard around the edges. One of the monks idly pulled a hunting horn from his belt, and putting it to his lips, blew a long dull note, as deep and ponderous as the day itself.

Philip heard it and knew his troubles were only just beginning. He tried to keep his eyes focused firmly on the rutted trail ahead, but could still feel the first sickly flutters of fear dance in his stomach as other monks, summoned by the horn, began to emerge from the surrounding woodland to watch him pass.

He imagined his father's voice growling inside his head. *"He has no piss in him."* The old knight had bawled many disparaging things at his young son over the years, but it was always this one failing he returned to time and time again. *"No piss I tell you. Put him to the trial and he'll always come up wanting. See, it's written on his face. No piss, no piss at all."*

Well, now they would see exactly how much 'piss' he had in him. Philip Mark, twenty two years old, violating safe haven on a holy feast day, and not a word of apology offered in mitigation.

"You're breaking the circle of refuge!" One of the monks angrily cried out to him. "Turn back now," another hissed. "Do you not see the sanctuary posts?"

Philip had no wish to pause and contest the point. He was in the wrong and he knew it. But his ship was due to sail in six days, and those wooden posts would remain planted in the ground for at least another forty. So he stayed silent and pressed on, ignoring their demands and curses.

Someone shouted *'sacrilege'* and hurled a stone which passed perilously close to his head. The second was aimed with more precision and drew cheers when it caught him on the right cheek just below the eye. His horse reared slightly, and the monks jeered in derision, but Philip reached down and patted him reassuringly. "Easy there. Easy."

In a forest clearing up ahead, he could see an angry reception committee of older Benedictines gathering outside the wooden Church of St Mary Magdalene. Despite the trickle of blood just below his right eye, and the other stones that now flew in at him from all directions, he maintained course and rode slowly forward to meet them.

Their spokesman appeared to be a tall black robed Abbot with a thin face and shrill voice. "What sacrilege is this?" he demanded, as Philip brought his horse to a halt in front of him.

Philip raised his outstretched arms a little higher to emphasise his good intentions. "Peace Brother and God's blessing on all here." He spoke steadily, and with a confidence he didn't quite feel. "My name is Philip Mark, eldest son to John of Touraine, a knight of considerable renown, and well known to the King."

The thin faced Abbot appeared wholly unimpressed. The fact Philip was here at all was bad enough, but to arrive with such boldness, not even pausing to first beg their mercy, only piled further grievous insult on top of injury.

"I care not a pig's tooth for your family name," he shrieked, the spittle frothing in his mouth. "This is holy ground and you are trespassing."

Philip remained calm. He sat high in his saddle, aware of the other monks closing in a hostile circle around him. "I come alone and unarmed," he reminded them. "Check if you will." And a note of defiance entered his tone. "But I have travelled some distance and I will have a hearing."

The Abbot looked fit to burst. "You have broken *God's truce*," he spat. "Any man who breaks God's truce is liable to His retribution."

There was an ominous murmur of agreement from the gathering monks, and they began to press forward dangerously. Fortunately one of the older Benedictines, a podgy and somewhat obsequious man, having noticed the impressive family ring Philip was wearing and sensing there may be more at play here than met the eye, stepped forward to take a more diplomatic hand in proceedings.

"We are all men of good reason," he purred, and Philip was glad to note he owned two shrewd eyes in that podgy face. "Let's not labour in pointless dispute. Tell us by whose authority you present yourself, and we will judge what kind of a *hearing* you should receive."

Philip slowly lowered one arm, reached carefully into his saddle bag and handed them a rolled scroll. The moment he saw the impressive seal, the podgy monk's face lit up. He handed it to the Abbot and Philip watched as they both read the contents. It was always gratifying to see the officious tamed by the very officialdom they toiled so hard to preserve. The Abbot glanced up after a second, still full of disdain, but aware he'd been out manoeuvred.

"God's peace," he said without much enthusiasm, "your journey is at an end. How may we assist you?"

Philip spoke equably, no wish to rub their noses in it. "You've granted refuge to a man called Robert Fitzooth," he said, "also known as Robin of Locksley or Robin Goodfellow. I would have an audience with him at your earliest convenience."

The Abbot raised an eyebrow, apparently surprised Philip had taken such a risk for apparently so poor a reward. He nodded at the podgy monk. "Brother Lucius will take you."

Philip carefully dismounted, handing the reins of his horse to one of the young monks who just seconds before had been roaring for his head, before following Brother Lucius into the church.

The chapel was still under construction and smelt pleasingly of freshly cut wood. The Benedictines had worked industriously since they'd arrived here a few months ago, reclaiming a large swathe of forest and setting about it with hammers and nails. He paused to watch as they tried to hoist a huge green bell up into the tower. The rope snapped after a couple of attempts and it plunged to earth with a deep and sonorous *clang*, causing much merriment amongst the adolescent monks.

The podgy brother handed him a perfumed piece of cloth to wipe the blood from his cheek. "The young no longer wish to study anything of merit," he lamented philosophically. "All reason has fled. I tell them daily, learning is a discipline. Take it willingly and you prosper, avoid it and you decline."

Philip nodded; just grateful this 'decline' hadn't been accompanied by an improvement in their aim.

Brother Lucius led him through the church and out into a fenced-off yard beyond, extemporising piously as they went, explaining how if he had his way there would be no 'bondmen, bastards or beggars in

Holy Orders', and why it was imperative candidates should have 'no physical defects' and always be of 'appropriate character'. Philip listened in silence. He knew the monk's type only too well. They were all the same these religious fellows, either at your throat or at your backside, and never pausing for breath in between. Now he'd clapped eyes on the scroll's impressive seal and read the official dictates within, Brother Lucius was falling over himself to be genial. Tomorrow he might just as easily pitch in with the first stone and think himself twice as admirable.

"A jolly hearted rascal this Robin fellow," he was opining airily. "I'm told he's a good finder of trails; and of fine appearance too. In fact you have his keen likeness I believe." He looked at Philip and made great play of perceiving something for the first time. "Yes, I see it plainly now, a very strong resemblance. Indeed you could be brothers."

Philip sniffed at the notion but inside he was deeply flattered. His father had always protested a healthy contempt for 'lathering' of all types. *Speak it false or speak it true but never make a blend of it.* That had been his doctrine. But Philip was different. He had a weakness for a 'good word well placed'. He glanced at Brother Lucius and attempted some affable humour.

"And if I told you I had come here to collect a bounty on him?"

The monk smiled munificently, he had Philip's measure now just as surely as Philip had his. "Then I would say 'good fortune Philip Mark', and I would pray for your soul. For Robin Fitzooth is swift to the sword and any man who takes him will have to move swifter still." *And you are quite clearly not that man*, he might just as well have added. But he preferred to let the pointed silence do it for him.

Philip smiled weakly. He cared even less for the monk now and tried to regain a little of his lost authority by opining haughtily: "A man is best judged not by his friends, but by his enemies. In their fervour you will find his true reflection."

Horse manure, Brother Lucius thought wearily, but nodded sagely all the same muttering "I believe it is so," with just enough gravity to suggest a great truth had been revealed. This pleased Philip no end and he was in high spirits again when they paused in front of a small wooden shed-like building next to the stables and the monk nodded at the door as if to say *in there*.

"Shall I summon him for you?"

Philip shook his head and fished a shilling from his purse. "For your many troubles," he said dropping a coin into the monk's hand.

Brother Lucius podgy fingers fastened around the coin and he inclined his head courteously. "My lord" he repeated as he slowly backed away.

Philip waited until he had gone and then tentatively pushed at the door. It eased open onto a small, windowless room, about twelve feet square and awash in watery shadows. The only source of light was a solitary yellow candle that dripped wax lazily from a tall stand nearby. In the middle of the room a man reclined in a wooden bath tub, his eyes closed, apparently fast asleep, with only his shoulders and head visible above the inky black water. In the far corner, just about discernible in the tawny gloom, Philip could make out the shape of a long bow propped up against the wall.

Philip closed the door behind him. The floorboards creaked slightly as he took a step forward. He paused; keen to make as little noise as possible. He stood in the rippling shadows and contemplated the figure in the bath tub. So this was Robert Fitzooth, the man he'd heard so much about. Like Philip, there was plainly no more than twenty two years in him, and like Philip he appeared to carry each one of them with an easy confidence. How else could he sleep so soundly?

And yes it was true what Brother Lucius had told him, there was indeed some resemblance between them. Both were fine bodied, and both blessed with good faces, though Robin's hair was a little longer and his beard slightly fuller. All the same, the notion of them being brothers was not as fanciful as it had first sounded, and Philip felt himself strangely improved by the association. He even allowed himself a moment of whimsy, conjuring an image of the two of them taking a jovial horn of ale together.

It was a quirk of Philip's nature that for all his pragmatism he was still prone to such sentimental leanings. And it was while adrift in these illusions of forest revels and brotherly larks that Robin suddenly spoke, taking him completely by surprise.

"Have your revenge in any way you deem fit," he invited casually, "I will not oppose you. Not in this holy place."

He said it without complaint or fear, without opening his eyes even; a man completely at ease with the world. Philip was immediately impressed. It was clearly true what they'd told him; here was a man unlike any other, someone of substance. A man he could admire, perhaps even emulate.

He cleared his throat awkwardly. "Why presume I've come to do you ill?" He asked.

Robin smiled, though his eyes remained shut. "What other purpose in hiding a dagger inside your boot?"

Philip was startled. How on earth had Robin known that? When he'd challenged the monks to check and see if he was armed Philip hadn't for a moment imagined they would. Just in case though, he'd hidden a small hunting knife inside the fur lining of his left boot. Saint Anthony in heaven wouldn't have been able to find it, yet Robin had known it was there without even opening his eyes. For a second Philip was speechless.

"You will find more things in forests than in books," Robin explained, turning his head with a tiny slosh of water and looking at Philip for the first time. "The sounds, the smells, even the shape of the shadows, all teach what the masters cannot." He had keen, purposeful eyes, and even in the amber half-light Philip felt himself wither slightly in their gaze.

"By movement alone a creature will often betray itself," Robin was saying. "The bend in every step, the weight of each footfall, from such things you will discern its true purpose." He closed his eyes again before adding, almost as an afterthought, "In time you will even be able to identify the type of weapon he has concealed about him."

For a brief moment Philip felt like applauding. Indeed had he not been charged with such a powerful sense of his own destiny, he would have sat right down there and then and asked Robin to teach him everything he knew. But Philip had a particular vision of the way things were going to be, and that vision involved Robin and him working together as equals, not as mentor and pupil.

He carefully removed the knife from his boot and placed it on the floor next to the wooden bath tub.

"My name is –" he began but in the same instance Robin sprang suddenly from the water, throwing him up against the wall and pressing a knife of his own to Philip's throat.

It all happened so quickly, Philip barely had time to draw breath let alone call for help. So much for Robin's not wishing to *'oppose him in this holy place.'* He'd obviously had the knife in his hand the whole time, carefully concealing it just below the dark water line. Despite this sudden reversal in fortune, Philip remained calm. Here after all was a man clearly after his own fashioning.

"If you read a man's heart as well as his movements," he advised evenly, "you'd know it was intended as a gift."

Robin didn't believe him for a moment but he admired Philip's pluck and was curious to hear what else he had to say. "I already have a knife," he reminded him.

"Mine is sharper and more suited to its purpose," Philip suggested. "Though in water I should be wary, less you accidentally remove something of value."

Robin smiled. "Your sense of humour serves you well," he told him, releasing his grip and lowering the knife.

Philip breathed out in relief, assuring him that he had no sense of humour whatsoever, only his 'father's bitterness' and his 'mother's fear', 'two hungry wolves' he explained 'who grappled daily for his attention', adding archly as he took in Robin's nakedness that 'both feed well today.'

"What do you want?" Robin asked, quickly getting back into the water.

"You are Robert Fitzooth, son of William, Earl of Huntingdon?"

Robin shook his head. "Northumberland's son Carrick is Earl."

But Philip had done his research carefully and reaffirmed what Robin already knew – that in this part of the world he was recognised as the rightful heir to the title Earl of Huntingdon by virtue of his mother and the Saxon line. Unfortunately the ruling elite had little time for Saxon heritage, and subsequently Robin now found himself forced to seek sanctuary with the Benedictines, accused of crimes he swore by every saint in heaven he hadn't committed. The trouble was, in forty days' time sanctuary would be lifted and guilty or not the men at arms would come for him.

Robin was moderately impressed by all this but took care not to show it, casually rolling a silver coin between his fingers. What business was any of it to Philip he wanted to know?

"The woman I gave my pledge to marry was kidnapped and taken overseas," Philip told him. "I intend to recover her by force of arms. To this end I'm putting together a ship's crew. But I need good hands. It's said you can shoot an arrow further and straighter than any man living, that you have rare ability with sword and quarterstaff, and can find a trail in the darkest forest."

"I also perform feats of magic," Robin said sardonically, "mention this also when you inscribe the words on my tomb."

But Philip was in no mood for humour. "My family are in good favour with the King," he assured Robin and produced the scroll that had so impressed the monks outside. "Commit to this enterprise and I promise all charges against you will be dropped." He took out his leather purse and deposited it with a heavy *clunk* on the stool next to Robin's bath tub. "I'll also fund you a substantial sum for your troubles."

Robin picked up the purse and balanced it in his palm. It had a pleasing weightiness to it. Philip watched him closely, trying to discern his response.

"Will you reap with me Huntingdon?"

The man from Locksley smiled. "Friends call me *Robin*."

"Friends I have in abundance," Philip informed him, "reliable men I have none. Forsaking all graces Robert, will you be that man?"

Robin shrugged, amused by the solemnity in Philip's tone. "For the sum you offer I will be him twice over."

Philip buried his fist in his hand, eager now to get on with things. "Then our business is well begun," he said with an air of satisfaction. "Gather your things. We leave immediately."

Robin suddenly realised there was still one important question he had failed to ask. "This woman," he broached, a little hesitant. "You say she was 'taken overseas'. But you fail to mention where exactly?"

Philip looked at him. Now comes the hard part, he thought. Best say it quick and keep it unfussy. He mustered a little frown, as if surprised Robin was even bothering with such an inconsequential thing. "Vinland"[2] He said casually, as though it were matter of no concern.

Robin gaped. Vinland! The great lost world of the Norse, where no Christian man had ever set foot. As a boy growing up in Locksley he'd heard the story many times over. How almost two centuries before, the North men had set sail in their long ships. Heading west, over the horizon, swept on by their own reckless greed and lust for adventure, until they'd discovered a place where the lands were wide, the skies were high and the inhabitants so savage that even the mighty Norse had gone in fear. *Skraelings!* Robin shivered inside. But surely it was just a myth.

---

[2] ***Viking word for North America.***

If such a place really did exist, someone else would have discovered it by now.

Philip returned the dagger to his boot, aware what Robin was thinking and already anticipating what was about to come next.

"There is no such place," Robin mused at length, more in hope than certainty, though he was careful to keep the concern from his voice.

Without a word, Philip produced the skraeling necklace. He dangled it from his fingers like a rosary, its assortment of polished white teeth *clicking* together disagreeably as it played in the candlelight. Robin stared in dismay at the collection of bony things, both animal and human, intricately laced together around a large bear fang, which curved into a sharpened point like a Saracen blade.

"Fortunately they have few decent weapons, and are easily charmed," Philip assured him, though Robin noted his eyes blinked many times as he said it. "I believe they are like mischievous children. As long as we stand firm we shall come to no harm."

Robin wondered if the Norse had laboured under similar misapprehensions. It was difficult to imagine those fierce northern warriors being chased back into the sea by 'mischievous children'. But he'd given Philip his word now, and Robin was nothing if not a man of his word. "I pray your confidence is well founded," he told him, without much enthusiasm.

Philip smiled. "Well founded *and* well funded," he replied. "We will lack for nothing Robert I assure you." And for a brief moment he fairly glowed with satisfaction. Robin looked at him, he hadn't noticed it before, but now he saw the terrible certainty of purpose in Philip's eyes. Christ who died upon his cross, have mercy on our souls, he thought.

TWO

The Great North Road, England
The feast of St Hygbald of Lincolnshire
18th September 1182.

Philip knew they were in trouble the moment Robin emerged from the nearby trees with blood on his hands.

The Great North Road had narrowed considerably since they'd set out on it four days ago. The old Roman track linking north and south, still ran down through England like a fossilised spine, but it was thorny and tangled in places, and without a tramping legion to keep you company traversing its length could prove a nerve racking business. Philip had already noted it had been some time since they'd passed a fellow traveller. And with the trees apparently growing thicker around them and the autumn sun waning mournfully on the horizon, he had the eerie feeling that the surrounding forest was slowly beginning to press in on them. He looked at Robin, and even without speaking, could immediately tell that something terrible had happened.

"Are you hurt?" he inquired, concerned there might have been an accident.

"No", Robin replied simply, not meeting his eye.

Philip felt a sudden prickle of fear. He watched as Robin bent down, scooped up some earth and began rubbing it liberally over his hands, taking great care to camouflage all traces of the blood. "Robert…?" he began timorously.

"Have you ever killed a man?" Robin asked suddenly, with an icy directness that turned Philip's stomach.

"Yes, of course," Philip lied, aware of the panic rising in his throat and doing his best to swallow it back down again, before adding quickly, just for good measure, "It's a dismal business." He wondered if Robin had heard the tremor in his voice, and momentarily pictured his father's shaking head, the sense of disappointment palpable. *No piss. No piss at all.*

But Robin was already thinking ahead. "You must know it," he stressed firmly, "know it in your eyes when you speak, and then they will know it too. And with luck we may be spared a fight."

Philip looked at him aghast, no longer able to keep the horror from his voice. "Spared a fight," he exclaimed. "Spared a fight with whom?"

Robin pointed to three figures in the distance, each one of them wearing a long cloak and hood. They were stood across the trail, apparently waiting. "With them," he replied evenly.

They'd set out from the Church of St Mary Magdalene three days before, travelling down the Great North Road towards Portsmouth where, Philip assured Robin, a fully rigged ship was waiting to carry them to Vinland. Apart from the bejewelled sword jangling from Philip's waist and the yew bow Robin shouldered with casual ease, there was little to distinguish them from the other travellers they passed along the way.

Thus far it had been an interesting and not altogether unpleasant journey. At various points they'd eaten succulent heron and wild boar, enjoyed an omelette made with sixteen eggs and flavoured with twice as many condiments, and drunk clove spiced wine with a group of cheery pilgrims recently returned from the Holy Land.

One evening at dusk they'd stood in companionable silence and watched a procession of peasants carry lighted torches through a cornfield to celebrate the feast of St Maternus. The yellow flames had danced and bobbed happily above the corn, weaving away into the distance like the long tapering tail of a dragon, leaving both Robin and Philip with a curious feeling of contentment as the day waned and a warm darkness settled around them.

The following morning they'd witnessed a far less edifying religious spectacle. Not long after having left the small tavern where they'd spent the previous night, a determined grey rain had set in; it filled every corner of the sky, and hammered purposefully in the puddles and streams. Robin had paused to shelter with the horses under a dripping oak, but Philip remained on the trail, his face tilted upward, the rain washing down his neck.

As they stood there, a long column of monks came trudging past, their bare feet stamping down in muddy unison, a monotonous chant upon their lips. *Atha Gebri Leilan Adonai.*[3] Each one was stripped to the waist and wore a small white cap marked with a red cross on his head. In their right hand they carried a scourge with three tails. And into each of these tails were knotted sharp nails or thorns. As they marched in file, one behind the other, they whipped themselves with the scourges, working in coordinated rhythm, until every naked back glistened with blood and rain.

Robin heard Philip quietly mutter something under his breath as the column wound slowly past. He looked almost pained, and when they were finally gone he shook his head at the folly of it and proclaimed, "It is not for any love of God that men perform such rituals." And then added, as though it was reason enough in itself for going there, "In Vinland I feel confident we shall witness no such displays."

Robin contemplated the tiny red rivulets, bubbling and frothing in the foot pools and channels the passing monks had churned into the mud but said nothing. He could read the omens as well as any man and this was clearly not a good one. He also noted that Philip had a habit of talking about Vinland as though it was only a matter of wishing it so and they would safely be there.

For his part, Robin continued to harbour grave misgivings. Sea voyages of any kind were notoriously unpredictable. And sea voyages of the type Philip was proposing were virtually unheard of. At best he reasoned they would spend a few days sailing in endless circles, before thinking better of it and

---

[3] ***Thou art mighty forever O Lord.***

returning to port. At worst they would be blown off course, and spend the rest of their lives wandering the oceans like Odysseus.

But what was the alternative. Dancing from a gallows on Castle Hill? Robin knew even half a chance was better than none at all. And so he mostly stayed silent, listening carefully as Philip described the arrangements he'd made, offering advice where it was sought, and keeping any reservations he had to himself.

Philip on the other hand was virtually effervescent with conversation. Now they'd begun he seemed determined to explain everything. It was almost as if, in some peculiar way, he was seeking Robin's blessing for the whole venture. And so, as the days passed and Philip talked, Robin quickly built up an exhaustive picture of his travelling companion.

Dark haired and sensitive Philip Mark had grown up on a large estate in France, the eldest son of John, a formidable knight who had gained the epithet 'Bloody' whilst crusading with the King in 1147. At 12 years of age, much to his father's disgust, Philip had given up the chance of following in his footsteps to become a religious scholar at the monastery of Sainte-Genevieve which was rapidly acquiring a reputation as a place for free-thinkers. He spent several happy years living as a child monk there and in many ways was ideally suited to a life in cloister.

"I could have supped happily from the chalice and been content," Philip mused wistfully as they rested one afternoon by a small stream, their horses tethered to a nearby tree. "I tell you true Robert," he insisted when he caught the little grin on Robin's face, "I know my own heart on this. It was learning and worship I was made for. Everything else has been a burden to me."

'Everything else' had begun seven years later, when his father died suddenly and Philip was summoned home by his mother, ostensibly to take up his seat as head of the family but primarily to rein in his younger brother Eustace who, thanks largely to his mother's indulgence, had developed an appetite for unruly behaviour and was running amok in the surrounding villages.

"By the time he reached sixteen Eustace had surpassed even our own wretched father in profligacy and sin," Philip informed Robin despondently. And though he'd finally brought Eustace to heel, the years that followed had proved a constant battle, with Eustace pursuing any course which begat its own pleasure or profit, and Philip more often than not having to clear up afterwards. Despite everything, Philip had tried his best to settle down. With the scholarly life now firmly behind him, he'd resolved himself to 'making the best' of things and pledged his future to a pretty young maiden called Marian.

He spoke with a disarming softness about Marian, how her skin was 'honey brown' and her hair the 'blackest silk'. A 'Saracen exquisiteness' he told Robin, that she'd inherited from her mother, a Sufi wanderer who had 'plied her trade' on the dusty trails of southern Europe, before meeting Marian's father, a 'most kindly and generous French Knight'.

Robin noted the concern in Philip's voice each time the subject of Marian's 'mixed blood' was broached. For a so called 'free thinker' he seemed completely preoccupied with the opinion of others, and drew his line of reasoning from what was being said in the taverns and the towns rather than what he felt in his own heart.

"I would not burden children with such a disadvantage," he reflected solemnly, going on to explain how his offspring might escape any 'stigma', provided he could secure a 'position' or 'name' for himself. After all he posited, hadn't the Bishop of Liege walked as 'boldly as Solomon', and that after fathering 17 illegitimate children, some of them barely human looking.

To Philip, the lessons were abundantly clear; a man's reputation was all that mattered. How he came by it and whether or not it was warranted counted for nothing. The most important thing was that it should be firmly established.

Robin was completely different. He neither sought his own image in the sight of other men, nor sat in judgement on theirs in return. For him life was simple. God had a plan. The details of it were unimportant. That it existed at all was enough.

Philip by contrast fretted excessively. Everything had to be weighed and counted. Nothing could ever be left to chance. His father owned lands in Derby and Nottingham he reasoned, as well as the estate in France. So why shouldn't a royal post be his for the asking? On the other hand he'd given his pledge to a woman with Saracen blood. There again, he had four years of monastery learning, and his family were still 'in good favour with the King', a claim Robin noted, Philip never seemed to tire of making. So maybe a 'noble position' wasn't entirely out of the question after all. And so it continued without respite.

"Perhaps even High Sheriff of Nottingham, Derbyshire and the Royal Parks," Robin suggested dryly, rolling a small silver coin between his fingers, as he had a habit of doing whenever he was mulling something over.

Philip paused. Was Robin poking fun at him? He caught the spark in his companion's eye and nodded. "You would not be advised to wager against it," he suggested. There was just one problem. "Eustace," he sighed cheerlessly.

Whether simply to spite him, or for reasons he was still unable to fathom, Philip's errant younger brother had seized Marian and with the help of an old Norse steersman called Holger, and a small crew of reckless friends, spirited her away to the mysterious world they knew only as *Vinland.*

"For over a year I had no idea where she was," Philip reflected bitterly. "And then Gilbert of York, a trusted associate of mine, located Holger in one of Winchester's 'stews'[4] and he showed us this." He held up the skraeling necklace.

Although Philip cut a fine picture of a man in torment, Robin couldn't quite shake the feeling there

---

[4] ***Officially sanctioned brothels, so named because the Bishop of Winchester collected rent from them.***

was something he wasn't being told. Even if, as Philip maintained, Eustace had always *'believed in Vinland',* why journey so far? After all, there must be a thousand different places where a man could just as easily hide, without undertaking such a perilous voyage. Thus far everything Philip had told him about Eustace spoke of childish impiety and cowardly self-interest. Yet here he was, risking his life on an apparent whim. And to travel to a place, that even if it did exist, almost certainly harboured terrors quite beyond anything he'd ever encountered before.

"It's the way things are set between us," Philip announced solemnly. "From the moment his eyes opened, he's made it his life's purpose to prove himself the better man. And he's not paused to draw breath since." He stared at the crows, picking their way across a nearby field and then added with a calmness which would have been chilling had it not been for the note of exhausted sadness in his voice. "While Eustace lives I will never have peace or see good days."

Momentarily laying his reservations to one side Robin found himself unexpectedly touched by Philip's plight. Better to meet a nameless foe on the road he thought, than find yourself shackled to a scheming sibling who blames you daily for his chains, and strives endlessly to use them against you.

"I believe," he said at length, "that the purpose of the Creator is revealed in all things. And though we don't perceive it at the time, even in the actions of our enemies, a reflection of His Divine wisdom can be found."

Philip looked at him. No need for any words now. In that small moment of compassion something quite profound had become known between them, and sensing his eyes beginning to smart, he turned away quickly lest Robin should see.

"When this business is finally done Robert," he promised a moment or two later, when he'd sufficiently gathered himself and they were both climbing back onto their horses, "I will make certain you share in whatever future I have." And he told Robin once again how his family were in 'good favour with the King', and swore a solemn oath on it by his faith in *Our Precious Lady, the Holy Mother Mary.*

Robin crossed himself devoutly. "And no better faith could a man ever have," he replied. And although neither of them realised it at the time, a strange kind of friendship had been born. Brotherly and fragile, it would be tested to destruction in the days and years to come, but something of it would prevail, right until the very end.

There was of course one further possibility Philip had failed to mention when recounting the tale of Eustace, Vinland and the missing bride-to-be. It was the major source of Robin's unease, and though he said nothing at first, it continued to gnaw away at him until by the third day of their journey he could stand it no longer.

"What if she went willingly?" He asked at last, with as much tact as the question permitted. "You say Eustace is a great deceiver of women. Is it possible Marian was deceived too? After all, a woman who imagines herself in love will risk anything. She'll abandon all reason." He paused and allowed the words to settle before adding, as sensitively as possible. "And if she doesn't believe herself abducted, she'll undoubtedly prove a great deal harder to *rescue*."

Philip tensed slightly in the saddle. "I gave her my pledge," he replied, in a tone that suggested the matter wasn't open for discussion. "And a man who gives a woman his pledge cannot afford to be mocked."

He sat up stiffly and made a show of looking composed. But Robin could sense the doubt in him. Clearly Philip also harboured a great deal of uncertainty about Marian's role in this. "If a woman plays him false he is already mocked," Robin reminded him gently.

Philip heard his father snort. *No piss. No piss at all.* He felt a sudden flush of anger in his cheeks. "Everything started must be finished," he declared irately, "would you have me turn back and leave the matter unsettled?"

And before Robin could reply he'd launched into a vindictive tirade naming Eustace as his 'mortal enemy', stating he would travel to Vinland on his own if necessary, and claiming Marian could couple with the dancing goat himself for all he cared, because he would bring her back regardless, even if it was to his own ruin, and if Robin judged him foolish then so be it, because he would be known for his deeds not his words, and why call into question a woman's virtue anyway when everyone knew women had no virtue to begin with…

His voice trailed off abruptly. Robin was looking at him askance, and to his horror Philip realised he had been ranting like a madman. "As I warned you," he mumbled apologetically, trying as best he could to make light of the outburst, "my sense of humour lacks for warmth." And then because he could still feel Robin's eyes upon him added, with an honesty he'd found elusive just seconds before. "It's true; I've seen her look at him many times. But I must know Robert…I must know for sure."

It was clearly a painful admission and Robin had no wish to tax him any further on it, so they rode on in silence for a while as twilight beckoned, and Philip kept his gaze fixed firmly on the tapering trail ahead.

At some point he became aware of a strange stillness in the surrounding forest. He wasn't sure exactly when the birds had stopped singing, or why the trees were suddenly so close. But as he looked up he was certain the jagged branches overhead were reaching across the divide towards each other. He glanced at Robin, who usually took an unfathomable interest in the rustling of deer or the cooing of wood pigeons, but on this occasion he seemed untroubled, and for fear of appearing foolish, Philip kept his anxieties to himself.

And that's how things had remained until Robin excused himself to attend the needs of nature, only to return from the nearby trees a short while later with blood on his hands. And now Philip found himself staring down the Great North Road at three ominous figures dressed in cloaks and hoods apparently waiting to do them no good.

"By Mary and all the saints Robert, what mischief is this?"

Robin tied his horse to a nearby tree, eased the long bow from his shoulder and carefully pulled an arrow from the quiver. He carried two types Philip noted, lighter hunting arrows and armour piercing bodkin points designed to do much greater damage. It was one of the latter he selected now. He didn't notch it, but gripped it in readiness, his thumb playing on the goose feather fletching. "Let's find out," he said, and to Philip's dismay he began walking towards the three hooded figures.

THREE

The Great North Road, England
The feast of Saint Theodore of Canterbury
19th September 1182.

Elizabeth knew he was watching her. She'd sensed him stir as she slipped quietly from the campfire into the surrounding woods. Now, as she settled into the small brook and began to bathe herself, she caught a glimpse of him, crouching behind a screen of leaves on the grassy ridge above. Pretending not to notice, she covered her body with her arms and hands and turned slightly towards him, letting the early sunlight play on her bare shoulders.

Men liked to watch her. Elizabeth knew that. Father Benedict had often lingered outside her room, peering through the crack in the door. *This is how Eve brought about Adam's ruin,* he'd tell her afterwards as he wiped himself with a cloth. But Philip wasn't like that. Philip was different. She could see it in his eyes. And for that reason alone, she wanted him to look.

As for Philip himself, he felt only shame as he peered through the leaves. Not since Marian had he experienced such a strong…but no, he didn't want to think about that. This is not knightly behaviour, he told himself sternly. And certainly not the doings of a man whose family are in good favour with the King. What would Robin say if he woke now and caught him lurking behind this hazel bush, rump stuck out, his neck coiling like a serpent in Eden?

Before he had a chance to calculate the disgrace, two hands shoved him roughly in the back, launching him head first through the bush and over the grassy ridge beyond. Arms flailing, he tumbled down the bank, completing several ungainly somersaults before landing on his backside in the small brook just a hairsbreadth from the startled girl who gaped at him as though he'd just dropped out of the sky.

The sound of laughter drew their attention back up the ridge, to where Robin stood looking down at them.

"By the faith," Philip exclaimed. "Are you shrunk in the head? I could have been killed."

This seemed to amuse Robin even more, and he called down. "Such things happen for folk's sins. Stand taller next time and be seen."

"I'll stand taller with a sword in my hand," Philip rejoined sharply, raising his dripping body from the water. "It's foolish play like this, with no regard for risk that'll bring the whole world to ruin someday."

At this, Elizabeth burst out laughing too, which only fuelled Philip's indignation and in a voice so bumptious it could have belonged to a monk he declaimed, "A man at his prayers should be left at his prayers." And he would have said more in a similar vein, had the absurdity of it not suddenly overwhelmed him.

After that, it was several moments before he caught his breath again, the laughter providing a release from all that had happened in the past few days. I'm alive, he thought. I'm alive and not only are my family 'in good favour with the King', but in saving the life of this young girl I've proved myself knightly too. And he was still chuckling as they made their way back to the campfire.

Although he now counted himself Elizabeth's 'protector', saving her life, or indeed anyone's life apart from his own, had been the last thing on Philip's mind the previous day, as he watched Robin walk up the Great North Road towards the three hooded men. He even briefly considered turning his horse around and galloping in the opposite direction. But ever mindful of his reputation, he secured his mount to a nearby tree, and scurried up the scrubby trail after him.

As he caught up, Robin appeared to be muttering something under his breath. At first Philip thought he was issuing him with instructions and strained to listen, only to realise he was in fact praying. *O Gate of Paradise, O Glorious Virgin, I pray thee succour and protect me at this dread hour…*

If Philip wasn't alarmed already, he most certainly was now, and his mind raced frantically. "This can be done with coinage Robert," he whispered desperately. "Let me negotiate a fee with them."

Whether Robin didn't hear or simply chose to ignore him, Philip had no way of knowing, but the last words he spoke as they came within earshot of the three hooded figures suggested he had already made up his mind. "Think of Eustace," he advised solemnly. "See his likeness in their faces and strike accordingly."

Before Philip could respond, Robin came to an abrupt halt, about ten paces from where the three figures stood waiting.

One glance in their direction was all Philip needed to confirm diplomacy was out of the question here. Despite the oafish grins, there was a palpable menace about them that even a blind man could have sensed. They stood three abreast across the trail, wrapped in the long cloaks and deep hoods favoured by travellers to the Holy Lands, although it was difficult to imagine too many prayers being offered up by this congregation. Apart from the disconcerting array of swords and axes they carried, all three bore expressions of dull eyed malice, and whilst two were pure bulk, the third stood so tall that even at this distance Philip had to raise his chin slightly to see his face. A movement he immediately regretted when he saw how full of gristle and spite it was.

"Peace fellow," the giant called out, greeting them with a jocular hail of the arm that spread his enormous frame even wider and put Philip in mind of the terrible Philistine Goliath. "Where do you travel?"

"To Portsmouth," Robin replied evenly. "And there take ship on a far pilgrimage."

"You don't look like pilgrims," snapped the bulky one to the giant's left, with a sourness that matched his expression.

Nor do you thought Philip, but knew better than to dispute the point. He could guess what had happened to the original owners of those cloaks and hoods and had no wish to end up the same way. He was trying to picture Eustace in their monstrous faces when he suddenly spotted her. A dark haired young girl, no older than sixteen, her clothing torn, her cheeks swollen from crying, tethered like a tame goat to a tree, just beyond the three brigands. She looked up, and her plight was somehow made worse by the glimmer of hope that registered in her eyes when she saw them.

Philip instinctively knew what Robin would be thinking, and whispered an anxious entreaty to him. "God is her protector Robert, not us. Whatever this is, leave it be. We have business elsewhere." Of all the things he'd said thus far, this was by some distance the most shallow-hearted and he felt himself immediately diminished by it. For his part, Robin made no comment.

"Shoulder that bow and walk easily if you'd pass among us," the giant was calling out.

But Philip was no longer listening. All he wanted to do now was find some way of redeeming himself in Robin's eyes. He looked at the huge lumbering ape, cleared his throat and addressed him in a tone that was both official and stern:

"We are the King's men and we go about his business. You've had your sport, now give us the road and allow us to be on our way."

The instant he spoke, Philip felt Robin tense alongside him and realised immediately that he'd made a terrible mistake.

The giant took a moment to digest the information. "King's men say you," he chuckled. "Then we are most fortunate indeed. For you are the very fellows we've been waiting for. You see, we are ‘guardians of the forest’, and whoever enters here must meet our challenge or pay us a token to continue on his way.”

“You’re men of the hood, made merry at our expense,” Philip cursed angrily.

The giant took a lumbering step forward but in a breath Robin had his bow up, arrow notched and metal point aimed directly at the huge gorilla’s head. It happened so quickly that even Philip was momentarily taken aback.

“Stand off,” Robin warned. “Or you’ll find your *token* on the point of this arrow.”

The giant looked at Robin with a wolfish grin that made Philip extremely uneasy. “*Stand off* says you. With one arrow notched and this princely wretch in tow”. He nodded contemptuously at Philip. “*Stand off* and where to then? To watch your maid soil himself before the arrow bites home?”

The two bulky brigands on either side of him laughed unpleasantly. The giant puffed out his chest. He was clearly one of those meat-faced brutes who liked the sound of his own voice, no doubt imagining a little lyrical flourish here and there afforded him gravitas. “The growing season is done,” he announced grandly, shifting the axe in his hand. “Now comes the time for reaping. Thus are the leaves of summer touched with gold.”

Robin’s fingers tightened on the drawstring, but he held his shot. “The two men you sent to flank us are dead,” he told the giant flatly, his voice unequivocal. “The third is badly positioned.” He nodded at a thick clump of trees off to their right.

"From that angle he'll have more luck striking you, than either one of us."

Philip looked and for the first time saw a shadowy figure hidden amongst the branches, arched in readiness, his bow drawn. How Robin had known he was there, let alone divined the angles, was anyone's guess.

The giant glowered suspiciously and, for the first time, Philip felt the balance of power subtly shift between them. With a thrilling rush of understanding he suddenly remembered the blood on Robin's hands and realised now how he'd come by it and why he'd taken so much care not to let it show. "By all the saints!" he exclaimed quietly.

The giant shifted awkwardly and cleared his throat, not quite finished yet. He flexed his enormous biceps, but his words were muted and betrayed a new uncertainty. "Play me false bowman and I'll tax you twice over."

Robin met his challenge with an even eye. "Give the signal," he told him calmly.

The giant hesitated, cowed by the confidence in Robin's voice.

"Give it!" Robin commanded loudly.

The giant threw back his large head and gave a great bellowing roar. They waited in silence for a moment but nothing happened. There was no answering call, no rustle of bushes, no sudden appearance of men summoned from the forest.

Robin cocked his head slightly, as if straining to hear. The giant blinked and swallowed nervously, and even though they were still outnumbered four against two, Philip knew they had won.

"Do we have the road?" Robin asked.

The giant nodded. "The road is yours," he acceded solemnly. "Let there be no more discord between us."

Philip breathed a sigh of relief but Robin kept his bow raised and what he said next plunged Philip straight back into despair. "We have made our peace then…but only once the girl is cut loose."

The giant braced visibly, as did the other two. Amidst all the drama, Philip had completely forgotten about the young girl tied to the tree, but clearly Robin hadn't. Philip glanced at the three brigands and saw immediately this was going to be a problem.

"Ask, and I'll willingly spread her for you," the Giant offered. "But there it ends. We have solemn business with this one."

"A fair proposition," Philip said quickly and with as much good humour as he could muster. "But we also have pressing concerns. Come Robert, our ship is waiting."

But Robin stood firm. "Cut her loose," he ordered, "or you'll have *business* with the devil."

Philip could hardly believe it. Having just avoided one fight, the quixotic fool now seemed intent on forcing another.

The giant scowled. "It cannot be done," he declared. "She took the life of a man most precious to me. A priest called Benedict, my own dear brother. Deceived him with her beauty, and then brought him to an end with a poison they say is created from the spittle of Cerberus." The giant's expression grew darker and a little snarl entered his voice. "And tonight," he concluded "when we're finally done with her, she'll dance in our fire."

Philip could feel events slipping out of control. The giant's resolve was hardening, and he could sense a restlessness in the two scoundrels on either side of him. They'd forgotten their caution of a moment ago and were drawing renewed strength from the stubborn gorilla's refusal to back down.

Philip turned to Robin, anxiously imploring him. "For pity's sake Robert, we have the road. Honour is satisfied here. Let's be on our way."

"Do you see him?" Robin asked calmly, ignoring Philip's plea and posing a question of his own. Philip frowned. What on earth was he talking about?

"Your brother Eustace," Robin prompted quietly, his eyes not straying from the giant's. "Do you see his likeness yet?"

Something gave in the pit of Philip's stomach, like a trapdoor dropping open, and with a sickly lurch, he felt himself fall through it. This is it, he thought. By all the saints in heaven, this is the moment! He looked at the three brigands stood in front of him, and at the fourth still crouched in the nearby tree. "I see it," he replied softly. "I see it clear as day."

It was a curious thing, Philip thought afterwards, but the violence when it came was startlingly brief. When he was younger, he'd heard it noised about authoritatively that in the midst of battle everything happened very slowly. It was not true.

Quite the reverse in fact, everything happened at an alarming pace. It was only afterwards, as you laboured to untangle the blurred sequence of events, that things became more protracted.

What he knew for sure was this: He and Robin had responded as one to the sudden sweep of the giant's axe. Philip had drawn his sword, and in a single movement sliced up and sliced down. And when he looked again, the two bulky men were prostrate in front of him. The first lay on his back, stomach torn open, guts wriggling free into the grass. Philip realised immediately he must have killed him outright with the first slice. The second was groaning on the ground next to him, the top of his head flapping open, hairy and red like an animal pelt. Philip surmised this was a result of the downward slice and instinctively thrust again, cleanly this time, running his sword straight through the man's chest. Mercifully, this stopped him groaning, though he twitched once or twice which Philip found equally disconcerting.

Philip paused and considered his handiwork. As he stood there he realised something else was amiss. The moment wasn't attended by a sudden urge to rush into the undergrowth and retch, as he'd been forewarned. Nor was he minded to shed any tears. What he felt now wasn't repugnance at all but a swelling of euphoria, pride even. By all the saints, if only his father could have seen him. No piss? He threw back his head and gave a whoop of joy. And if there'd been anyone else to kill he'd have happily set about it.

He'd not seen Robin dispatch the other two, but he'd got a vague sense of it from the shiver of movement he'd glimpsed from the corner of his eye as he drew his own sword. A swift shifting of arm and shoulder and a tiny hum as drawstring sped its arrow.

He'd assumed Robin had emptied his entire quiver but in fact he'd released just two shafts. The first had punched clean through the giant's forehead, the armour piercing bodkin point passing into his brain and carrying a portion of it out through the back of his skull. The second, which Robin must have notched and loosed in almost the same movement, had brought the hidden archer crashing from the tree and was still protruding from his chest when they found his body a few moments later. He was no older than fourteen, and for the first time, since the whole bloody business began, Philip felt a shudder of pity. "Should we bury them?" he asked. "I can fashion a cross from some sticks."

Robin shook his head. "The forest will carry them off," he replied simply. Philip looked at him aghast. He could see the grim poetry in it. After all, these rascals had lived happily off the forest so why shouldn't the forest now live off them? But where was the Christianity?

Robin seemed to read his thoughts. "You're right," he mused philosophically, pulling his arrow from the chest of the dead boy. "*It is* a *dismal business*."

The sun was almost down now, and as they stood there, Philip felt something stir in the woods around them. It came as a breeze, but Philip knew immediately it was something else. Robin felt it too. It lingered in the trees for an instant, rustling in the leaves and swaying in the branches, before coming upon them in a sudden rush. They steadied themselves as it swept clean past, carrying the first heavy leaf fall of autumn in its wake. For all their masculine affectations, both men were deeply superstitious, avidly interpreting dreams and premonitions, and attaching great significance to everything from a sudden breeze, to the flight of a raven or the unexpected toll of a bell.

Perhaps it was just their imagination, sharpened by the violence, or perhaps in the unsettling gloom they'd caught a glimpse of Tomakin and the terrible shadows that awaited them in Vinland. Either way, it changed their mood.

"We have made a treaty with death," Robin said at length, a sombre fatalism in his tone. "Whatever awaits us in Vinland, this is sure proof heaven lays no blessing on it." He shouldered his bow and turned back towards the Great North Road and the young girl whose plight had set them to battle in the first place.

With nothing of purpose to add, Philip muttered a brief prayer to the Virgin and hurried after him.

The young girl whose life they'd saved was beside herself with joy. She was a graceful, dark eyed beauty, well shaped for a sixteen year old Philip thought, though he immediately reproached himself for noticing. As he also reproached himself for noticing it was Robin's arms she gratefully fell into and not his when they finally cut her loose. However, she was so appreciative, and so overflowing with dark eyed, well shaped gratitude that he quickly forgot about this, just as he quickly forgot how ready he'd been to abandon her only a short while before.

Having saved her life they now had little option other than to take her with them. And some time later, when they'd found a place to rest for the night, and brought her some new clothes, the girl told them her story.

With both parents dead and no one else to raise her, she'd been entrusted to a local priest called Benedict, ostensibly to serve as his 'hearth girl'. This was the 'precious brother' the giant had spoken of, the man she was accused of poisoning.

"It was God's will," she stated defiantly when Robin put the charge to her. "And God's will shall set it right in the end."

She told them Benedict had deliberately sent unsuspecting pilgrims to their doom, spying out the weaker ones before informing his brother and the other 'guardians of the forest', and then sharing in the spoils afterwards. Worse still, he'd 'disgraced himself' and his 'priestly mission' in the sight of God, working her 'most cruelly with stick' by day and imposing his 'shameful manhood' on her by night.

"Who mourns the passing of such a rogue?" Philip reflected casually. "They take their chance with the devil and the devil pays them out in kind." He shrugged it off, as if to say 'and a good thing it is too'.

He liked the girl. She had spirit. Even better, she clearly had expert knowledge. And it struck him that her 'knowledge' might prove useful on their trip to Vinland. "Tell me," he enquired, "was it root or herb that did for him? And more to the purpose, how did you get the old goat to sup it down?"

But she wouldn't say, other than to briefly murmur something about it being an *'old recipe'*, adding coyly that a good hearth girl always knew how to *'kindle the fire'* , before reassuring them that Benedict had died peacefully, an *'entreaty to the Holy Virgin'* on his lips.

Like all good lies it contained a great deal of truth, and like all good liars she not only told it well, but clearly believed most of it too. It was very similar in fact to the story she'd told the giant. Unfortunately for her, he'd seen his brother's corpse, prompting him to enquire whether or not Benedict's 'entreaty to the Holy Virgin' had included a request that his 'shameful manhood' be severed after his death?

She'd fixed him with a glittering eye and told him the same thing she now told Robin and Philip. "I do the Lord's work. Father Benedict often told me so himself. And when someone does the Lord's work, He guides them accordingly."

"Well spoken," Philip proclaimed, and for a second Robin thought he was going to hug her. But instead, he showed her the skraeling necklace and told her about Marian, Eustace, and the great Vinland crusade, remarking how someone with her 'special learning' might 'serve good purpose' on such a trip.

The girl looked at the necklace and said it sounded like a 'most commendable expedition', adding that she had remedies and tonics for 'all kinds of malady' and would consider it an honour to accompany them on such a 'noble quest'.

Robin smiled, and thought to himself, if we do find ourselves adrift at the end of the world, this one will surely ensure our suffering is mercifully brief at least.

"My name is Robert," he told her, as they properly introduced themselves, and then added, with a wry glance in Philip's direction, "however, *friends* call me Robin".

The girl beamed happily. She'd never had any proper 'friends' before. Her name was Elizabeth Paston, though she would later change her surname to the more fanciful 'de Stainton', and twenty nine years later, on December 24th, 1211, she would kill the man who had just saved her life.

FOUR

Nine Months Earlier...

North East Vinland, the 'Great Eastern Woodlands Region'
(Somewhere inland from what is now the New York/Connecticut coastline)
The Feast of the Holy Innocents
28th December 1181.

They called him *Cloud Man*. It wasn't his name but it described the way they felt about him. Pale skinned, weak, always changing... a *clouded man*. He would have preferred something a little more venerable, but as he stood opposite the cave and watched the last few spokes of sunlight poking through the rafters of a heavy grey sky, he realised none of it really mattered anymore. In just a few moments he would surely be dead.

He closed his eyes and tried to picture the last time he'd seen her. The grassy cliff top they'd stood upon, the white-capped waves curling onto the sandy beach below, the orange sun melting slowly into the trees behind them, the play of twilight in her eyes as he leant over to kiss her.

They were happy then. He was sure of it. With a gentle breeze ruffling their hair and the ocean glittering dreamily on the horizon, the world had lost its severity and for the first and last time in their lives they'd felt completely safe.

"It's just like paradise," she'd sighed contentedly, "our very own Garden of Eden." And he'd watched as she'd breathed in deeply, filling herself up with the beauty and tranquillity of it all.

A starry dusk had started to settle and though he'd been reluctant to let go of the moment, he knew the others back at the settlement would be getting worried. "We have to go," he'd told her softly, "they'll be waiting to post the night watch."

The breeze had started to pick up as they'd made their way back through the tall grass that grew in vast swooning ripples along the coastline. And it was as they were pushing their way inland, through the long, willowy stems, trying not to lose their way that he'd first begun to suspect something might be wrong.

To begin with it was no more than a vague sense of unease, a prickling disquiet that he'd initially put down to a drop in the temperature. But as they sighted the small wooden settlement in the distance, and saw the orange glow of cooking fires twinkling in the dark, a terrible fear had suddenly taken hold of him and he'd stopped dead.

He remembered how she'd frowned at him in bewilderment and gone to speak, and how he'd gathered her quickly to him, covering her mouth with his hand.

"Don't make a sound," he'd whispered anxiously as he strained to listen. There'd been a tiny rustle in the grass off to their left, a ghostly movement so slight it was almost imperceptible. And that was when he'd known for sure. Something was out there, something malevolent, and it was gathering itself in the surrounding darkness, slowly tightening its unseen grip on them.

She'd stared up at him, her eyes wild with fear. They could hear the settlement preparing for nightfall. Faint sounds carried lightly on the wind. And he'd thought to himself, *they don't know yet!* They're cooking and laughing and happily singing songs, and they have no idea of the terrible danger slowly creeping up on them. And his mind had raced frantically as he'd tried to think of a way to warn them without betraying his own position.

Whether she'd chosen that moment to slip from his grasp and run, or whether he'd released his grip and told her to run, he'd still not properly resolved in his own mind. All he remembered was they were both suddenly racing towards the settlement, waving their arms frantically and shouting desperate warnings, and the next thing he knew he was face down in the long grass, blood trickling from his mouth and everything around him was in flames.

Lying there in the darkness he'd quickly realised that any movement, even the twitch of an eye, would alert them to his presence. And so he'd kept as still as was humanly possible, listening as the terrifying whoops and screams slowly faded, only to be replaced by the grisly sounds of tomahawks and scalping knives going to work. At one point he thought he'd heard her call out his name but even then he hadn't dared stir from his hiding place.

Eventually they'd grown bored of the chopping and carving and several had started to relieve themselves. This quickly developed into a competition to see whose arc could stretch the furthest, and with some proving considerably more adept in this capacity than others, he'd rapidly found himself saturated by the powerful whips of urine that came scything through the tall blades of grass.

After what seemed an age, when they'd finally exhausted the possibilities of this game, not to mention the considerable contents of their bladders, they'd wandered off laughing, no doubt to search for any stray *swannuken*[5] they'd failed to murder and mutilate the first time around.

Long after they'd gone he'd continued to lie there, partly out of fear and partly out of shame, wet strands of hair plastered to his neck and face, the spit and crackle of the flames the only sound in an otherwise ghostly silence. Finally he'd mustered enough courage to open his eyes. And that was when he'd seen him.

At first it was nothing but a shape, something muscular and undefined hunched over in the smoke, its head and shoulders working in frenzied motion. And as he'd heard the sound of flesh being torn and crunching bone he'd thought to himself that it must be a wild scavenger called to feast by the scent of fresh blood. He'd reached slowly for his sword, determined to put an end to this sacrilege at least.

---

[5] ***Native American Indian word of unspecified origin meaning 'salt water people' and used to describe the very first European settlers.***

And then all of a sudden it had paused and stood upright, arching its back, and stretching out its arms, uncurling long spindly fingers, a strange moaning sound in its throat, and to his horror he'd realised it was a man.

Tomakin! The other skraelings had warned him about the terrifying shaman but he'd chosen not to pay them any heed. They played so many practical jokes and told so many tall tales, he'd felt certain this was just another one. After all, how could something as monstrous as they'd described exist in a land as beautiful as this?

Now he watched in appalled silence as Tomakin straightened up, his powerful body silhouetted black against the burning settlement. He saw that the shaman wore an all-encompassing headdress that sat snugly upon his shoulders. Made from the upper front portion of a human skull, the internal bones that had protected the mouth, nose, and eyes had been carefully removed as had the entire rear and lower portions of the cranium, leaving just the upper face and forehead, which had been skilfully amalgamated with a leathery skull and appended with a shaggy abundance of human hair, all knotted together with beads and feathers.

As if this weren't intimidating enough, some further spidery strands of black hair had been added to the portion of skull immediately below the eye sockets and nose, to form a gruesome mask from which the wearer could issue a fathomless stare and the observer could imagine himself gazing into the face of death itself.[6]

For a brief moment Tomakin had appeared to look in his direction, and he'd been filled with such panic, that he'd soiled himself without even realising it. But then the shaman had turned and slowly walked away, disappearing once more into the thick swirls of sooty grey smoke.

That had been almost six months ago. Six months since they'd found him sobbing wretchedly in the blackened grass. Six months of following an endless succession of trails and rumours through the thick leafed forests of Vinland. Six months constantly convincing himself she was still alive, only for his courage to desert him all over again now they were finally here.

He kept his eyes firmly shut. He could sense the restlessness in them as he tried to pray. Brave warriors every one, noble men without a doubt, but they'd made their preparations already and now they just wanted to get on with it. He tried to concentrate, speaking the words aloud and with an even greater gusto than before. *Have mercy on me, O God, according to your unfailing love; according to your great compassion blot out my past transgressions.*

But it was no good. He opened his eyes and looked about him, taking a slow survey of the scene. To his right the huge pine forest bristled thickly as far as the eye could see, covering every rise and fold in

---

[6] ***Such a device did not simply allow a shaman to impersonate whatever or whomever the mask represented; it allowed him to become that entity, a concept of transformation quite alien to medieval Christians.***

the land like the prickled back of a hedgehog. To his left a dozen warriors stood waiting, bows and hatchets at the ready, faces colourfully striped with war paint, heads shaved bare except for a single tuft of hair which ran the length of their scalp like a well-tended hedge, from the middle of their forehead to the nape of their neck. And finally, directly in front of him, his eyes came to settle upon the one thing he didn't want to see, the entrance to the cave. *His cave. Tomakin's cave,* opening up in the rock face like the mouth of a roaring bear. Black and impenetrable, it stood waiting to swallow him whole. He should have listened to *the old woman who knew how to heal*, he told himself. With one of her potions he would have been immune to anything by now, even death.

A silvery rain had started to fall, pattering gently in the leaves and undergrowth and lending everything a shimmering lustre. He tried to console himself with the thought that Tomakin might not even be in there. After all, they'd followed enough false trails in the past few months.

Kocoum walked over. The muscular young warrior had been watching him closely as he prayed and he understood most of the words now. Indeed, he'd mastered Cloud Man's tongue far quicker than Cloud Man had mastered his. But it wasn't the words Kocoum found so interesting, as the display that went with them. In all his life he'd never seen a grown man exhibit such fear in the face of death before. It was bewildering. Was it part of a ritual he wondered, to disgrace oneself like this? Part of the death rite, like a dance or a chant? Did this strange God Cloud Man worshipped, who made such a virtue of dying, require his followers to ritually humiliate themselves before they gave their lives, a final gesture of subjugation before He allowed them to join Him?

"Did you talk to your God?" he asked brusquely. Cloud Man nodded, though Kocoum noted he didn't appear any happier for it.

Nearby one of the other warriors, his face painted white and decorated with jagged black stars, was softly tramping the wet earth, his feet moving in tiny circles.

"Is that for me?" Cloud Man asked.

The young warrior nodded. The set of his chin denoted a firm will and his eyes blazed with an intelligence the other warriors credited as mystical. "He's making the necessary preparations," he informed him, "just in case your own God wasn't listening."

Cloud Man watched the 'death dance' for a moment. It was a melancholy little ritual, accompanied by an incessant chant that seemed not the least bit likely to improve the mood of any discerning god. But he knew the skraelings attached great significance to such things. Indeed they had a reverence for death that even the most pious of priests back home couldn't hope to match, so he said nothing and waited for the ceremony to finish.

The moment it had, one of the warriors deployed a small fire-making kit of iron pyrite and flint. When he had a decent blaze, the other warriors dipped their arrows in the flamc and launched a succession of blazing shots into the mouth of the cave, each time with the same result, a brief flourishing of light as the shaft disappeared into the darkness and then nothing. Almost as if someone was waiting inside and deliberately snuffing each one out as it landed.

Kocoum frowned. "The fire is afraid," he muttered unhappily.

Cloud Man ignored this as he struggled to put on his chain mail. The skraelings believed nature was alive with spirits. Both humans *and* animals possessed them, as did virtually everything else, including mountains, streams, trees, and even rocks. But if he was going to die, he was going to die a Christian death, untainted by any heathen superstition. "The fire has good sense," he grunted with a gruffness that gave no indication of how he really felt inside.

The rain had grown much heavier now; it spilt down over the entrance to the cave and drummed relentlessly in the trees and rocks nearby, seemingly intent on beating out a single name. *Tomakin, Tomakin, Tomakin.*

The warriors stood in silence, listening. "Even the rain whispers his name," one of them remarked.

Kocoum cleared his throat and spat defiantly into the weather, keen to show his contempt both for the shaman and his supposed 'power'. He turned to Cloud Man. "Are you ready?" he asked.

Cloud Man nodded and took up his crossbow, fumbling to load a foot long bolt into the groove at the front of the weapon. He knew they thought little of him as a warrior and with good reason. Endemic warfare was a way of life in Vinland. Tribes fought all the time and young boys lived for the day when they could join their fathers and older brothers in battle. It was unthinkable that any warrior worthy of the name would hide whilst his friends were being slaughtered. That's why they were sending him in first. It was an opportunity to expunge his shame and at the same time cleanse his orenda[7].

And there was another reason too. Tomakin had placed a line of patterned stones across the entrance to the cave. As the warriors believed the shaman to be endowed with preternatural powers, it followed that the stones were enchanted too, and that anyone stepping over them would immediately suffer some misfortune. Thus a volunteer was required to gauge the strength of that enchantment and with his defiance perhaps even shatter it.

In many ways it was a great honour. The way he behaved in the next few moments would determine the way they spoke and sang about him for years to come.

Unfortunately the more Cloud Man thought about the cave, the more reluctant he was to confront whatever lay inside it. "I would pray a little longer," he told Kocoum, unable to keep the fear from his voice or prevent the childish tears from welling in his eyes.

---

[7] ***A person's own inner spiritual power, used to combat the forces of evil. Although each individual's 'orenda' was small, Native Americans believed it contributed to the much larger 'orenda' of the whole clan and as such was highly prized.***

Kocoum shook his head. “No more praying” he told him firmly, “this is your day Cloud Man, seize it with both hands.”

“I can’t do it Kocoum,” he whimpered. “I can’t go in there.”

The warrior slapped him hard across the face. “Lead the way or I will take your scalp myself,” he shouted, and the other warriors growled their approval. They all liked Cloud Man but none of them could abide these displays of cowardliness.

He stood there miserably, the sting of Kocoum’s hand still burning on his cheek. He realised there was nothing for it. If he tried to run they would hack him to pieces without compunction. He pulled himself together as best he could, put on his conical ‘Norman’ helmet with its long protective nose piece, and took a first faltering step towards the cave.

By the time he reached the line of painted stones he was dizzy with fear. *If I am to die then let it be with thoughts of you my love*, he told himself, and with a flinch he stepped gingerly across the line. He’d half expected a bolt of lightning to split him in two as his boots squelched down noisily in the mud on the other side, but nothing happened. He was right outside the cave entrance now. He peered into the darkness but it was impossible to see anything. “Marian?” he called out, “Marian it’s me, Eustace.”

There was no answer. He walked slowly forward, his crossbow raised in readiness. From across the small clearing, Kocoum and the others watched as he disappeared into the cave.

Nine days later Kocoum was discovered by his eleven year old sister Chepi, washed up on the banks of a muddy river, not far from their village. Barely alive, he was covered in grisly cuts and bruises and two of his fingers were missing, seemingly torn at random from his hand by some sharp toothed predator.

Chepi screamed to see her beloved brother in this condition and was deciding whether she dare run and fetch *the old woman who knew how to heal* when Kocoum suddenly opened his eyes and looked at her.

"Oh sweet brother," she cried. "What have they done to you?"

He stared at her in bewilderment. He had no idea how he'd got there or what had happened to him. But, he did remember one thing.

"Wendigo,"[8] he told her in horror, "*wendigo!*"

---

[8] ***A malevolent cannibalistic spirit which could possess or transform a human.***

FIVE

Atlantic Ocean
The Feast of Saint Ursula and the Eleven Virgins
21st October 1182.

The arrow came out of the dark, winging its way through the storm and striking the ship's mainmast, just inches above Philip's head. He stared in disbelief. Gilbert was right; someone on board *had* been hired to kill him.

Another huge wave washed over the ship as he sought for some glimpse of the assailant, but the weather was in a thunderous black mood now, and it was impossible to see anything. "Many congratulations," he shouted above the tempest, summoning a defiance that was pure bravado, yet still feeling a little disappointed Alyne wasn't on hand to record it. "I grant you're most uncommonly devoted to your work."

A second arrow flew down the ship, nicking his arm and taking a piece of his cloak as it passed. He eased his body around the mainmast, seeking more cover, yet taking care not to lose his footing in the treacherous conditions. Just a few moments earlier he'd watched in horror as Alyne was carried away in the rushing slurry of an enormous wave. I can't die, he told himself. Not yet. Not like this.

"I know who you are," he shouted into the weather. It was a lie but it made him feel better. "I'll hang a piece of you from every tree in England. My family are in good favour with the King."

He waited for the third arrow, but it didn't come. Had the attacker lost their nerve? Even better, had they lost their balance and been swept overboard in the torrent? He pictured the faces of his fellow crew members. Which one could it be? He crouched lower and prayed for the weather to calm.

The powerful sea storm had taken them completely by surprise a month into their journey. It broke upon them from the west without any warning and raged for two whole days and nights, and when it finally abated on the third, almost as suddenly as it had begun, Philip Mark knew for sure that Robin of Locksley had just tried to kill him.

Up until that point the weather had kept a begrudging distance, brooding only occasionally on the horizon, and Philip had dared to hope they might get all the way to Vinland without any significant disturbance.

For the first three weeks they'd travelled slowly and in relative comfort, hugging the coastline as they followed the old Norse route, sailing first north to Greenland, where they rested for a few days and took on extra provisions before setting out into the open sea again.

For a day or two the going was easy. The waves lapped cold and green against the hull, and Philip found himself enjoying the fresh sea air and constant play of light on ocean. The rising swell however made it clear the weather was slowly closing in, and soon they encountered much heavier seas, accompanied by driving grey rain and flying spume.

As conditions worsened, and they rode the crest of each new wave, plunging suddenly down and then slowly rising again, Philip found himself wondering if perhaps he hadn't been a little too hasty in vowing to pursue Eustace to the ends of the earth. And this feeling only increased when he found himself struggling with a heavy bout of seasickness.

Robin on the other hand was faring much better. He enjoyed the great surging waves, the wind bellowing in the sail, and even being flung from side to side, whilst wielding a bailing pan. Philip watched him with envy. How could anyone take pleasure in this? The world in disorder, skies raging, seas broiling, your guts in your mouth, the fear of death in every heave? Even facing the brigands on the Great North Road seemed preferable in comparison.

Robin lives upon the moment, Philip thought, he takes joy in every breath. *This* is the difference between us he told himself glumly. I by comparison barely live at all, save in memory and regret. Robin knows contentment, whilst I brood and scheme, always looking forward or back, but never to the side. Always craving things beyond my reach, but never seeing what is next to me.

He caught the eye of seventeen year old 'Alyne of the dale', the fresh faced young Irish troubadour he'd hired to chronicle the journey. He was clutching onto a piece of rope for dear life, and looked even more wretched than Philip.

"This is what comes of it," Philip shouted above the ceaseless howl.

"Comes of what?" Alyne shouted back.

"Too much prayer and contemplation and not enough learning how to swim," Philip told him with a smile.

And the ocean rose up in fury on all sides, huge volcanoes of sea, brimming with water that poured over the deck and washed away anything that wasn't fastened down.

"We've raised the dragon," Holger shouted, grappling his way along the ship's main rail, his eyes blazing wildly. "We've raised him up from hell, and now he wants to feed." He laughed offensively, enjoying Philip and Alyne's discomfort. All this was honey to him, Philip thought to himself. The old, wizened Norse man with the bedraggled beard and white hair, every bit as unkempt and ferocious as his manner, was clearly having the time of his life.

Robin had been surprised when they'd arrived at Portsmouth and Philip had informed him that Holger would be their steersman for the journey. Wasn't this the same navigator who'd steered Eustace to Vinland just over a year before? Holger was a 'man of the sea' Philip explained brusquely. He had no 'allegiances'. You paid his costs and he took you where you wanted to go.

"If this North man makes his way back and forth so readily, why not seek a proper commission for his troubles?" Robin asked.

At the time it had seemed a reasonable question. After all, Holger professed knowledge of an unknown world. If he really knew how to get there, why not take an official crew, with flags and maps, to chart the place and claim it for the King?

Philip assured him Holger had tried many times, but no one would ever listen. And the moment Robin met him he knew why. This old grizzled Norse man, who proclaimed himself a great grandson of Viking explorer Bjarni Herjolfsson,[9] had a stormy madness in his soul. Its ferment could be seen so clearly in his misty sea eyes, that no one in their right mind would risk time and money on a steersman so obviously unstable.

Fortunately for Holger, the Mark family with all its complicated rivalries had long since passed the point of being in their 'right minds' and had supplied him with not just one, but two willing sponsors in the last eighteen months alone.

At least the vessel they put to sea in was worthy, something Robin hadn't always assumed would be the case, especially on their trip to Portsmouth, when it became apparent Philip himself knew precious little about ocean travel. As ships went, this one was fairly inconspicuous, with a large square cotton sail at the mainmast and a spare sail of canvas for stiffer winds, but none of the usual colourful pennants and ensigns fluttering to show who was aboard. In excess of a hundred and fifty feet long, it had raised platforms at both the prow and stern,

---

[9] ***Bjarni Herjolfsson sighted the eastern coast of North America in AD 985. Approximately 175 years* before *the birth of Robert Fitzooth, a.k.a Robin Hood, in AD 1160.***

where a few trusted men at arms were posted. Directly underneath the stern was a small cabin with tiny windows facing rear, which served the beautiful Rosamond of Navarre and her two female attendants. It was essentially a sailing vessel, though there were rowlocks for sixteen pairs of long, narrow bladed spruce oars, each one cut to a differing length so it could strike the water in chorus with the others, delivering a series of rapid, short, choppy strokes.

The rest of the ship was crammed to bursting with every item conceivable, including additional timbers to affect repairs at sea, piles of extra rope and canvas, smoking braziers, bundles of warm clothing, sacks of almonds which would be crushed to make milk for cooking, herbs and spices, salted fish, sacks of fruit, fresh water, casks of ale and wine, barrels of live lobsters, eels and crabs, and a whole stockpile of cages for laying hens. There was also a complex system of 'rain funnels' to capture and store fresh drinking water.

At night, Robin, Philip and the others bedded down on straw mattresses under a large canvas awning which, when raised, provided them with shelter, usually in a corner of the deck near the capstan or the permanent altar on the quarterdeck.

As for the ship's 'crew', they were as disparate a bunch as you'd expect to find on such a voyage, their reasons for being there every bit as strange and complicated as the people themselves.

Some of the younger ones, especially the high spirited knights, thought of it as a chivalrous adventure. Others, such as the ruddy faced Oswald of

Norwich, who was always ‘in ale’, and the ever watchful Roger of Doncaster were strictly there for the money.

One or two like the anxious Gilbert of York, whose long face was always attended by bad news – and true to form upon rendezvousing with them at Portsmouth he’d told Philip that one of the crew had been hired to kill him – had known Philip from childhood and had come out of genuine loyalty. And a few, like Harold of Leicester, a jolly rascal with a good fund of obscene jokes, had unfinished business of their own with Eustace.

The young monk Brother Geoffrey, whose sharp features burnt with sincerity, and whose ordination at the tender age of nineteen had preceded his ‘calling’ to a more frugal way of life, dreamt of founding a new Benedictine Order in Vinland. Whilst the sullenly handsome Guy of Gisbourne, who had a burgeoning reputation as a swordsman, and was already uncommonly well-travelled for a 21 year old, kept his reasons to himself, sardonically noising it about whenever asked that ‘unicorns and flying dragons roamed plentiful’ in Vinland and he had a desire to see both.

Gisbourne had an aloof, aristocratic manner and rarely opened his mouth without insulting someone. Be it Rosamond’s beloved Basques: “They make noises like dogs and are so keen on base congress with animals that mares and mules have to be given chastity belts.” Or Alyne’s skill as a troubadour: “I advise you to master the whistle and fart. Your songs lack for melody. Learn both with spirit and you'll keep us at least in good humour if nothing else."

He also seemed compelled by a strange need to touch or repeat things a requisite number of times, and always in the same sequence, as though it were part of a ritual. Thus if he spilt a drink or dropped some food, he would stamp his right foot three times. And after practicing with his sword, he was unable to sheath it without first turning once on the spot and giving a gruff little cough. During moments of extreme stress, he'd accompany this behaviour with an involuntary little shoulder twitch or occasionally by emitting a tiny yelping sound. That he tried to disguise these compulsions only made them more noticeable, and soon everyone on the ship was imitating him, albeit not in front of Gisbourne himself. Given his ability with a sword, that would have been far too dangerous.

There were also the wayward sons like Ralph of Shrewsbury who'd pressed the purses and patience of his own family long enough and now fancied trying his luck with some of the fabled skraeling women, whom Holger assured him, coupled 'willingly and in great numbers with any man who took their fancy.'

Of the rest, one in particular would prove particularly memorable, though not for the reason he might have wished. Crispin of Lincoln was either 'mute' or 'observing a vow of silence' depending on who you asked. And as Crispin wasn't speaking, no one bothered to ask him. It was widely rumoured that he'd undertaken the journey as an act of penance after inadvertently killing his twin brother. A fact fiercely disputed by Harold of Leicester who claimed he'd lost heavily at dice and was simply attempting to escape his debtors. Whatever the truth, his ultimate infamy would reside not in his silence or his contribution to the expedition, which was negligible, but rather in the manner of his death, which when it came would prove once and for all that the inhabitants of Vinland were anything but 'harmless children'.

SIX

Atlantic Ocean
The Feast of Saint Donatus of Fiesole
22nd October 1182.

Apart from Holger, the most important person on board was 19 year old Rosamond of Navarre. When Philip had assured Robin the expedition would be *'well funded'*, he hadn't been joking. Rosamond's money was financing the entire trip.

The only daughter of the immensely wealthy trader Godwin of Navarre, Rosamond had been indulged from an early age. Widowed and remote, Godwin had sought to win the affection of his children with lavish gifts, and extravagant entertainments, the consequence being that Rosamond had quickly developed into a petulant young woman who tired easily of things and was constantly on the lookout for new and exciting ways to spend her time.

When Godwin died unexpectedly, from a surfeit of 'wine and misery', Rosamond's older brother, the fey and sickly Bernat had become heir to his vast empire. Not surprisingly, it had all proved too taxing for such a 'feeble soul' and Bernat had immediately taken to his bed, where he'd remained for the past two years, 'neglecting Mass and staring gloomily at his toes', allowing Rosamond complete mastery over their father's enormous fortune.

A large retinue of 'experts' were retained to advise her, but it quickly became apparent Rosamond had her own ideas. The carriage of her head alone, with its imperious blue eyes, and scornful yet strangely kissable red lips, told you that here was a young female who'd never sought permission from anyone in her life. And she certainly wasn't about to start now.

All the same, it was Rosamond's ailing brother Bernat, Philip had originally travelled to Spain to meet. Godwin's family had a reputation for philanthropy, and Philip was hoping to secure finance for his Vinland expedition.

Bernat lived on a large farm in a remote part of the countryside, where the sun kept a constant vigil and everything laboured in a permanent haze of heat and dust. It felt so barren and isolated, Philip wondered as he approached on horse whether he might even entice Bernat to go with him.

Once inside however, it quickly became apparent what a forlorn hope this was. Bernat had lain on his bed the entire time, listless and pale, his watery eyes fixed on some distant point, as Philip described in great detail how he intended to travel to the unknown world and recover his bride to be. Whether or not Bernat heard him, it was impossible to say. But he didn't speak until Philip was about to leave, when he roused himself suddenly, and out of the blue enquired as to whether Philip had ever imagined himself to be a piece of fruit, and if so what kind of fruit exactly, and just how big were the pips?

As Philip hurried away, one of the young maids in attendance approached him and whispered. "Speak with the blonde child. She is mistress now."

The 'blonde child' was Rosamond of Navarre and it took Philip several weeks of careful petitioning and a journey to England to get an audience with her. When they did finally meet, he quickly discovered everything he'd heard about her was true, including the strange attachment she displayed to a scrawny little dog called Lycomedes, which she carried around in her arms, wrapped up in fine silks, as if it were a human baby.

Unlike Bernat, Rosamond held court on a busy estate in York, with its own glassy blue lake and a travelling fair which was already pitched and trading when Philip arrived. Trotting his horse through a flock of squabbling geese with minstrels and dancing bears performing on either side, whilst two men flogged a pig tied to a cartwheel and dressed in human clothing, he began to wonder if perhaps he might have been better lingering a little longer in Spain and answering Bernat's question about the piece of fruit.

Like the regal women of Aquitaine, Rosamond painted her cheeks red, lined her eyes with charcoal and wore exotic perfumes from the east. And like the women of Aquitaine she pursued men with vehemence, even though she considered most of them brutal and tiresome.

As Philip was shown into a long room lined with expensive tapestries, she was having her left hand intricately patterned in henna by a young Mesopotamian girl, whilst clutching Lycomedes to her bosom with the other, and casting the occasional bored glance out of the window at the archery contest being held in her honour in the meadow below.

“What purpose in hitting a piece of wood,” she lamented wearily. “It would be of more interest if they took aim at each other.”

She glanced up at Philip and evidently liked enough of what she saw to shoo the girl away and get to her feet. With arms and ankles loaded with bangles she jangled pleasantly as she moved, though not pleasantly enough to drown out the screams of the unfortunate pig outside.

“They say it takes human shape at night and goes about making mischief with their daughters,” she told him, entertained by his apparent discomfort.

“No doubt taking to the sky once fully sated,” Philip rejoined dryly. He had no particular love for animals, but he had no particular love for people either, and of the two he knew which was in greater need of a flogging.

She smiled and presented him with a limp hand, which he took and kissed with the kind of practiced obsequiousness only an ambitious cardinal in Rome could have bettered.

Though Rosamond encouraged the artists she commissioned to portray her as a barefoot Guinevere, in behaviour and disposition she was much closer to a teenage Messalina. And it was in the spirit of the latter that she gathered her flowing robes around her and sank back into a plush chair to hear what he had to say.

The secret in dealing with someone like Rosamond of course was to quickly capture her attention and then boldly hold it by adding intrigue and excitement to your tale. Unfortunately Philip’s wordy preamble, detailing Holger's ability to navigate by means of stars, smells and a 'magnetic needle in a bowl of water', did neither, and only a short way into his appeal she held up a hennaed hand to stop him.

"Are you wanting in the head?" she demanded, mildly amused. "Watching fish and counting waves. What kind of fool wastes their time in such pursuits?" She glanced at one of her maids, who giggled at the absurdity. Rosamond gave her dog a little kiss and then whispered into his ear, loud enough for Philip to hear and much to the amusement of the maid, "Are you listening to him Lycomedes? He talks of Vinland as though it were a real place."

"It *is* a real place" Philip replied dryly, a note of tardiness in his voice. She glanced at him, and her smile faded as she saw the skraeling necklace he took from his pocket. He poured it slowly from one hand into the other, allowing the threaded teeth to clatter together as they collected in his palm.

She eyed the necklace cautiously. She knew a lot about jewellery and this was certainly of a type she hadn't seen before.

"I'll wager everything I have you'll not find another like it," Philip informed her, with a furtive glance over his shoulder, a practiced little affectation he reserved for just such occasions. Her eyes widened. He definitely had her attention now. He held up the necklace for her to take.

"Is it charmed?" she enquired warily.

"Only with good fortune," he assured her.

She lifted it gingerly from his palm, playing it through her fingers and holding it up to the light to examine the polished white teeth. She even put it in her own mouth for a moment to bite down upon and taste.

"My Lady," Philip intoned softly, as he watched her matching the necklace with her own jewellery. "This is but a sample. Many others are fashioned in gold and precious stone. Do me this good service, and I promise I will return the favour tenfold."

She put Lycomedes down and told the maid to fetch them some brandy wine, and by the time she returned a few moments later, Rosamond had agreed to fund the entire expedition, with just one stipulation. She wanted to go too.

Philip refused outright. The journey alone would be far too hazardous. And who knew what dangers they would face once they got there. But she was adamant. And the more Philip protested, the more she made it a condition of her support.

"Have it as you will," she told him finally. "But this is my offer and I will not move on it."

He was reminded of a petulant Eustace, who as a boy had once demanded to be taken on a picnic in return for saying his prayers. Philip looked at the scrawny Lycomedes who was nuzzling at his mistress's feet. How long would the dog last at sea he wondered if Holger and the others got it into their heads food was scarce? He wondered too at his own capacity for finding women like Rosamond both objectionable and desirable at the same time.

"You seek for love. I seek for adventure," she told him, the deep blue in her eyes pooling seductively with his. "Why deny either? And we would travel uncommonly well together. Both Lycomedes and I feel most confident of it."

So it was eventually agreed, and Philip told her he would make the 'necessary arrangements'.

She had originally wanted to bring an entourage of over twenty but space on-board was limited to thirty nine in total and Philip needed fighting men so in the end they agreed on three. Two of these, one rather more comely than the other, were young female maids to 'attend her', whilst the third was a rather languid 29 year old called Walter of Malmesbury, who did little aside from take her arm when she strolled on deck, and scold the two maids whenever they did something wrong.

Her luggage included clothes, furs, jewellery, veils, goblets, washbasins, soaps, food, and an impressive looking silver crossbow which had apparently belonged to her father and on which Walter nearly garrotted himself just two days into the journey.

With the crew assembled and ready to sail, Holger gave an address in his own coarse style, scratching and spitting and sparing no detail as he listed the trials and tribulations they would face at sea. "Expect to be miserable most of the time," he growled. "Food rots. No one washes properly, storms rage and when things are finally settled, the endless horizon and the gentle swell are apt to induce a strange melancholy."

He could have added that in warm weather the deck stank of urine, faeces and vomit, not to mention the smell of rat piss, which as far as Robin could discern was virtually constant.

"You will not sleep much," he continued, adding to his litany of woe. "In high seas the timbers grind so hard you'll think the ship's being torn asunder. And sometimes it is." He paused and gave a gruff laugh. "In the morning when you get up and your bowels begin to heave you will join queues at the bow head, where there are two seats projecting out on each side of the prow. Do not tarry long in the execution of your duties here, the queue is constant, your position is vulnerable and the waves are quick to rise."

Robin leant over and whispered into Philip's ear. "Our steersman's homily wants for sunlight. I feel not the least bit warmed by it."

Philip smiled wryly. Amongst other things, the two men shared a similar sense of humour.

"Above is the rigging, the shrouds, the stays and the sails," Holger was telling them. "Take great care when stoking the cooking braziers. I have no wish to perish at the hands of a hungry fool." He glanced at Walter of Malmesbury, who instead of listening was whispering and giggling furtively behind his hand with Rosamond and one of the maids. Holger's eyes narrowed. "Men will lose their tempers," he warned darkly. "They will perceive themselves slighted and seek for revenge." He glowered at them with the authority of Moses come down from the mountain. "I caution you now, master these urges, for any man who raises his hand to another will be dragged through the ocean three times over. And any man who takes the life of another will remain there."

Gisbourne stifled a yawn and looked out to sea, eager to be on his way.

"If the ship is becalmed or driven off course you may find yourself with insufficient food and fresh water." Holger paused to pass wind, something he did with offensive regularity. "Should this happen, I advise you now, settle all differences with your fellow travellers. Ask for their prayers and put yourself in God's hands. With any luck the end will come quickly. If not, I have a sharp knife to speed the process."

For a moment there was complete silence, and then Brother Geoffrey gamely spoke up, his voice full of boyish enthusiasm. "How soon before we begin?" Everyone laughed and his good humour earned him a round of applause.

As they prepared to cast off, Rosamond prevailed upon Walter to chaperone her around the ship so she could personally greet and introduce herself to each crew member, joking and flirting with them as if she were the hostess at some extravagant banquet. She took a particular shine to Robin, dipping her eyes suggestively as she petted Lycomedes and cooing "Welcome are you Robert Fitzooth. I trust we shall ship well together." And then, aware Philip was nearby and sensing an opportunity for a little mischief, added in a voice that made it sound almost like a veiled invitation. "There is little comfort in lengthy travels. We must rely on our close companionship to distract us from the hardships."

Alyne and Elizabeth watched from a distance as Rosamond fluttered from group to group. "She has great beauty," Elizabeth opined at length, though in a manner that was anything but complimentary. Alyne glanced sideways at Elizabeth, but wisely kept whatever thoughts he had to himself.

Robin had initially been surprised by the inclusion of the young Irish troubadour. He could see the sense in having someone around who could sing songs, but this lad's commission, to provide a 'complete account in rhyme and song' of 'great deeds done beyond the seas' confirmed a vanity in Philip, Robin had hitherto only suspected.

Philip himself had resisted being drawn on the subject, claiming airily that the "Bishop of Lincoln is never separated from his biographer." And adding, with an equal lack of conviction, that it was 'only proper for men of good fortune' to set down a 'narrative of their achievements,' if only for the benefit of future generations.

Not that Robin minded. Alyne's compositions were sound enough, he sang the 'Song of Troy' as though he'd actually been there, and he maintained a devotion to the Holy Virgin that even Robin himself couldn't rival.

Alas, the same could not be said of Rosamond. If Elizabeth hadn't cared much for her back in Portsmouth, it was nothing to the way she would feel about her once they were properly at sea, where Rosamond and her small retinue behaved as if they were on a pleasure trip, laughing and drinking and promenading around the deck in a dazzling array of outfits.

"She is impelled by want," Brother Geoffrey scowled disapprovingly, and went on to give a lively imitation of all the grisly horrors that would be visited upon Rosamond and her 'daughters of Eve' when they finally arrived in hell.

Not surprisingly for a man who, as a symbol of humility, wore a shirt of the roughest goats hair under his monk's habit, Brother Geoffrey had taken an instant dislike to Rosamond and her 'prancing creature' Walter of Malmesbury. And over the next few days, he kept up his tirade against them, seething against the iniquity of a 'Christian woman borrowing the skins of squirrels and the labour of silkworms to lend herself superficial beauty', and thundering out "Daughters of Belial" every time Rosamond or one of her handmaidens walked past.

"You think you have begun the process of sainthood," Walter rebuked him disdainfully. "Linger a little longer at the altar of life and then pronounce upon our sins." And this began a heated debate between the two men that didn't properly finish until one of them lay dead in the woods of Vinland and the other stood over him, sobbing like a lost child.

Holger also declared himself to be 'wholly unimpressed' with the young woman from Navarre and her 'limp fig' of a 'friend', though he was undoubtedly speaking for virtually every man on board when he went on to add, much to Brother Geoffrey's disgust, that his disapproval, however, wouldn't prevent him from 'mounting her many times over' and with an 'unholy zeal' should the opportunity ever present itself.

Philip was aware of the disruption Rosamond and her entourage were causing but having accepted her money was reluctant to do anything about it, hoping instead that things would settle down once they were further out to sea.

Right now, he also had more pressing concerns. His old friend Gilbert of York had arrived out of breath at Portsmouth with news of a traitor in their midst. This traitor he informed him, 'proficient in the arts of subterfuge and murder' had been hired to make certain no harm came to Eustace, primarily by ensuring that a great deal of 'harm' came to anyone who might pose a threat to him, starting with his own brother.

"It's whispered by all who know," Gilbert told him anxiously. "A large bounty has been placed on the head of Philip Mark. As to the identity of the traitor, nothing is known. Some say he's a knight turned bad, other's that he's a renegade monk from the Holy Land, all that seems certain is his skill, given the amount of money at play."

Gilbert was a distrustful, extremely humourless young man, whose loyalty extended only to Philip. He would have been handsome had it not been for a blotchy brown birthmark that dominated his left cheek, prompting the old rogue Harold of Leicester to suggest with a snigger that Gilbert had been 'caught in the middle of a dung slinging contest'.

Philip wondered if perhaps they'd already confronted the mysterious 'traitor', and told Gilbert about the brigands they'd encountered on the Great North Road. But Gilbert shook his head. "This thing is to be done elsewhere," he said. "It's a godless business and it seeks for a godless place of execution." He looked at Philip, the sentiment of old friendship welling up in his eyes. "You have my sword" he assured him. "But I am one in twenty. If something happens to me, who shall stand in my place?"

Philip ruminated for a moment, though in truth he already knew the answer. "There may be one other," he said, thinking of Robin.

Thirty two days later, as the storm raged and he crouched by the main mast, waiting for the fatal third arrow to arrive, Philip began to wonder if he'd made a terrible mistake.

SEVEN

Five Years Later...

Jerusalem
The Feast of Saint Michael and All Angels
29th September 1187.

The city was falling. All day long the huge windmill arms of Saladin's catapults had hurled great knuckles of rock into Jerusalem's ancient walls. Now, in the ruins of daylight, they rained down yet more fire and fury, enveloping the city in thick choking smoke, and sprinkling it with showers of blazing cinders. To the procession of barefoot pilgrims, who wound their way through the mazy streets, beseeching God to spare them, it was as if the world itself was on fire.

Yet even as the city prepared to embrace its death, high above the conflagration, two hooded figures flitted across the open rooftops. They wore the distinctive white tunics adorned with a red cross that set apart the Knights Templar from all other crusading warriors in the Holy City, and they moved at incredible speed, plunging repeatedly into the smoky abyss as they leapt from roof to roof.

'Alyne of the dale' led the way. Twenty two years old and no longer the fresh faced young troubadour whose lullabies had taken him all the way to Vinland. Now there was a worldly toughness about him, and his once pretty face bore all the hallmarks of a battle scarred veteran. Robin followed a pace or two behind. Twenty nine years old, his hair a little longer, and his beard a little fuller, but still the same handsome *Robin Who Wears the Hood* who'd made such an impression on the skraelings five years before. Only these days he was known as 'Sir Robert of Locksley', his nobility restored as Balian of Ibelin made good on his promise to create sixty new knights to defend the city.[10]

For several days they'd both fought courageously at the walls, wielding sword and bow as Saladin's lumbering siege machines had rolled forward like wooden giraffes to spill their armies down onto the ramparts. Now as the bloody sunset mingled with the flames and chaos in the tiny streets below, they'd deserted their post and were striking out on a quest of their own.

They paused briefly in the smouldering half-light to confer, their white tunics torn and bloody from many days of combat and their unshaven faces sweaty and blackened by the smoke. Alyne pointed to a complex of brightly lit buildings in the distance.

"Bernat of Navarre leases it from the Templars," he said. "The man you seek has a room on the second floor."

Robin nodded. He hadn't slept for almost three days, but now he drew fresh breath for one final effort.

---

[10] ***Finding there were fewer than 14 knights in the entire city, Balian of Ibelin who'd been charged with the defence of Jerusalem by its Patriarch Heraclius, immediately set about creating 60 new ones.***

He took a small silver coin from his tunic and rolled it thoughtfully through his fingers.

"There's no purpose us both leaving our spirits in the outremer,"[11] he told Alyne, "hurry back now, and when the time comes, make your escape as best you can."

The young Irishman remained where he was, clear white teeth in a thick black smile, "do you really think I'd travel this distance and not see it properly finished?" he asked.

Robin's jaw tightened and he shook his head firmly. "You don't understand," he said, looking at the coin, "there are things that need to be done. Things you want no part of."

Alyne gripped his arm. They'd been like brothers these past five years and he wasn't about to desert Robin now. "A curse on all traitors," he declared with boyish enthusiasm.

Robin looked at him, a weary sadness in his bloodshot eyes. "*A curse on all traitors*," he rejoined softly. But it sounded more like a lament than a call to arms.

They travelled further along the roof, following one of the tiny streets that split through the city like deep crevices in a slab of rock. Near the ruins of Solomon's Temple they paused briefly again, before leaping across the small divide to an adjoining building and dropping down into a walled courtyard below.

---

[11] ***A crusader word for the Kingdom of Jerusalem – 'The land across the sea'.***

The desperate screams and lamentations that had sounded like a single ghostly wail up on the rooftops were much louder and far more disconcerting at ground level. Individual voices could be distinctly heard above the bombardment. An angry old man called down curses on the *heathen* Saladin, a desperate mother begged God to spare the life of her child, and someone shouted that the much feared Mamelukes[12] were already inside the city.

With burning embers drifting like fiery snowflakes in the smoky dark around them, Robin and Alyne notched arrows in readiness and moved cautiously towards the large building directly in front of them. There was an eerie lack of movement as they approached the arched doorway, and in the huge hall beyond they discovered the remains of what appeared to be an abandoned banquet. Half eaten food lay strewn across the floor and spilt wine pooled around discarded goblets.

Alyne picked up one of the goblets from the floor, filled it with more wine and raised it in a good humoured toast. "Waes hael[13] Robin," he said with a smile, "peace and plenty attend all your days."

Suddenly there was the sound of sluggish movement from the room immediately above. They stopped to listen. It was as if something heavy was being dragged across the floor. Robin put a finger to his lips, and without speaking, they quickly located a broad stone staircase that led up to the second storey.

---

[12] ***The best and most feared soldiers in Saladin's army.***

[13] ***Anglo Saxon toast meaning 'be in good health'.***

And it was here, in a richly adorned suite of rooms directly over the main hall that they finally found him, a gaunt faced man of indeterminate age, hastily packing a sack of silver and gold artefacts looted from churches all over the city.

"You're late," he told them tetchily without bothering to look up. "The others have already gone. Bernat of Navarre has envoys in Saladin's camp negotiating safe passage. There's no time to lose."

Robin watched him for a moment. Had they passed in the street he would barely have recognised the man. It was amazing to see how much someone could change in just five years. Long haired and heavily bearded, his face withered to the bone, he was the very ruins of the man he'd once been.

"I have a cart waiting by the Damascus Gate," he informed them, "but we must hurry."

When neither of them responded he huffed irritably as men do when dealing with idiots, and looked up. The moment he set eyes on them his expression changed. The hoods, the bows, and the fact they weren't selling their lives dearly at the wall told him everything he needed to know.

"Take whatever you desire," he invited nervously, "there's enough for all."

Robin stepped into the room, his boots crunching down on some broken glass. "What makes you think we've come to rob you?" he asked.

The man frowned. The voice sounded familiar, but he couldn't identify the hooded face.

"State your business," he commanded, "I have no time for games."

Robin slowly pulled back his hood so the man could see him properly. If there was any surprise in that gaunt face, it certainly didn't show, though Robin noticed the man's Adam's apple bobbed appreciably as he silently assessed the situation.

"They told me you were captured at Hattin," he said after a moment.

Robin nodded, mildly amused by the rumour. It wasn't the first one he'd heard and it certainly wouldn't be the last. "Saladin himself took my head," he told the man.

The gaunt face smiled with no mirth at all. "You're a warrior Robin," he mused, "you don't slay unarmed men."

"Only *friends* call me Robin," the man from Locksley reminded him, and with a flick of his thumb he sent the silver coin spinning through the air. It landed with a '*ting*' at the man's feet.

A sudden iciness descended, and the man saw immediately how his life depended upon what he said in the next few moments. "We *were friends* once," he ventured modestly. "At least, I like to think we were."

Robin made no comment. The man shifted uncomfortably, little beads of nervous sweat beginning to break out on his skeletal brow. *Think of something,* he told himself anxiously, *think of something quickly, or he will have blood!*

"Bernat of Navarre has put a price on your head," he blurted out hurriedly, as though he'd been greatly incensed to hear it.

"I know," Robin replied quietly, his tone suggesting he wasn't unduly troubled by the idea.

“He’s confused,” the man babbled, trying to keep the rising panic from his voice. “He blames you for what happened.”

“I wonder why,” Robin replied, slowly removing the arrow he’d notched and replacing it with a flint headed one he’d brought back from Vinland.

The man swallowed nervously when he saw the new shaft with its distinctive skraeling feathers and designs. “Let me talk to him for you,” he suggested, though it sounded more like a plea. “Even if you escape the city, he has men all over Europe. I know Bernat. I can speak to him, explain what really happened.”

“I’ll speak to him myself,” Robin told him evenly. “Have no fear of that.”

The man turned in desperation to Alyne, appealing to him directly. “By Him that died on the tree,” he implored, “do you not say a word to this? What wrong have I done that you should stand idle whilst this brigand commits murder?”

Alyne hesitated, caught between his loyalty to Robin and his clear discomfort at the way things appeared to be unfolding.

Robin spoke up for him. “The skraelings believed we had no souls,” he told the man. “They thought we were dead inside already.”

“They were savages,” the man shouted bitterly, huge tears of despair brimming in the red and white of his eyes. “The entire expedition was a nightmare. You know that as well as any man.”

Robin raised his bow and took careful aim. “Do you remember what I told you that night on the ship?”

The man nodded reluctantly, and his throat made tiny whimpering noises. *Blood demands blood*, he thought desperately.

"Say it," Robin told him.

The man looked at Alyne, one last fraught plea in his eyes. Alyne was confused, the two men spoke as if they'd been on the trip to Vinland together, but he'd been there also and he had no recollection of the man.

"Say it!" Robin commanded.

The man tried to gulp only to find there was no more phlegm in his throat.

"You told me…" he began hesitantly, his voice virtually a whisper, "…you told me to be wary, because one day soon you would surely call upon me."

Robin's fingers tightened on the drawstring. "And that *day* is finally come," he said pointedly. Without further comment, he released the arrow and it flew across the room, striking the man powerfully in his right eye, and felling him like a tree.

Alyne gasped in disbelief. "By all the saints," he cried and rushed across to where the man lay, his legs jerking spasmodically, as the sharp flint head destroyed his nervous system.

He turned on Robin accusingly. "You said he had information," he shouted, "information that could lead us to the traitor."

"He *is* the traitor." Robin told him flatly.

To the young Irishman's horror, Robin reached into his tunic, took out Kocoum's hunting knife and roughly jerking the man's head back, set about his scalp with the sharp blade.

Alyne turned away from the grisly spectacle in disgust. From Vinland to the walls of Jerusalem he'd witnessed death in all its many guises but nothing he'd seen had distressed him as much as the cold blooded killing that had just taken place in this room. "May Christ's mercy save us," he mumbled disconsolately.

It was perhaps a further unfortunate complication that the removal of his long hair had somehow brought the gaunt man's face into much sharper focus so that when Alyne looked again he realised to his horror that he *did* know him after all.

"By the faith," he exclaimed, slowly beginning to piece it all together, "I do recognise this fellow. He was with us in Vinland. We fought the skraelings together."

Robin didn't reply. He had the scalp off now and looked set to embark upon the next stage of the ritual mutilation which involved cutting open the man's stomach and removing his entrails. This was too much for Alyne and he grabbed up his bow and levelled it purposefully at the man from Locksley.

"Stand off," he shouted angrily, "stand off now Robin and leave him be or I swear by the Holy Mother I shall lay you at his side."

For a moment Robin didn't move, and then he slowly put down the knife and turned to face him. The bow trembled dangerously in Alyne's hands and his face was wrought with emotion.

"I warned you," Robin reminded him calmly, "I told you there were *things* that needed to be done. *Things* you'd want no part of."

"You told me you sought for justice not revenge." Alyne snapped back, so upset he was barely able to sight his arrow.

"This man did more evil than you dare imagine," Robin told him, "by means of his treachery I was almost put to death."

"And now you practice the same treachery on me," Alyne rejoined bitterly.

"What would you have me do?" Robin asked him in exasperation.

"I would have you tell the truth," Alyne replied, "I would have you declare *'It is butchery we are come to do'*. And in stating it I would have you say his name. That even as you perform these desecrations, he is granted one final Christian courtesy."

Robin flew up angrily, knocking the bow from Alyne's hand and throwing him back against the wall. "His name is washed away," he yelled and his eyes were blazing with fury. "Don't speak it again. As long as you live, don't ever speak it to me again."

They stayed like that for a long moment, Robin breathing hard into his face, Alyne with his back pinned to the wall, Saladin's catapults pounding down on the city. Alyne finally broke the silence, his voice filled with sadness.

"I gave you my solemn pledge," he began, "and much I thank you for the many kindnesses you've shown me these past five years." He paused, and the pain of what he was about to say next was almost palpable. “But sometimes master, I fear we do nothing but the work of outlaws.”

Robin made no reply, but something in his expression changed. He let go of Alyne and turned away, pausing to retrieve the silver coin from the floor. The young Irishman slid slowly to the floor and buried his head in his hands. It was Vinland, he thought to himself. No matter what they did, it was always Vinland.

EIGHT

Atlantic Ocean
The Feast of Saint Romanus of Rouen
23rd October 1182.

Shortly after Gilbert had told him about the traitor, and some time before the great storm broke upon the ship, Philip sought out the only other man on board he believed he could trust. And that night, as Elizabeth lay on her mattress straining to hear, he stood at the far rail with Robin, their faces obscured by shadow, their words buried under the ships relentless creaking and groaning.

"I am betrayed," Philip quietly informed him. "A large bounty has been raised on my life, and the man who seeks to claim it is already on board. Worse still, I have no way of knowing his identity."

"You say *betrayed*," Robin enquired calmly. "Betrayed by whom?"

Philip smiled dryly, though his words seemed much heavier with fatigue than usual. "If I told you it was by the hand of my own dear mother, would you be surprised?" he asked.

As ever, Robin's expression gave little away. "A strange family tree," he mused at length, "with tangled branches."

Philip gave a snort of derision as if to say you don't know the half of it. "Tangled and thorny," he replied bitterly, "and grown out of all proportion to the slights and misdemeanours that first gave it root." He paused, aware that his voice was rising. He took a deep breath and settled himself. "She has always favoured Eustace," he said evenly. "And now she makes the choice in blood. So be it. In time I will pay her out in kind. Until then I need to know who I can trust."

The man from Locksley looked out over the tranquil ocean. It was too dark to see very much, but here and there he caught a shimmer of movement as the light from the ship's two lanterns repeatedly dissolved and took shape again in the rippling swell. "Friends call me Robin," he reminded Philip at length, his tone gently chiding.

"*Friends* I have in abundance," Philip replied. "What I need now are men who'll take my part."

"And catch an arrow for their troubles?" Robin asked cagily.

Philip opened his mouth to say something and then stopped. He looked up at the moon, a fingernail clipping of light in the black sky. "It's true," he conceded quietly, a dignified resignation in his voice. "I told you I needed a 'good hand', not a shield to protect me from my own family. I had dared to hope that somewhere along the way we might find ourselves of one brotherhood. But such journeys are not begun with a fee. And by any reckoning you've already stood your part in our agreement. I will not press you further."

He turned to walk away. It was a masterstroke of honesty and humility and Robin, who like Philip could be surprisingly sentimental at times, felt himself unexpectedly moved by it.

"Tell Gilbert we'll sleep in shifts," he declared abruptly. "One to remain with you at all times."

Philip affected surprise at this sudden change of heart. "And risk *catching an arrow for your troubles*?" he repeated wryly, a little glimmer in his eye.

Robin gave a good humoured shrug. "My 'troubles' keep me in debt with the Lord," he replied. "Better I start paying them off now than in Purgatory."

Thus it was agreed, and Robin and Gilbert took it in turns to keep watch over Philip. Privately, Gilbert would have been much happier with Gisbourne, whom he secretly admired or Harold of Leicester, whose enmity for Eustace was well known, even the so-called 'mute' Crispin of Lincoln would have been preferable, but Robin was a noted bowman, and had already proved himself once on the Great North Road, so Gilbert kept any lingering doubts he had to himself.

And for the next week all went well. The seas were calm, the winds were good and for the most part the weather kept its distance. Indeed, things went so smoothly that Philip began to wonder if perhaps Gilbert's information about the traitor had been wrong. And when by the end of the second week, still nothing had happened, Philip felt virtually certain of it. Even Robin seemed to relax.

With little to disturb them, they quickly settled down to a comfortable routine, tending the ship, playing the occasional game of dice, and watching Rosamond and her entourage as they took their daily 'parade' around deck. At night they would sit by the glowing braziers and listen as Holger regaled them with tales of Vinland and what they could expect to find there.

"It is the most beautiful place on earth," he sighed wistfully, "great forests, unlike any you have ever seen, and lakes and valley's so wide and deep that only the mighty Odin could have dug them out."

"What about the skraelings?" Rosamond trilled impatiently. She'd heard they ran free, like 'savages in the Garden of Eden' and the prospect of watching and perhaps even joining in with them excited her greatly.

Holger took a sip of ale, his eyes growing distant. "They are a people of great beauty," he said. "Ferocious in battle, but loyal too, and brave, always brave. I tell you, no man or woman on earth has a greater love of liberty, and no warrior in history has ever defended it with such prowess."

Gisbourne, who always chose to sit on the fringes of these gatherings, seemingly lost in his own thoughts, scoffed audibly at this.

Holger looked across at him, his grizzled old face as imperturbable as ever.

"Take good care young Gisbourne," he counselled gravely, "or your boldness may lead you into a peril from which you will not easily escape."

"My *boldness* will lead me to the biggest skraeling I can find," Gisbourne replied angrily. "And then we shall see who's 'love of liberty' is greatest." He raised himself up and stalked off towards his mattress at the ship's stern.

"At his end few will mourn him," Alyne mused after he'd gone, giving voice to a sentiment already widely shared amongst the ship's crew. Ralph of Shrewsbury stamped his foot three times and gave a gruff little cough, and Rosamond laughed so noisily, Robin knew immediately it was an attempt to bring Gisbourne charging back to the brazier. He glanced at her reproachfully, and she stopped though a girlish wickedness continued to linger in her expression.

Holger stared into the brazier, the crackling orange light twinkling in his boggy eyes. On his last trip to Vinland he'd wandered off on his own while Eustace and the others made camp for the night. Not far into the forest he'd happened upon a young skraeling girl called Chepi, sat calmly in a tree watching them. Surprisingly, the girl possessed a few words of Old Norse, most probably passed down from her grandparents, and she and Holger had conversed affably for a few moments. She'd told him about a powerful new war priest called Tomakin; a monstrous figure who could 'bend shadows to his will', tore fingers from the hands of his enemies with his own teeth, and boasted two arms like huge turtle claws.

Holger brooded quietly on that now. If he had his way, Gisbourne and Tomakin would find each other in Vinland's great forests and afterwards he would sail for home one hand lighter. "*Mourning* is the least of it," he opined after a moment. "At his *end*, few will even recognise him."

Things continued in a similar vein until the thirty third day of the journey, when the great storm took them completely by surprise and two arrows flew out of the dark, the second passing so close it drew blood from Philip's arm. Just moments before he'd looked on helplessly as both Alyne and Gilbert were swept away by a huge wave. He'd assumed at the time they'd both perished but it transpired they'd simply been deposited at the other end of the ship where they'd managed to cling on until the tumult passed.

Although both arrows had narrowly missed, there was no doubting thc ability of the man who had despatched them. In such conditions, even putting an arrow in flight would have been beyond most archers, yet this one had loosed two in quick succession, and on both occasions come within a breath of striking his target.

Philip knew of only one bowman on board who could shoot like that. He had watched him many times during the preceding four weeks, bringing down sea birds for the cooking pot with a single arrow attached to a long piece of thin rope. It always began with a slow, almost lazy stretch of the arm, followed by a sudden flurry of hand and shoulder as the arrow was loosed. Often, what had seemed speculative revealed itself as anything but, as the arrow dipped sharply in mid-flight and gathered pace until it struck its target with deadly intent. Could it really be that this bowman, who Philip had dared to think of as a friend, had in reality been planning to kill him the whole time?

When the storm finally abated on the third day, Philip dug the imbedded arrowhead from the mainmast and confirmed what he already suspected, an armour- piercing bodkin point. There was no longer any doubting it. Robin of Locksley was the man his mother had hired to kill him.

Quite amazingly, despite its ferocity the storm hadn't incurred any fatalities. Alyne had been swept to the stern where, despite a fierce battering, he'd managed to hold on. Brother Geoffrey had sprained an ankle, Ralph of Shrewsbury and one of Rosamond's handmaidens had briefly managed to render each other unconscious, though what they were doing in such close proximity in the first place was never properly explained. And Oswald of Norwich had acquired a black eye, though he couldn't remember how he'd come by it. Apart from that everyone else was fine. Even scrawny little Lycomedes had survived in one piece.

A quick inventory of the damage showed the ship, barring a few minor repairs, was largely intact too. Which meant Philip was left with just one immediate problem. What to do with the man who'd just tried to kill him?

Philip's preferred method of dealing with any problem was to sit down quietly and carefully evaluate all the options. This was the process that had led him to wait over a year before heading off in pursuit of Eustace. But Gilbert, who had no love for Robin, urged him to 'act swiftly', before the 'serpent has a chance to strike again'.

And when Philip continued to hesitate, Gilbert took matters into his own hand. With Roger of Doncaster and a couple of the younger knights, he fell upon Robin a few moments later. After a violent struggle in which Roger of Doncaster had his nose broken, Robin was beaten unconscious, and young Elizabeth, who flew to his aid with commendable energy, was roughly thrown to one side, Robin found himself dragged across the deck and roughly shackled to the mainmast.

"Gather his other arrows," Gilbert told Roger of Doncaster. "I want everyone to witness his guilt."

Philip lingered on the edge of things, wary of this headlong rush into judgment yet reluctant to intervene. A twinkling of light caught his eye and he bent to retrieve Robin's silver coin from the deck, noting how worn and smooth it was. He squinted at the inscription, barely decipherable even in this light. Charlemagne? No, surely not. Baldwin the Third perhaps? Either way it was a relic from another age. He slipped it into his tunic, and waited to see what Gilbert and the others would do next.

He didn't have to wait long. Roger of Doncaster had returned with the arrows and as Robin struggled at the mainmast, Gilbert was already taunting him with his guilt. "Stand beggar. Why in such haste to get away?"

Like most suspicious men, Gilbert's mistrustful nature paid out both good and bad in equal dividends. He negotiated well at prices, could spot a liar at a hundred paces, and was rarely surprised by treachery of any kind. On the other hand he seldom smiled, had few friends and very often, as was now the case, employed his raging paranoia in the pursuit of personal vendettas.

It had all started way back in Portsmouth, right from the moment he'd heard about the fight on the Great North Road. As bizarre as it seemed, Gilbert had felt a pang of jealousy. As Philip's oldest and truest acquaintance it should have fallen to him to defend his friend. Instead of which, Robin was now being hailed as 'champion.' For the first time ever, Gilbert felt excluded. And though he'd tried hard to ignore it, the feeling had steadily grown in him until soon it seemed as though the man from Locksley had not only saved his best friends life, but also supplanted him in his affections too. He watched as they sat huddled together in private discussion, and found he was constantly reminded that it was Robin's counsel Philip now sought, rather than his. Robin's opinion he seemed to value above all others.

In an effort to redress the balance, Gilbert had quietly poured scorn on Robin's 'faux nobility', particularly his claim to the title 'Earl of Huntingdon'. He'd denounced it as 'preposterous', declaring his mother 'deranged', his father a 'liar', and Robin himself a 'common poacher'. But if anything the bond between the two men had grown even stronger.

And then, as if in answer to his prayers, an arrow had flown out of the storm and suddenly all he needed to do was get Robin to admit his guilt and everything in the world would be well again. For the first time in weeks Gilbert actually felt happy.

Fortunately, he had no notion just how fleeting his moment of triumph would prove. In just over four weeks the coast of Vinland would rise majestically on the horizon, Rosamond would scream and clap her hands in glee, the keel would touch sand, and Robin would still be at Philip's side as they vaulted ashore. Moreover he would be there when Philip knelt on the soil of this strange new world and offered up a prayer for the soul of his 'most trusted friend, Gilbert of York', whose body they had consigned to the ocean twenty days before.

NINE

Twenty Nine Years Later...

Kirklees Nunnery, England
The Conception of the Blessed Virgin Mary
8th December 1211
(Sixteen days before the death of Robin Hood).

They were calling it a disturbance of the soul, a creeping confusion which made him restive and uncertain. They said as long as he took respite and was regularly bled, he would soon be well again.

But Elizabeth knew that wasn't true. She'd seen this type of malady before, and it always started the same way. First a fogginess of thought, the sufferer forgetting what they wanted to remember and remembering what they wanted to forget. This was invariably followed by a surfeit of inappropriate emotion and behaviour, a combination of cruelties that quickly led to a kind of madness from which there was no hope of escape.[14] If you were lucky, death would quickly follow, but not until the last vestige of dignity had been stripped away. It was a final trial they said, one last test of faith before the Lord claimed you.

In Elizabeth's experience it was a 'trial' usually reserved for the very elderly, but just occasionally, as if to prove a point, it sought out younger victims too. There was no pattern or sense to it. Robin, it seemed,

---

[14] ***Clearly some form of Alzheimer's.***

had just been unfortunate. The only thing she could do now was keep him as comfortable as possible and pray for a swift delivery.

Not that she said any of this of course. No one did. The pretence that 'respite' and 'bleeding' would provide a cure was assiduously maintained by all. But each and every one of them knew the truth. That was why the big fellow they called John Lyttle fell into such a fitful sob the moment they set foot outside the room, and why Alyne lingered in the corridor after the others had gone, his eyes seeking out hers in a private understanding.

"All these years we've kept our distance Elizabeth," he sighed, "yet now it seems you have some part to play in this after all."

He didn't need to say any more. She knew exactly what he meant. Outside, two ravens were squabbling noisily, whilst a thin drizzle clung to the ragged trees. Even with those little sprigs of holly, it was hard to imagine anything joyful in such a wretched season.

"I shall remain at his side," she assured him, "until the very end."

He jangled a small bag of coins but she shook her head. "I can accept no payment for doing what I've been entrusted by the Lord to do," she explained. "This is God's work, and God's work requires only truth and love."

Alyne put aside his bow and ceremoniously knelt on the cold stone floor in front of her. He kissed each of her bare feet in turn before getting up again and pressing the bag gently into her palm, closing her fingers around it with his own.

"Then give it to the priest," he advised solemnly, "and tell him to distribute it amongst the poor, so all will know what a noble man he was."

"You are a mirror of charity," she told him, bowing her head courteously, before stowing the bag in her robe.

Alyne was no fool. He knew that despite her show of piety, Elizabeth had already accepted a much larger sum from one of the Sheriff's emissaries. That was why he'd come to her. He needed a villain to help him finish the song he was writing. And not just any villain either. This one would have to sit comfortably alongside Judas, Brutus and all the other reprobates whose treachery down the ages had brought about a good man's demise.

Having reassured himself she was up to the task, Alyne promised to return again in a few days. He'd baited the hook, now he'd have to wait and see if she took a bite. The moment she did, he'd have his villain, and the song would have its ending. Not a happy one perhaps, but a memorable one. And that was all that really mattered.

Alyne had become increasingly preoccupied with endings and beginnings these past few weeks. Many songs and stories were already being sung and told in villages and towns all over the land and somewhere in their rhymes Alyne had started to discern the threads of a single narrative. It didn't matter that the skraeling Tomakin, or the traitor they'd caught up with in Jerusalem, or indeed many others continued to elude that narrative. Let those who came afterwards squabble over particular details. The important thing now was to secure the legacy.

And as he melted back into the forest with John Lyttle and the rest of them, Alyne was already writing the final verse in his head. *'By the wicked prioress he lay, and there was betrayed good Robin Hood, in Kirklees on a snowy day.'*[15] He glanced up at the sky. Maybe there really would be snow, he thought. Who could tell?

Had she known what Alyne was planning, it's unlikely Elizabeth would have been quite so accommodating. But the truth was she'd waited almost twenty nine years for the chance to feel special again, and she wasn't about to pass it up now. Besides, something about Robin's plight had deeply affected her. And in the days that followed she rarely left his side.

Since returning from Vinland, Robin and Elizabeth had met only intermittently. Usually he'd arrive late at night, when most of the other sisters were sleeping. Occasionally it was to seek a cure for some ailment, but mostly it was to visit Marian. Elizabeth would always rush to the kitchen to prepare him something to eat and drink, but invariably he'd be gone by the time she returned. Sometimes they'd exchange a few words at the gate, but he was always

---

[15] ***Whilst the first literary allusion to Robin Hood dates back to the 1300's, the first printed account of his death doesn't appear until the late 1400's, though it's widely accepted this version is based on much earlier accounts.***

on guard. Elizabeth was known to have links to Philip Mark, and very few of the outlaws trusted her.

One morning however, with spring gathering at the high arched windows, and mild sunlight collecting in the empty quadrangle below, she'd found him sat alone in the chapel, his eyes fixed on the large bronze cross above the altar.

"The skraelings believed their Great Spirit sent them a messenger," he told her quietly as she sat down on the wooden bench next to him. "His name was Deganewidah and he was born of a virgin." He smiled thoughtfully, as if struck by the notion. "They said he was the Great Spirit's incarnation on earth."

Elizabeth made no comment. As she recalled, Robin had always been partial to these kinds of musings, both extravagant and inflammatory and invariably the herald to something more personal. As it turned out she wasn't wrong.

"I miss it Elizabeth," he reflected earnestly, after a moment or two. "I miss the great forests and the huge tumbling rivers. I miss the smells and the tastes, I miss the uppowoc."[16]

"And Tomakin," she enquired pointedly, "do you miss him also?"

He fell silent, and she knew he was thinking not just about Tomakin, but about Chepi and the traitor, and probably all the others too.

"What happened," she asked sensitively. "Philip and you were gone for so long. We thought you were lost…or worse."

---

[16] ***Native American Indian word for tobacco.***

Robin stared up at the cross. It appeared to slowly change colour, the dark bronze gradually turning gold as the sun slipped effortlessly from one window to the next. "You would not believe it," he said distantly, "even if I told you. For sometimes I hardly believe it myself, and I was there."

He reached into a sack he had at his feet and with the air of a man ridding himself of an unwanted gift, handed her a remarkable silver arrow, telling her he'd won it the day before in an archery competition. "Make what use of it as you can," he advised nonchalantly, "I have no further purpose for it."

She held the arrow in her hands, closing her fingers around the long shaft. The shiny silver caught a ray of sun, throwing a glinting band of light across her eyes. She had little doubt the competition had been arranged by the authorities with the sole intention of apprehending him. She imagined the tension of the shoot as she fastened her grip on the sleek stem, the village girls screaming in adoration, the bloody melee as he made his escape. How typical of Robin she reflected, that he should risk his life and the lives of others for something he neither valued nor wanted.

That had been almost seventeen years ago. The silver arrow had vanished soon after. No doubt taken by one of the flighty young oblates who, having discovered a life of prayer and servitude was not for them, routinely disappeared over the walls at night, usually taking something of value with them. Or there again, maybe there was some truth in the rumour that it had been stolen to order at the behest of Bernat of

Navarre, who it was said, had developed a strange obsession for all things pertaining to the outlaw Robin Hood.

Either way it was long gone, as was the fearless outlaw who had won it. As indeed was the woman he'd come to visit. All of them, long gone over the wall and into the forest, never to return. Now there were just the shadows and the people lost in them, fearful and bemused, struggling to remember.

As each day passed, Elizabeth did her best to keep him active. Sewing and reading seemed to help, but for long periods he remained locked in his own thoughts, rolling a small silver coin between his fingers, or silently brooding at the window, watching as the winter outside thickened, the thin drizzle giving way to the first billowing flecks of snow.

At night he was troubled by bad dreams and would wake up shouting that *'Tomakin had come for him'*, convinced the skraeling shaman was crouching in the shadowy corners of the room, ready to pounce. To stop him from rousing the entire nunnery, she would hold him in her arms, rocking him gently to and fro, whilst stroking his hair and making soft, soothing noises, until eventually he'd fall asleep again.

Sometimes during the day the mist in his eyes would clear and he'd ask her a multitude of questions, mostly about Marian, and she would answer as best she could and then he would abruptly fall silent again and return to brooding.

During these long periods she would find herself wondering at the strange path which had brought them back together again after all this time. Slowly, the notion that God was giving her a second chance began to take hold, and she started to picture the two of them living happily in the Gatehouse for years and years to come.

"We've been blessed," she told him as she pressed her lips to his cheek. "God has made a room for us." And the romantic idyll continued to unfold in her mind. *I am May*, she told herself, *the maiden of spring. I stand at the gates of summer and wait for my Green Man to return.*

She held his head gently between her two hands and slowly turned his mouth to hers. "Live on my love," she whispered, her cheeks wet with tears. "Live on and be my bounty."

On December 14th, Brother Barnabas, an elderly Benedictine with leathery skin and arthritic fingers paused in his travels to take ale with the Sisters at Kirklees and join them in celebrating the feast of Saint Fingar of Hoyle. As he was preparing to leave, Sister Euphrasia, who was second cousin to the late Guy of Gisbourne, and generally considered one of the most devout women at the nunnery, paused in the execution of her duties and whispered something in his ear. The old monk looked at her and then hurried on his way.

Outside, with no sunshine to soften its grip, a hard frost had taken hold of the surrounding countryside, producing a white stillness that even the hunched crows seemed reluctant to disturb. Sister Euphrasia watched from a small window as Brother

Barnabas made his way back along the frozen track. It was God's will she told herself.

Two days later, with a spiteful dawn ushering in the feast day of Saint Adelaide of Burgundy, Brother Lucius wrapped himself in a thick fur cloak and travelled to Nottingham to meet Philip Mark. The two men had crossed paths many times since their first encounter on Holy Rood Day in 1182, though every subsequent occasion had only served to reinforce the original misgivings each shared about the other.

"There's talk of Kirklees," Lucius told Philip confidentially a short while later, as he warmed his hands at the fire in Nottingham Castle's Great Hall. "A stranger kept in the gatehouse, a man of some fifty years. They say the Prioress herself attends him."

Philip stopped stoking the burning logs and looked at him. "He is ill?" He said it almost in surprise, as if such a thing was virtually impossible.

Lucius shrugged. He was Abbot now, with 'power of jurisdiction' over a large swath of territory, much of which also fell under Philip's remit as Sheriff, and the twin misery of dealing with both had turned his youthful pudginess to sagging melancholy. "Why else retire to such a place?" he asked jadedly. "Death or glory, these sisters happily dress a man for both. Whatever ails our friend, it can only be a matter of time."

Philip shook his head vigorously. "I don't believe it," he declared, "your spies are deceived. And you are deceived along with them." He poked at the fire with renewed venom, filling the hearth with a swirl of burning embers.

Lucius watched him with a mixture of pity and contempt. "My 'spies' are not *spies* my lord," he observed calmly. "And the only deception here is the one you practice on yourself."

Wounded by the remark, Philip turned on him, his words spiked with accusation. "How is it you dare speak to me thus, when all these years, I've sought nothing from you but your friendship?"

Despite the roaring fire and embroidered tapestries, there was a pervading darkness to the Great Hall. It circled restlessly like a ghost in the vaulted hollows of the ceiling, swooping down suddenly to fill a man's heart with blackness and poison. It had long since claimed Philip, and now, with smoke in his nostrils and the wind howling at the stone battlements outside, Lucius felt it bearing down on him too.

"It is for the sake of that friendship I speak as I do," he replied, weighing his words carefully, aware of his own shortcomings and no longer wishing to bury them under diplomacy. "You told me once *'a man was best judged not by his friends, but by his enemies'*, that *'in their fervour you would find his true reflection'*. I have to tell you now, that reflection serves you poorly, and you do ill to pursue it."

Philip stared at him in disbelief, amazed not only that Lucius had remembered, but that he'd chosen this moment to quote it back at him. Mistaking the monk's counsel for insolence he flared up again, railing like a scorned child. "How many times am I to say it? He took something from me.

And I will have it back, by whatever means. Do you hear Lucius, by whatever means!"

Philip's features, already reddened from years of excessive drinking, had become taut and distorted, and Lucius could see there was no point in arguing any further. He inclined his head courteously. "Then I pray God grant you success in your endeavour my lord. As for Kirklees, I suggest you take a large force of men. There are rebels in the woods as well as outlaws and both seek ways of advancing their cause."

Philip had expected more objections, a stern warning about the enduring appeal of martyrs perhaps, or even another sermon on forgiveness. In short, the same argument they'd been having for the past twenty years. But the monk seemed drained of argument, and his weariness was so disarming Philip found himself nodding meekly, the anger in him suddenly gone too. "Like water, I boil over," he offered awkwardly by way of apology. "Nevertheless I thank you for your advice Lucius. I shall travel to Kirklees in person, just as you suggest, and whatever 'reflection' I find there, I assure you I shall wear it proudly as my own."

Lucius wondered if Philip had heard the latest songs they were singing. The *'brave and noble Robin Hood, may he continue in good health'*, the *'weak and cowardly Sheriff, let him forever rot in hell'*. It's the songs they'll remember, he thought. Everything else will fade away. Only the songs will remain. "Yes my lord," he said sadly, "I fear you shall."

For a long time after he'd gone, Philip remained stood by the fire, his back straight, his eyes fixed on the dancing flames. The old monk was right he thought. Only a madman would embark on such a journey without a heavily armed escort. And he looked at the tiny stub on his left hand where his small finger had been torn from the bone. *Only a madman* he thought, and for the first time in weeks he found himself laughing.

On December the 17th Elizabeth woke with a start at the sound of footsteps in the corridor outside the door. She sat there listening as they receded, and all at once she was filled with a sense of dread. *She knew!* There was no doubting it, she told herself. Sister Euphrasia *knew*. That's why she'd looked so sheepish at Mass this morning, and why Brother Barnabas had set off at such a pace for Barnsdale three days ago.

She pictured the likely outcome in her head. Philip would be sure to arrive in person this time. And he'd probably bring soldiers too. She thought about the money he'd paid her. A vast sum of money, and all he wanted in return was the answer to one simple question. *Where?* I must tell him, she thought. I must explain. The longer I keep it to myself, the worse it'll be, for everyone.

But what was she going to do about Robin? She couldn't let Philip take him. Not like this. She bit her lip and tried to think. And suddenly she heard the voice inside her head. No, she told herself. Please, not yet. Not me. *Not me…*

December the 18th was the feast day of Saint Winebald of Wessex. The other sisters filed dutifully into the chapel, but Elizabeth stayed in the Gatehouse, glowering at the small arched window. It might as well have bars, she reflected sourly. At least that way no one would bc left in any doubt.

She looked at her hands and found they were bunched tightly into fists. Alyne would be back again tonight with his anguished sighs and jangling purse, and she would of course tell him to 'have faith'. But she knew it had nothing to do with faith. A few days ago she'd convinced herself that God was giving her a second chance. Now she realised He was just playing a trick on her, another of His little jests to set alongside all the others. I've been abandoned, she thought. Nothing I say will ever be heard. No one I love will ever love me in return. The world has turned its back on me, and so has heaven.

Robin was awake now, and she realised he was muttering something. He was already badly weakened from the blood she'd taken, and she had to press her ear to his lips to hear what he was saying.

"I must see her," he implored softly. "I must see her one last time."

Her eyes narrowed. "Do you know the way?" she asked him, a clipped brittleness in her voice.

He stared at her, his eyes uncertain, like a child who's been admonished and doesn't know why. She immediately softened. "Have no fear," she assured him, "I know where she is."

Mass had finished, and somewhere in the grounds outside, the younger sisters were singing as they prepared the trees for Christmas. Elizabeth listened. The songs they sang had nothing to do with shepherds or angels or sleeping saviours. They were all about a brave forest outlaw who *'allowed no woman to suffer injustice, nor would he steal from the poor.'*

She felt a sudden stab of jealousy. Let them sing of me she yearned. Let them tell my tale. And again the words echoed inside her head. She reached across and tenderly stroked the side of Robin's face. *By my own hand* she thought.

TEN

Atlantic Ocean
The Season of Hallowmas: All Souls Day
2nd November 1182.

It was Guy of Gisbourne of all people who saved Robin in the immediate aftermath of the storm. With everyone gathering around expectantly, sunshine once again breaking through the clouds, and Gilbert waving the 'matching arrowheads' above his head as though they were nails from the Holy Cross itself, the atmosphere had rapidly taken on the curious air of premeditated murder and jolly May revels that usually attended a village lynching.

Thus Oswald of Norwich, who always called for ale, now called for it more vociferously than ever, Roger of Doncaster brandished his sword and declared he would 'cut out the traitor's heart', Brother Geoffrey raised up a sermon, the so-called 'mute' Crispin of Lincoln remained watchfully silent, Ralph of Shrewsbury punched Robin in the mouth before disappearing beneath the canvas with one of Rosamond's handmaidens, and Walter of Malmesbury was even seen to dance a little jig.

Everything was going splendidly in fact. Even Alyne, though ostensibly appalled by the whole spectacle, had secretly felt the first stirrings of a bold new composition.

And then Gisbourne had stepped forward and ruined the whole thing, declaring loudly, "Huntingdon was with me the whole time." And going on to describe how the two men had sought refuge at the ship's bow, roping themselves together as the waves rolled in, and holding on for dear life as though the 'Virgin Herself was willing it'.

"From the first swell to the last, I had him in sight," Gisbourne affirmed. "Therefore he couldn't have loosed those arrows. And any man who claims otherwise is a liar." As with virtually everything else he said, Gisbourne words were unequivocal and carried with them the implicit threat that anyone wishing to dispute the matter should expect to do so at the sharp end of a sword.

With no apparent takers, Gisbourne instructed Elizabeth to unshackle Robin and 'tend his wounds'. He then concluded proceedings with one of those involuntary little shoulder jerks that Ralph of Shrewsbury had become so adept at imitating, and headed back to his own solitary position at the ship's bow.

Gilbert could hardly believe it. Every bone in his body had told him Robin was the traitor. More than that, he *wanted* Robin to be the traitor. Now, as it began to look like his quarry might escape him, he turned in desperation to his old friend for support.

"Philip," he implored, "by all that's holy, tell them. Make them understand. You said yourself no man alive could have launched those two arrows with such precision."

It was true, Philip had said precisely that and more besides, and at the time he'd believed it too. Even worse, he'd stood meekly to one side whilst

Gilbert and the others had seized Robin, set about him with their fists and feet and shackled him to the mainmast. But now, as it began to appear their judgment may have been flawed, he had no desire to implicate himself further in the affair. So instead of backing Gilbert up, he turned away awkwardly, damning his friend's claim with silence.

Gilbert stared in dismay and then rushed after Gisbourne, chasing him back up the ship towards the bow, wielding the matching arrowheads, and proclaiming them 'clear evidence of Robin's guilt'. If there was no connection he insisted, 'how by all the saints in heaven' did Gisbourne explain these?

Gisbourne stopped walking and turned to face him. "I explain them by means of simple roguery," he countered flatly, making no attempt to mask his disdain. "You know as well as I that any man here could have taken those arrows and used them for his own purpose."

"And executed that 'purpose' with such precision?" Gilbert demanded, his tone becoming increasingly shrill.

Gisbourne fixed him with a baleful eye. "The only 'purpose' at play here is your own," he told him scornfully. "You seek for Huntingdon's blood not because of any guilt you discern in him, but because of the guilt you discern in yourself."

It was a fairly shocking allegation, even by Gisbourne's standards, and all the more so for being true, which was why it drew such an audible gasp from Rosamond and the others, and why Brother Geoffrey leapt to his feet shouting "recant", and why even Ralph of Shrewsbury popped his head out from under the canvas to see what was going on. But it was what happened next that really took everyone by surprise.

For a moment Gilbert did and said absolutely nothing, and the old rascal Harold of Leicester whispered "for shame" just loud enough for everyone to hear. And then all at once Gilbert gave the most tremendous cry of despair and threw himself not at Guy of Gisbourne as might have been expected, but at his 'friend' Philip Mark instead. He flew at him in such rage, that Philip was on his back with Gilbert's hands fastened around his throat before anyone could react.

Whether Gilbert intended to kill or simply punish him, Philip never knew for sure. In later years he would continue to review the incident in his mind without ever quite resolving it to any degree of satisfaction. Suffice to say the hands at his throat felt determined enough, and there was undeniable anger in them too. Yet perhaps they weakened when they should have strengthened. And perhaps there was something else too. Something he saw in Gilbert's eyes as Geoffrey and the others desperately tried to pull him off. And perhaps that was why he pondered so restlessly on the episode in later years, and why, despite Philip's best efforts, the two men were never to speak in friendship again.

As for Robin, following Gisbourne's dramatic intervention he now found himself cast as the unlikely victim of the piece, with everyone falling over themselves to make amends, most notably Roger of

Doncaster who loudly offered to forgo his rations for the next few days in order to speed his recovery, and Rosamond who airily brushed Elizabeth aside, instructing her two handmaidens to take Robin to her cabin so she could 'personally tend' his wounds, a duty of care which she undertook with a great deal of devotion.

Privately however, many of those on board continued to suspect that Robin and the hired killer were one in the same. This was partly due to Robin's renowned skill with a bow, partly due to Gilbert's presentation of the 'evidence' against him, which had been strangely compelling, and partly because they all felt cheated out of a good lynching. There was also the matter of Gisbourne, who was so disliked by now, that everything he said was immediately treated with scorn. Indeed, Ralph of Shrewsbury was soon whispering that Robin and Gisbourne had in all likelihood concocted the entire episode between them in order to discredit Gilbert and enhance their own reputations. All of which left Robin himself in a slightly vulnerable position, which is why he meekly submitted to Rosamond's vigorous ministrations and said very little of consequence for the next few days.

Meanwhile, with calmer seas, and a steady wind, the real traitor continued to move freely amongst them, protected by the false identity he'd established at the journey's outset, quietly biding his time whilst revelling in the mood of suspicion his attempt on Philip's life had created.

As for Philip, his troubles were only just beginning. Gilbert failed to join them at the cooking brazier that night, and in the days that followed he neglected his ship duties and was more often than not to be found stood alone at the stern, wrapped in a thick cloak, his back to everyone, staring out into some private infinity. When he didn't appear at Mass for the third consecutive morning, Philip reluctantly approached him.

"You were deceived," he informed Gilbert sympathetically, "we all were. And the *deceiver* remains among us still. Help me Gilbert. Help me catch this traitor and put him to the sword before we reach Vinland and he wreaks more havoc."

He was attempting to appeal to Gilbert's sense of duty, but the young man continued to gaze forlornly out at the ocean, his eyes darkening as he touched the blotchy brown mark on his cheek that Harold of Leicester had found so amusing.

"When I was a young," he began quietly. "I asked my mother if she could wash this stain from my face." His voice faltered slightly as he remembered the painful conversation. "I asked her with the hope that only a small child can muster. She told me, *'it is God who has put it there, and it is His purpose that it serves. But as you travel you will find many who will not notice, and many more who will not mind, and of the others, there will be many who carry birth stains of their own, even though some remain invisible to the eye.*"

Philip lingered at his side, awkward and uncomfortable and no longer completely sure what it was they were talking about. "Gilbert," he implored conciliatorily, "if we leave this business as it stands, I fear a great distance will open between us."

Gilbert smiled sadly. "The distance between us is already great," he replied. "And now I am humiliated. And a man humiliated serves little useful purpose."

Philip went to place a consoling hand on his sleeve and then clumsily checked himself as he remembered Gisbourne's accusation. Gilbert noticed but said nothing. And feeling the shame burn in his cheeks, Philip turned and scurried away.

And there it might have ended. Gilbert broken, Gisbourne triumphant and a good friendship brought to ruin by a tiny act of reticence that was as feeble as it was graceless. However, Walter of Malmesbury had other ideas, and the following day, with the afternoon far advanced and the wind slackening in the sail, he approached Gisbourne as he sat on the quarterdeck, polishing his sword.

"A strange pretence," he observed conversationally, "to play a lesser man with such conviction."

The two had never spoken directly before, and Gisbourne's demeanour made it clear he didn't welcome the development now. But Walter persisted. "And to what profit I wonder?" he posited, "to live a life of shadows and yearning, cloistered away in one's own disapproval, like a forest hermit with no faith to persuade him?"

Gisbourne worked his sword fiercely, not a muscle moving in his taut face as he listened.

Walter lowered his voice. "You and I eat from the same dish," he whispered knowingly. "But I do so with no shame."

Gisbourne stopped polishing the sword and got slowly to his feet. He looked Walter directly in the eye. "Be cautious with your words," he warned, "for I will forgive your womanly insolence only once."

Walter snorted. "I'll be as cautious with them as you were with your own, when you condemned Gilbert for a crime you have committed many times over in your own heart."

Gisbourne's eyes narrowed menacingly. "Do you dare threaten me?"

"I do more," Walter told him defiantly, his voice rising sufficiently to furrow Gisbourne's brow. "I forewarn you. Raise such a tide again and I will spill your secret for all to enjoy."

Gisbourne shifted uncomfortably. It had been a long time since anyone had dared speak to him like this. He opened his mouth but before he could respond, the ship lurched suddenly as it rode a wave and he lost his footing. Falling forward, he instinctively grasped hold of Walter, locking the two men in a reluctant embrace. Walter seized him tightly, gripping him close as he whispered in his ear.

"I see all," he told the young knight. "You both love and hate yourself in equal parts, and the dispute between the two is never finished. But I will finish it. I will stand you bare so none shall be left in any doubt. Not even you."

Gisbourne flailed desperately, trying to push Walter away. "I would see you dead first," he snarled angrily.

"Then you had better kill me whilst I sleep," Walter advised him undaunted, "for the moment you draw a sword I shall shout it aloud for all to enjoy. Sing it like a monk with psalm fever. And even as I'm run through I shall swear it on the Bible, swear it with my last dying breath, so all will know I speak the truth."

The ship settled again, and the two men broke apart. Gisbourne looked around anxiously to make sure no one had been watching. The sun was almost done now, and its dull orange glow left both men's faces masked in shadow.

Walter picked up Gisbourne's sword and handed it to him. "And should you think further on the subject," he warned, "be advised, I sleep more lightly than most, and given your predilection for extraordinary noises and movements, I doubt you shall catch me unaware."

He gave Gisbourne's cheek a playful squeeze and then headed off to join Rosamond and the others who were already gathering at the cooking brazier. Had he lingered a moment longer, he would have seen Gisbourne check one of those involuntary little shoulder movements he'd just spoken of, before turning his face to the sea and swallowing back the tears that had started to prickle in the corner of his eyes.

I am not to blame, Gisbourne told himself furiously. *I am possessed by a demon that is yet to make up its mind. And this demon torments me with questions I cannot answer.* He braced himself, clenching his fists and grinding his teeth. *Have courage,* he thought, *no man can survive without courage.* But the tears came anyway.

With Gilbert sulking silently at one end of the ship, Gisbourne brooding unhappily at the other, and the seas becoming choppy again, a poisonous atmosphere began to develop on board. Petty squabbles became more frequent, small cliques formed, and even Rosamond's daily parades failed to arouse much interest. What had seemed like a great adventure just a few weeks before now increasingly felt like a terrible mistake, with many privately wondering if Vinland really was just a myth after all, and Ralph of Shrewsbury even hypothesizing that Holger was deliberately sailing in circles as part of some diabolical plan to turn them all into cannibals.

To add to the gloom a dispute broke out between Rosamond and Elizabeth, over an item of jewellery Rosamond claimed Elizabeth had stolen from her. The quarrel quickly involved the entire ship. And with the two young women squaring up to each other, Harold of Leicester shouting encouragement and Ralph of Shrewsbury calling for the loser to be 'tossed into the ocean with no clothes on', Philip was forced to intercede.

Despite her protestations, it immediately became apparent Elizabeth was guilty. Three people had seen her enter Rosamond's cabin, and even Elizabeth herself admitted taking the piece, though she maintained it had only been to 'borrowed for a while'. This was a risible explanation, even by her standards, and Rosamond – partly because she was bored and partly because she'd taken to despising Elizabeth with a vengeance – wasn't minded to accept it.

The item in question was little more than a shiny trinket, almost insignificant when compared to some of Rosamond's other jewellery, but Philip didn't want to upset the young heiress, and therefore had little option other than to prevail upon Elizabeth to make a full and unreserved apology, something Rosamond insisted she must do in front of the entire ship.

Unsurprisingly, Elizabeth wasn't happy about submitting herself to such a public humiliation, and Philip had to stress its necessity if she wanted to avoid one of Holger's more drastic 'punishments'. Finally she agreed, and the whole crew was assembled to witness her opprobrium.

It started badly, with Rosamond keeping everyone waiting whilst a squally rain shower passed. When she did finally emerge from her cabin she sauntered haughtily along the deck, attended by Walter of Malmesbury and flanked on either side by her two handmaidens. She presented herself in front of Elizabeth, whose expression had darkened considerably by now, and grandly announced "I'm ready," before settling herself on the chair provided by Philip, languorously arranging her various silks, and turning her painted face up in expectation.

For a moment there was no sound at all apart from the flap of the wind in the sail above, and Philip began to fear the worst. He gave a prompting little cough, but Elizabeth continued to stare straight ahead, not *at* Rosamond exactly, but *through* her. Phillip felt his stomach tighten. "Elizabeth," he whispered imploringly, just loud enough for the sixteen year old to hear. She blinked suddenly, looked at Rosamond properly for the first time, then gracefully bowed her head, apologised for her 'mistake', begged the young heiress's 'forgiveness', and pledged herself to do whatever was 'necessary' in order to 'make amends'.

That she was able to utter the words at all was a marvel. That she was able to utter them in front of such a large audience, let alone in a manner suggesting genuine contrition, was a minor miracle. And Philip was just thanking God that she'd seen good sense, when *it* suddenly happened. Rosamond puckered those full red lips, looked Elizabeth directly in the eye, and proffered a smile. *A smile!* Like a spiteful child with a sharp stick who continues to provoke the wounded animal long after it's down, she couldn't resist one final jab. True it wasn't a particularly big smile. Had you blinked you would have missed it. But Elizabeth didn't miss it. And therein lay the seed of what was to follow. Because it wasn't a smile of thanks or empathy, it was a sign of triumph. A direct message to Elizabeth from Rosamond, that she flourished as all others waned. And Philip knew in that dreadful moment that everything was lost.

As soon as he could, he took Elizabeth to one side, and desperately tried to impress upon her the need for magnanimity. "If we give our peace, even to a dog," he insisted, "that peace must be kept inviolate Elizabeth. *Inviolate*, do you understand? "

She looked at him with eyes that seemed worryingly full of intent. "Yes," she said calmly, "even to a dog. I understand."

Philip felt a sudden shiver of apprehension. He was too late and he knew it. Thus it came as no surprise to him when a hysterical Rosamond appeared on deck the following morning, cradling the limp body of Lycomedes in her arms and screaming about 'witchcraft'. He'd seen the glint in Elizabeth's eyes the day before. No doubt the same glint Father Benedict had seen as she mixed him a final 'potion'. *If only you hadn't proffered that smile,* he thought to himself.

"Your young maiden has her revenge I think," Holger told him with a knowing grin and an approving little nod in Elizabeth's direction.

Philip shook his head vigorously, Elizabeth had already proved her worth by concocting a remedy for their seasickness, and he was adamant it shouldn't get out that his young protégé was also a poisoner. "No, no", he breezed authoritatively, as though it was just one of those things, "the poor animal was always weak. It was the hardship of ocean life that finally did for it."

Holger raised an eyebrow but said no more. The dog had been irritating, and his only regret was that Elizabeth had cheated him out of a good stew.

They buried poor Lycomedes at sea the same day, with nearly everyone in attendance, and Brother Geoffrey officiating. Philip had feared the young monk might not enter into the spirit of things, having taken against Rosamond and her entourage from the start. But now he finally had something useful to do, he seemed to revel in it and set about the prayers with heartfelt gusto.

By the time they lowered Lycomedes to his rest, the waves were already lapping hungrily at the ship's side, as if in anticipation, and Philip watched as the ocean rose with one mournful heave to take the limp body under, turning it once, as if to taste it first, before quickly swallowing it down whole.

Rosamond gave a little cry of despair as the dog disappeared, thick black charcoal tears rolling down her pale white cheeks, like inky raindrops on the face of the moon. "God's blessings my Love," she cried out in a voice that suggested she wasn't entirely immune to the theatrical possibilities of the occasion.

Philip caught Elizabeth's eye as she stood nearby, silently contemplating her handiwork. She held his gaze coolly; her chin raised slightly, the twitch of a smirk on her lips. *I must talk to her*, he thought. *I must stop this now, before something terrible happens.*

But he never got the opportunity. Because the following day something terrible did happen, and Elizabeth was the only one who could help him.

ELEVEN

Atlantic Ocean
The Feast Day of Saint Martin of Tours
11th November, 1182.

After it was done, and the sun was setting, Brother Geoffrey approached him as he stood alone at the stern. "Make your confession now," he advised gravely, "and beg God's forgiveness. I swear by all that's holy your soul is in great peril if you don't."

Philip lifted his head and gazed out at the darkening horizon. Holger was right he thought. There was an endless monotony in it that tempted a man to melancholy.

"It was murder," Geoffrey persisted dolefully. "Call it by no other name."

The young monk looked stern and nobly anguished at the same time, a bearing he seemed to have perfected since they'd set sail from Portsmouth seven weeks ago.

Philip closed his eyes and let the gentle breeze soothe his face. "How wonderful," he mused wearily, "to be as absolute as Caesar in everything you say and do."

Geoffrey stiffened. "It is not for my sake," he insisted, with an air of pious satisfaction. "You are accounted a wise man, and hitherto you have acted prudently. So again I urge you, repent now, while there is still time."

Philip exhaled heavily. Even the scent of Brother Geoffrey was pious. A condition he seemed to achieve through a combination of natural inviolability and a mysterious lemon coloured balm he applied to his face each morning, the purpose of which was never fully explained. Indeed, it was only because Gilbert had insisted on taking someone who could attend their spiritual needs that the young monk had been included in the first place. A decision Philip now bitterly regretted.

"I will not trade Bible words with you," he told him firmly. "What I did, I did for all. And all are saved because of it," he looked the young monk directly in the eye, "*even* you."

The two men stared at each other. "He was a veritable martyr," Geoffrey responded evenly, "May God have mercy on his soul. And may God have mercy on your soul too, for you are already stood at Satan's gate." He turned with a sanctimonious swish and walked away.

The moment he'd gone, Elizabeth placed herself at Philip's side. She'd watched the encounter from across the ship and could guess what Brother Geoffrey had said to him. Without a word, she lightly took hold of Phillip's hand, a gesture at once both reassuring and supportive. "Have faith," she whispered, "God will see the reason in it."

More than anything in the world Philip wanted to believe this, and just hearing her say it gave him hope. He took the skraeling necklace from his pocket and carefully slipped it over her head. "I pray it brings you better fortune than it has brought me," he reflected wistfully.

The sun had all but disappeared now, leaving nothing but a few scratches of pink on the horizon. She reached for his hand again, but he withheld it this time.

"I try to love my fellow man," he professed unhappily, "but the truth is I neither care for him nor his brothers. True friends I can number but..." He held up a hand and considered his fingers, trying to determine an honest number. And in that moment he had a sudden memory of Gilbert and himself, as carefree young boys, running freely together in the soft haze of a distant French summer.

Elizabeth stroked the sharp bear tooth. "You have more friends than you know," she assured him, abstractedly pressing the tip of it into her thumb until it drew a tiny bead of blood. "All they ask is that you acknowledge them."

He looked at her again and saw there was something powerful in her expression. *Kiss me* her eyes seemed to say. *Kiss me now,* and all will be right with the world. *Kiss me* and we can both be saved. But he blinked instead and the moment was lost.

"The monk has a poor way with words," he reflected solemnly, "but there's truth in them just the same." He glanced back to where Holger was lighting the ship's main lantern. He could feel the darkness pressing in on them again. "Gilbert *was* a martyr," he said with a look of shame, "and I am just as surely damned to hell."

How different it had all seemed just eight days before. With an unexpected catch of fish, Robin once more taking exercise on the main deck, and Alyne performing a jolly new composition about two lascivious women called Dido and Lavinia who were both shamelessly in love with the same knight, the fog of gloom which had threatened to engulf them now appeared to be lifting. Even Rosamond had recovered sufficiently from her 'loss' to swing recklessly on a rope chair Ralph of Shrewsbury and Roger of Doncaster had erected for her. And with Gilbert now preferring the isolation of his mattress to his lonely post at the stern, Philip had pushed all thoughts of treacherous shipmates to the back of his mind and dared to hope things might slowly return to normal.

It was Elizabeth who spotted it first. "He has the sweating sickness,"[17] she informed Philip gravely, after Gilbert had again waved away her offer of food. "In a matter of days it will consume him completely. We must find land and put him ashore."

Philip stared across to where Gilbert sat wrapped in a bundle of clothing and blankets, no human part of him visible except for a hand that even from this distance appeared to shake uncontrollably as it clutched a water flagon. "Holger says we're some way yet from sighting land," he whispered anxiously, trying to keep the rising panic from his voice.

---

[17] ***Tuberculosis, considered highly contagious and for which there was no known cure.***

"Then we must quickly find some other solution," she replied calmly. "Delay any longer and we shall all be put at risk."

Philip needed time to think. As a boy at Sainte-Genevieve he'd enjoyed solving difficult problems, weighing one imponderable against another. Indeed, it was this scholarly approach that had made him such an outstanding pupil. The trouble was the world moved at a different pace, and away from the monastery such deliberation began to look like indecisiveness, something they could ill afford with Gilbert's condition rapidly worsening.

Seeing the uncertainty in his eyes, and fearing any failure to act now would only hasten their demise, Elizabeth took matters into her own hands and went straight to Holger, who quickly summoned the others. Not surprisingly their verdict was unequivocal.

"The longer he remains on board, the more chance there is of the sickness spreading," Harold of Leicester told Philip. "The matter must be settled now."

"What would you have me do?" Philip implored unhappily, "we're Christian Knights and we live by our faith in Christ. Gilbert is our brother."

"Your faith in Christ won't save you and it won't save your *brother* either," Holger replied with typical bluntness. Despite Brother Geoffrey's best efforts, the grizzled steersman had clung doggedly to the Old Norse gods of blood and thunder and by their lore there was only one solution. "He must be thrown overboard or made to jump," he proclaimed. "And either way it must be done quickly."

When Philip shook his head and told them he needed 'more time to think', the blustery rogue Roger of Doncaster drew his sword, as he had a habit of doing on such occasions, and volunteered to 'finish it now, with one swift thrust.' At which point Brother Geoffrey, who'd hitherto said very little, grabbed up a crossbow and furiously declared Gilbert's suffering to be 'holy in origin', and a 'divine test of their faith'. Announcing he would 'strike down' the first man who dared 'raise a sword' against his Christian brother, he urged them all to return to their duties where he recommended 'fasting and prayer' as a means of 'invoking God's mercy.'

Holger looked ready to set upon the monk right there and then, but the bolt in the crossbow was loaded and whatever else he might have been, Geoffrey wasn't the type to make idle threats.

"He has a dog shaped demon in his lungs," Holger snarled angrily, "and when it starts to cough, each and every one of us shall feel its bite!"

"Then the sooner we get to praying the better it will be for all," Geoffrey answered firmly, crossbow raised, daring any one of them to make the first move.

And that's how things remained for the rest of the morning, with the young monk stood guard over Gilbert, whilst the others attended the ship, occasionally pausing in a huddle around Holger, their voices low, their eyes furtive, as if waiting for the right moment to strike.

At some point the wind dropped, and with no one inclined to row, and nothing in the sky but a few wispy scraps of cloud, the ship lingered becalmed, as if stubbornly refusing to continue until the matter had been properly resolved.

Shortly before midday, Gisbourne further complicated matters by buckling on his sword and taking up a position alongside Geoffrey. Whether this was out of genuine sympathy for Gilbert or simply because he felt compelled to put himself at odds with everyone else, it was impossible to say. Even Oswald of Norwich, stumbling past Philip with his umpteenth ale horn of the day was prompted to observe. "One part of him shepherd, one part of him fox, and all parts contrary to the point of spite."

With Gisbourne's sword now added to Geoffrey's crossbow, an uneasy truce prevailed, with the ship effectively divided between those like Holger, Roger of Doncaster and most of the others, who wanted a quick 'solution' to the problem, and Geoffrey who saw any such 'solution' as a direct challenge to the will of God.

In such a febrile atmosphere, it became increasingly difficult for Philip to chart a diplomatic course between the two factions. And fearing it was only a matter of time before he'd be forced to take sides, he sought out Robin, who sat alone, plying the drawstring on his bow, seemingly oblivious to the crisis unfolding around him. The two men had not spoken to each other since the incident at the mainmast eleven days ago, and Robin's behaviour since had made it clear he was in no hurry to renew the acquaintance. But Philip was desperate, and Robin seemed the only one on board not galvanised by some form of hysteria.

“What am I to do?” he implored miserably, the quiet despair in his voice matched only by the wretched expression on his face.

“Why seek my advice?” Robin asked calmly, strengthening and adjusting the drawstring. Before adding wryly that Geoffrey hadn’t felt similarly inclined to grab up a crossbow and stand guard when *his* life had been threatened.

“There is justice and there is murder,” Philip rejoined sharply, “and the two are not to be confused.” It was a poor answer and it did little to ease the tension between them.

Robin flexed his muscles and stretched the bow, making great play of how the bruising to his ribs made this extremely difficult. “You’ve already made your decision,” he told Philip with a grimace, “all you seek now is my approval for it.”

Philip ignored Robin’s discomfort and looked at him. “Do you approve?” he asked hopefully.

Robin put down his bow. “No,” he replied flatly. “And even if I did, two minds in accord don’t make a thing right.”

Philip dropped his voice and moved closer. “Then you would happily die here, with the dog in your lungs?”

“I would *happily die* anywhere,” Robin answered evenly, “that is the difference between us.” And he rested his head against the side of the ship and closed his eyes, the pale sun bathing his face, a man completely at peace with the world.

Philip stared at him, incredulous, then with a huffy snort turned away. *No piss,* he told himself disdainfully, *no piss at all!*

As Gilbert's oldest friend, and virtually the only other person on board not intent upon his murder, Philip was the one crew member, apart from Gisbourne whom Geoffrey would permit near the beleaguered young knight. He arrived at regular intervals with food and water, sometimes pausing to wipe the fine sheen of sweat from Gilbert's brow, though he was careful never to remove the protective silk mask Rosamond's maid had fashioned for him.

"How many days do I have?" Gilbert asked, as the sun waned on the third afternoon.

"How many days are there in a lifetime?" Philip quipped, with an awkward chuckle that was neither comforting nor convincing.

Gilbert reached out and shakily pulled aside the silk mask, trying to discern an answer in his friend's eyes. Philip met his look evenly, not even a flicker of concern in his expression. In a braver man such composure would have been commendable, in Philip it was nothing short of extraordinary. Unfortunately it also told Gilbert exactly what he wanted to know. He replaced the mask and smiled grimly. "I see." He pushed the food away with an air of resignation and slumped back against the side of the ship. He understood perfectly now. "Am I to jump, or do you intend to throw me in?"

"Don't be foolish," Philip urged with a hail-fellow heartiness. "By tomorrow morning you'll be well again."

"By *tomorrow morning* I'll be barking like a dog," Gilbert responded bluntly. "Any fool can see that."

Philip picked up the bowl of food and told him it was strength he needed and that everything else could wait. But Gilbert knew it couldn't wait, and took a firm grip on his friend's arm. "I would drink something first," he said, the gravity in his voice forestalling all objections. "Have Elizabeth prepare me a tonic." He paused to glance at Gisbourne and Geoffrey, before adding in a whisper. "Tell her it must be swift and leave no trace. I would hate for Gisbourne to seek revenge on my behalf." His face crinkled in amusement as Philip feigned shock. "Come now Philip," he cajoled, "no false dealing here, the thought is already in your head. I simply give voice to it."

Philip looked away in shame. *Let this cup pass from my lips* he thought. "You speak of murder," he whispered solemnly.

"I speak of friendship," Gilbert replied, the wind rousing suddenly in the sails, as if stirred by the sentiment, "one life given, so many can be saved."

Philip started to shake his head but Gilbert cuffed him smartly on the cheek. "We are out of time." He said. "Do as I say. And afterwards, when it's done, look to Huntingdon, he is your man now."

Brother Geoffrey and Gisbourne glanced around to see what was happening, but Gilbert held up a trembling hand to allay their fears. "All goes well," he called out, "just two old friends making plans for the future."

That evening Philip found Elizabeth at the cooking brazier, and took her quietly to one side. "The dog Lycomedes," he began awkwardly, "after he'd taken the measure, was there much suffering?"

She frowned and told him she had no idea what he was talking about. But Philip was in no mood to play games. "I have it in my power to change your status on this ship Elizabeth," he warned her irately. "In the blink of an eye I could turn you into a rag for Holger and his boon companions."

She stared at him in defiance, and with the barest hint of a tremble on her lip, reminded him that surely it was to 'save' her from precisely such a 'fate' that Robin and he had intervened 'so bravely' on her behalf in the first place.

She had a guile with words and Philip was immediately shamed. "Forgive me," he croaked unhappily, "this business with Gilbert..." his voice trailed off and his head slumped disconsolately as his eyes came to rest on the sturdy timbers at her feet.

She stepped closer. "But if you require my help," she reassured him softly, "you have only to ask." And with the tips of her fingers, she gently lifted his chin so that their eyes met in silent complicity. There was no going back now and he knew it.

"I *do* ask," he whispered quietly.

After it was done, and the sun had set and everyone had fallen into a fitful sleep, apart from Oswald of Norwich who stood watch at the bow, ale horn in hand, Robin joined him at the stern. They stood alone in the darkness, beneath a shimmering infinity of stars, neither one of them quite sure where to begin.

Philip was first to break the silence. "If you seek for justice," he said without turning. "I ask only that you show patience. A line is forming and you are not at its head."

"A line," Robin raised a playful eyebrow, as if impressed. "And we still have some distance yet to travel."

Philip stared into the shapeless night. "Have you not heard," he announced dryly, "I am already stood at Satan's gate."

Robin tilted his head towards the heavens, endless and unfathomable and twinkling with mystery. Had it been like this on the very first day he wondered? "We are all stood at Satan's gate," he ventured quietly, and there was genuine sympathy in his voice this time.

Philip closed his eyes, more grateful than Robin would ever realise. "I wish only goodwill between us Robert," he replied wearily, trying to keep the emotion from his voice, "if such a thing is still possible."

Robin smiled, even though it hurt his bruised jaw to do so. "Friends call me *Robin*," he reminded him for the umpteenth time.

Friends, the word creaked accusingly in the timbers beneath them, sloshing lightly up against the ship's hull, rocking them to and fro with its gentle insistence. *Friends* complicate things Philip thought. They make demands that are unreasonable and then let you down when you need them most. *Friends* are buried at sea, with dogs and effluent, and rotten food.

He swallowed heavily as he remembered Gisbourne holding the wooden goblet to his nose and sniffing suspiciously. He'd been so angered by the insinuation that he'd grabbed the goblet back and raised it to his own lips. *"Damn you Gisbourne, if it's proof you need!"* He would have drained it too, such was his mood. But Gisbourne had laid a restraining hand on his sleeve, his eyes filling with childish emotion as he proclaimed *"friends have no need to prove their love."*

Perhaps it was because Gisbourne had no friends himself, that he placed such sentimental value on their importance. Or perhaps it was because deep down he knew what Gilbert was about to do for them. *What greater love hath a man?* Philip shut his eyes. He saw two boys playing together in the haze of a distant French summer. *Friends I have in abundance.* And he saw Gilbert's smile slowly fade as the goblet slipped gently from his hand. *God wash this stain from my soul.*

Philip kept his eyes closed. He could feel the darkness growing around him again, only this time it felt like it was growing inside him as well as outside. In the morning he would speak to Alyne. The young Irishman would find a suitable verse for Gilbert in his history of 'great deeds done beyond the seas'. In word and rhyme they would put everything right. Gilbert's eyes would shine again, his days would grow brighter, and even the birth stain on his cheek would disappear. But until then Philip had an overwhelming urge just to tell someone the simple truth. He handed Robin the small silver coin he had retrieved from the ship's deck the day Gilbert and the others had shackled him to the mainmast. "You don't want to be my friend Robert," he said softly. "Friends fare badly where I am concerned. A man is much better judged by his enemies. In their fervour you will find his true reflection."

TWELVE

North East coast of Vinland
The feast of Saint Catherine of Alexandra
25th November 1182.

Fourteen days later and they finally had their first sighting of land. It rose without warning on the horizon, grey and indistinct, like the dark humps of a great sea monster. Shimmering on the curve of dawn, it gradually took shape, before disappearing abruptly into a squall of messy weather, briefly re-emerging a short while later, only to vanish again as more rain swept in. It continued to play this maddening game of hide and seek for the rest of the morning, leaving Philip and the others increasingly frustrated as each 'sighting' proved more fleeting and illusory than the one before.

As the day wore on, and their enthusiasm for the 'hunt' began to wane, Robin found his thoughts wandering back to his childhood days in Locksley. Things had been much simpler then. A young man learnt to rely on his instincts in the great forests of Sherwood and Barnsdale. He learnt to trust God and accept each day for what it brought him rather than what he wanted it to bring, even when what it brought him was almost unendurable.

With a sudden pang, he remembered his mother, the rot already in her bones, her lips moving soundlessly as she beckoned to him. *"The sickness in her is like rust,"* he'd heard them telling his father.

"It does not abate or relént." And when he'd shut his eyes to pray he could picture it spreading through her body, eating its way into her heart like a black fungus.

He stared into the grey clouds bunched on the horizon and forced himself to picture her last day. He saw the priest and his father stood at the hearth, heated whispers in an orange glow. *"The designs of the Almighty are unknowable William, and woe to him that casts a shadow of doubt on them."* And he saw himself, some fifteen years younger, walking slowly past them, oblivious to everything apart from the summoning finger that drew him weakly to her bedside.

Her face had become sunken and pale, but her eyes burned as brightly as ever. She caressed his wet cheek with a soft hand, smiling in gentle reproof at his distress. *"Don't be anxious Robert. I'm going to the most wonderful place."* And because she knew he didn't trust himself to speak, she told him the story again. The one he always loved to hear.

"When our dear Lord was dying on the cross, the Robin flew to His side and, to give comfort in His pain, sang sweetly into His ear. With his tiny beak he picked at the sharp thorns in Our Saviour's brow, prising them loose one by one. Until that day the Robin had been a plain brown bird, but the Holy Blood stained his breast. And because God was so impressed, He decreed that from that day on, every Robin would bear the mark of Christ upon them, so all would know that not even the smallest act of kindness goes unnoticed."

He felt her tremulous fingers weave through his hair, ruffling it proudly one last time. *"Pick at the thorns Robert. No matter how many you find. Pick at every single one."* Her face seemed to glow with love for a moment, and all the puzzlement and fear which had oppressed him for so long suddenly vanished. She pressed something into the palm of his hand, and when he looked he saw a small silver coin, the same one she had placed there on the morning of his birth. *"The child who receives always gives. And the child who gives always receives. Promise me Robert. Promise..."*

He opened his mouth to promise, but it was already too late. And even from this great distance he felt his eyes mist and his throat tighten as he remembered the weight of his father's hand on his shoulder and the throb of grief in his voice. *"Be still now son. Let her be. She's passed from this world."*

"I see it!" Elizabeth's sudden cry yanked him abruptly from the dark clutches of memory and dumped him firmly back on the ship's deck. He looked up, and there it was, a thin band of misty blue hills and deep green forests, rising from the ocean like the battlements of an overgrown castle. He drew breath sharply, not quite sure whether to believe it or not.

All around him people were rushing to the rail and stabbing fingers at the horizon, and suddenly there was no longer any doubt and everyone on board was cheering and hugging each other. And before they knew it, Robin and Philip were embracing too, and Philip was shouting above the commotion, "I told you

Robert. I told you we would find it." And in all the excitement Robin forgot about the small brown bird picking at the thorns, he forgot about his mother's fingers in his hair and why he always insisted that friends call him *Robin*, he even forgot about Gilbert's sword at his throat. Instead he found himself swept along on a wave of unbridled emotion. And as he embraced Philip he found himself embracing the notion that in facing adversity they'd become firm friends again. And that nothing or no one in the entire world was ever going to change that.

* * *

Marian wondered if the priest had heard her. She waited a moment and then said it again, much louder this time. "I don't love him father." And she suddenly realised it wasn't a confession at all. It was a plea for help. "I love his brother. I love Eustace." There, she'd finally said it. Now let the heavens fall. She braced herself, but still there was no response from behind the small black grate opposite.

Marian squinted into the gloom, and for the first time she began to notice something strange about the small confessional booth in which she was knelt. For one thing it kept changing shape. And then there was the smoke, thick, grey ropey coils of it, drifting out through the grate. She knew *that* smoke, knew what it meant. And even though she couldn't see him, she felt his eye upon her, as she'd felt it upon her every day since he'd destroyed the settlement and taken her captive almost a year ago.

She looked up to discover the curve of the church roof was suddenly gone and she was staring at open sky instead. She got unsteadily to her feet and in the same instant found herself stood at the edge of a glistening pond, the same one she'd waded in as a child. *I'm dreaming* she thought. But she wasn't dreaming, she was *drifting*, floating on a temporal mist through a landscape of memories and half memories, one moment walking across the furrowed soil of her youth, the next lying on her back in the long grass near the animal traps, Eustace at her side, church bells peeling in the distance.

She watched the birds circle above them. I'm not here she told herself dreamily. And none of this is here either. It's all a lie, an illusion. Something *he* wants me to see.

No sooner had the thought entered her mind, than the entire tableau in front of her disappeared and she found herself back in the longhouse, blinking up at the uppowoc smoke which hung in the hollows overhead like a thick fog. She knew where she was now, and more importantly, she knew where *he* was too. She could hear him breathing, feel the heavy rise and fall of his chest as he lay next to her, *dreaming her dreams*.

She tried to lift her head, but it was no use. The sacred herb had filled her with such a lethargy that even raising an arm required more strength than she possessed. She stared up at the barrel shaped roof high above. I'm trapped inside a beehive she thought, too heavy to fly, a drowsy bee, weighted down with honey.

She closed her eyes, and with the tips of her fingers felt blindly for the hunting knife she knew he kept at his side. *But this bee can still sting.* And though she was barely able to move, she willed herself to find it, long fingers creeping spider-like through the dark. *Picture it in your head* she told herself, *feel your hand close around it.* She sensed him stir anxiously next to her. Good, she thought. Now he can scramble in his dreams to make sense of things. From out of nowhere, Eustace appeared, and they were back in the long summer grass again. But she bit down hard upon her lip, the sudden pain forcing the vision from her head. In the same instant her hand closed on the knife and she heard the sleeping figure next to her emit a tiny cry from his throat. She smiled.

"Tomakin", she whispered into the dark. "Tomakin, I have something for thee." And with a tremendous effort she rolled over and thrust the knife deep into the sleeping shaman's chest.

* * *

Though he'd said nothing, Holger had known they were close to land for several days. He'd heard and felt it's 'signs' everywhere, from the distant screech of an unseen bird soaring high overhead, to the tiny pinch of an insect crawling on the back of his hand. Yet now they were finally here he seemed more irascible than ever. It was almost as if having got this far, he suddenly resented the prospect of sharing his secret world with them. And as Rosamond jumped up and down, excitedly clapping her hands, he interjected sourly that there was ‘still some distance yet to travel’ and that ‘no one was to put ashore’ until he’d found a ‘suitable place to weigh anchor for the night,’ adding that he would turn the ship around and head for home should his orders not be observed.

Yet after nine largely joyless weeks at sea, not even Holger’s crabbiness could dampen their spirits and it was Brother Geoffrey, ever ready with a prayer on his lips who best encapsulated their feelings as he raised his arms to heaven apostrophising loudly, “at the beginning of the world, there were no slaves and there were no masters. The land was unspoilt and all upon it had plenty.” Whereupon many of the young knights, Robin and Philip included, fell to their knees, crossing themselves devoutly and beating their breasts as they gave fulsome thanks for their delivery. Even Walter of Malmesbury, who usually scoffed at such displays, found himself crying uncontrollably on Rosamond’s shoulder as he promised her that in this ‘sacred place’, they would ‘make the world anew.’

Unfortunately Holger appeared in no particular hurry to help them, and spent the rest of the day traversing the endless coastline with all the trepidation of a mouse who knows there’s a hungry cat waiting. When he did finally find a suitable spot to weigh anchor, it was already getting dark and the general consensus was that any trip to the shore would have to wait until the following morning.

Perhaps to forestall a growing sense of anti-climax, Rosamond and some of the others, Ralph of Shrewsbury and Oswald of Norwich most notable among them, decided it would be a good idea if they drank and sang a little to 'celebrate' their safe arrival.

Not surprisingly Brother Geoffrey disagreed, citing prayer and reflection not 'ribaldry' as the best preparation for the day ahead. And for once he had a point. Apart from Holger, no one on board had the slightest idea who or what they might encounter once they stepped ashore. A keen eye and steady hand would be the least of their requirements, neither of which were guaranteed by a night of heavy drinking and dancing. Something both Robin and Gisbourne recognised as they stood by the ship's main rail and surveyed the mysterious coastline opposite.

"Banishing him from our thoughts won't dull his blade," Gisbourne opined soberly, "nor stand him idle when the time for battle comes." He tightened his hand around the rail, suppressing the flurry of involuntary jerks and twitches that shivered up and down his spine. He glanced back at Rosamond and the others, his eyes narrowing in contempt. "And making high revel only brings him quicker to our table."

Robin kept his eyes focused on the land opposite, rolling his mother's silver coin thoughtfully between his fingers. A thicker darkness was falling now, cloaking the woods and mountains in even deeper secrecy. "There cannot be worse things in forests, than there are in castles," he mused quietly. "And men remain men, wherever they roam."

Gisbourne smiled at the note of apprehension in Robin's voice. "So long as they *roam* on two legs and their blood runs red, you'll hear no complaint from me," he said teasingly. "Until then, I'll speak to the one whose *family are in good favour with the King*, and have him put a stop to this Navarre witch and her merrymaking."

But the idea of 'merrymaking' had already found favour with the rest of the crew and Philip, remembering how Gisbourne had undermined him during the dispute over Gilbert, refused to support the imposition of a curfew, warning it would lead to 'certain discord' should he or anyone else attempt to enforce it. Adding slyly, that the 'spectacle' of Christian Knights arguing with each other would surely give more succour to any watching enemy than a little harmless revelry. As usual, his words were diplomatically weighted to make them sound both reasonable and disparaging at the same time, leaving Gisbourne uncertain whether he was being placated or reprimanded. And seeing the carousing was already well underway and that neither Robin nor Brother Geoffrey appeared ready to back him up, the young knight slunk away, somewhat despondently, to his mattress.

Now there was no longer anyone around to disapprove, a strange, almost anarchic spirit took hold of the revellers, and nine weeks of pent up frustrations were finally released in one glorious surge. With Walter wearing his brightest colours, Ralph of Shrewsbury giving a bravura imitation of Gisbourne at the last supper, Alyne singing with a lustiness he'd hitherto suppressed, and Rosamond and her two handmaidens dancing as if their very lives depended on it, Oswald of Norwich was left with the simple task of ensuring the whole thing was washed along on a copious tide of ale, a purpose for which he might have been born.

Philip watched from a distance. This is madness, he thought. But after everything that had happened since that first day in Barnsdale Forest, it was a madness he could cope with. Even Robin seemed to be enjoying himself, and as the revelry grew more raucous, Rosamond gathered him suddenly by the arm and swept him quickly away from the main deck, the swirl of her dress giving the impression that she floated as they ascended the few steps to her small cabin below.

The moment they were inside she wrapped herself around him, smothering his face in drunken kisses, and forcing her tongue deep inside his mouth. When she felt him begin to resist, she redoubled her efforts, working her hands feverishly until he broke away completely. She seized hold of him again, grappling franticly to return her mouth to his, only for him to pull away more forcibly this time. She stared at him in bewilderment. "Is it not to your liking?" she asked, genuinely perplexed.

Robin shook his head, telling her they were both "muddled" from "too much ale". He turned for the door, but she moved speedily to block his path. She'd waited too long to let this moment slip from her grasp now.

"Am I not shaped according to your taste?" she enquired coyly. When he didn't reply, she took a step forward. "The timbers on this ship hold few secrets," she said moving herself slowly against him, "I hear everything you men say," and she put her hands gently to work on him again, "how you pry into the secrets of my body, how you desire to put each part of it to the fullest use." She smiled as she felt him stir. "My knight has raised his sword," she whispered, "now let Guinevere show him how to joust."

But Robin pulled free of her once again, this time pushing her hands away when she tried to restrain him. This was too much for Rosamond and her face changed suddenly, its elfin prettiness transformed by anger. "Perhaps you'd prefer it if I summoned Walter of Malmesbury," she cried. "Maybe he has something to offer that is more to your favour!"

"Summon whoever you will," Robin replied bluntly, "I shall not bed with you,"

"Then we shall both die wondering," she snapped heatedly, adding that the 'wondering would profit no one', whilst predicting that many years from now he would 'tug himself dizzy' in frustration as he remembered the opportunity he'd spurned tonight.

"It may well be the case," he confessed solemnly, "and I would not wish to cause offence. But I have given my word to the Virgin, and I dare not break it now."

"What *virgin*?" she demanded irritably, as though the woman might actually be hiding on board somewhere. Seeing Robin smile at this she was about to shout again when her eyes suddenly lit up with understanding. "You seek for love," she declared in amazement. "Robin Goodfellow seeks for love and has made his pledge to the Holy Mother not to weaken until he finds it."

She was laughing at him now, but it wasn't her derision Robin minded so much as what she said next. "You think yourself a man of will, but deep inside, you're just like him. A charmless cotter."[18] She didn't use Philip's name, but they both knew who she meant. "You crave something you cannot have. And the more it eludes you, the more you search for it, blaming everything and everyone but yourself for its absence."

Her words stung because in many ways they were true. Philip's strengths, his tenacity and guile, his notions of chivalry that bordered on the romantic, were Robin's strengths too. But so were the many shadows they cast, the stubbornness and pretence, the need to create one's own myth. Something Robin was only dimly beginning to appreciate.

"I seek only truth," he told her with as much grace as he could muster; though he struggled to keep the hint of pique from his voice.

She laughed bitterly. "There is no such thing," she stated. "*Truth* is a myth, a grey song of the heart. It dulls our passion for life and refuses us comfort when we need it most."

He'd never heard her speak so cynically before. Up until now he'd considered her immature and occasionally even stupid, but never cold. "Who told you such a thing?" he enquired softly, with a sudden

---

[18] ***A class status barely above 'serf'.***

pity in his voice that suggested he was picturing the large, empty, motherless rooms of her childhood.

This was too much for Rosamond. There was only one reaction she wanted to see in Robin's eyes when he looked at her, and it certainly wasn't pity. "Go swill ale with your shepherd girls," she sneered dismissively, shooing him from the cabin with a flurry of her hand, "there are plenty of other men here with grit in them."

She was right too. There were plenty. And Ralph of Shrewsbury was one of them, though even as they tumbled back onto her mattress a short while later he was beginning to have second thoughts. It wasn't that Rosamond was lacking when it came to the rigours of the *'joust'*, quite the reverse, and he might even have enjoyed himself if only she hadn't spent the entire time talking about Robin and his wretched 'pledge of abstinence'. It got to the point where he had to conjure up biblical images of his own, albeit ones from Sodom and Gomorrah just to complete the encounter.

"Any fool can seek for love," she declared tetchily as he brought their brief union to an unsatisfying conclusion. "Is it not enough for a man to pledge his soul, why must he pledge his body also?" And as they rolled apart, she announced that if Vinland proved a 'disappointment', she would return to England and find herself a "husband worthy of the name."

Realising this immediately ruled him out, Ralph of Shrewsbury responded with customary good humour, and proclaimed his 'utmost faith' in her ability to find such a man, adding that even if she didn't he was confident there were 'men aplenty, already wed' who would quickly make up for it.

He'd meant it as a compliment of course; the barefoot beauty no red blooded male could resist. Yet for a compliment to find favour, it must also contain a kernel of truth, which was why she struck him so hard across the face. Because she knew it *was* true. And therefore it was no compliment at all.

Much earlier that day, far beyond the great swathes of forest, Robin and the others could see from the ship's rail, Tomakin woke with a sudden gasp, his heart racing. He looked down, half expecting to find the knife still embedded in his chest. But there was nothing, not even a bloodstain. He felt with his fingers and discovered it still lay by his side, sheathed and unused.

He turned to look at Marian. She lay on her back, arms limp, lifeless eyes staring up into the smoky gloom. He prodded her with his foot. When she gave no response he raised himself sluggishly and reaching across, dug his long black fingernails deep into her cheek. Still she didn't move.

He frowned. Was it really possible? Had she crept into his dreams while he was sleeping and turned them against him? For the first time he noticed the tiny curve of a smile on her lips. The wendigo in him snarled angrily and bared its teeth. *Finish her* it growled. *Use the mask. Gorge on her!* But Tomakin told the wendigo to be still. *Father* will decide, he thought. *Father* will know what to do next. After all, it was *father* who'd told him to take the woman in the first place. As soon as she could stand, he would take Marian to his cave, and if *father* willed it, he would cut out her heart and eat it right there in front of him.

Long after the 'merrymaking', with the ship rocking gently at anchor and everyone on board sleeping, the one who still sought to betray them felt something warm move against his legs. Lifting his head, he discovered one of Rosamond's handmaidens, the younger and more comely of the two, clambering on top of him.

"Have no fear," she whispered, the slur in her voice indicating she was still heavily 'in ale'. "I wish only to tell you something." She sat herself astride him, like a rider taking the saddle. "But first I would kiss you." She leant forward and pressed her lips to his, though it was more of a wet splodge than a kiss. "There," she sighed drunkenly, "now Judas is repaid, and the *traitor* finds himself kissed in return."

His blood ran cold, though he feigned amusement. "Bold humour," he chuckled nervously, "and twice as funny for being said with such sincerity."

She smiled down at him, her long hair tickling his cheek. "Five summers ago you came to my village and won a prize for shooting arrows. Afterwards you lay with my sister in the meadow by the river. I hid in a tree nearby and watched. I've carried your face with me ever since. You went by another name then. Shall I tell you what it was?"

The traitor hurriedly glanced around, but only Roger of Doncaster, stood watch at the far end of the ship, was still awake. "I have a hefty purse," he began anxiously, "and the sum in it will double once I return to England."

But she hushed him with a second wet kiss. "Take breath," she whispered soothingly, "I have no mind to betray you. Quite the reverse, I seek your help."

Despite this assurance, he sensed the unspoken addendum *'or else!'* in her voice and decided it was probably best to play along. "Tell me," he began cautiously, "how may I serve you?"

She drew closer, until their lips were almost touching again. "*Serve* me with justice," she purred, and proceeded to tell him about Rosamond's father Godwin, and how through 'cruel usury'[19] he'd brought about the ruin of her own family and driven them all to beggary.

"I watched my father finish his days in the manor fields," she told him quietly, "roped to a heavy plough like a workhorse, whilst I was forced to wait hand and foot on the daughter of the man who'd put him there." She rested her head on the traitor's chest and shut her eyes. "I care not how you finish your business with Philip Mark and his bowman," she reassured him candidly, "all I wish is that you make sure a great tragedy befalls my mistress. And that I am present when it does to witness to it!"

---

[19] ***Taking excessive interest on a loan.***

The following morning, as soon as Brother Geoffrey had said Mass, they unsheathed the oars and rowed eagerly for the headland, singing God's praises as they went. After nine long weeks, they had finally arrived in Vinland.

THIRTEEN

North East Vinland, the 'Great Eastern Woodlands Region'
The feast of Saint Crispina of Tagora
5th December 1182.

They were being tracked. Robin had known it from the outset, but now the others were beginning to sense it too. Hand signals had replaced spoken words. Trees were no longer marked to guide the way back. And Roger of Doncaster, whose crunching footfalls had scattered the woodlands at the start of their journey, now trod with the deftness of an angel. Yet still the feeling persisted. Someone or *something* was watching them.

As the day wore on, their imaginations grew increasingly feverish, until eventually each rustling leaf or tremulous branch was transformed into something more sinister. Only Philip remained impervious to these delusions, pressing ahead with the zeal of a young Moses, pausing only to chide them for their caution.

Since the death of Gilbert, a remarkable change had come over Philip. Gone were the lengthy periods of deliberation. Now he did everything at speed, pouring himself into each task as though it were his last. It was almost as if the loss of his friend had engendered in him a new spirit of recklessness, chasing away all wistful notions of 'great deeds done beyond the seas,' and replacing them with a grim-faced determination just to get the job finished.

"We have our end in sight," he snorted irately as Robin drew them to a halt for the umpteenth time that morning, "yet you continue to go about it like a gong farmer[20]. Raise a song and walk boldly. We have nothing to fear from this place but our own anxiety."

Robin stared into the dense woodlands. Here and there a shaft of sunlight had penetrated the towering conifers, piercing the shady brown aisles below with misty columns of gold. He riveted his eyes on the display, wondering at its subtle beauty. On the crossing over there'd been a paucity of such colours. Now there was a deluge of them, and he was struggling to adjust.

"We'll sing when the job is done," he said presently. "As for having 'nothing to fear'…" His eyes wandered between the trees, trying to locate the source of his unease. "…There are shadows in these woods and they move of their own accord. When we know their business, then we'll know how much we have to fear."

Phillip scoffed. Unlike Robin, he had no interest in familiarising himself with the vagaries of this strange new land. He cared little about its smoky blue hills or billowing grasslands, and certainly had no wish to acquaint himself with any of its abundant wildlife. As to whatever poetry was to be found in its boundless woods and rivers, he'd happily leave that up to Alyne. All that concerned him now was finding Marian and getting her back to the ship again, preferably as swiftly as possible. A purpose in no way

---

[20] ***A serf employed to clean out castle cesspits.***

assisted by Robin's insistence on stopping each time a twig was heard to snap.

"How many times am I to say it?" he sighed wearily. "Your *shadows* are as children. They play at hiding but they offer no threat. And the longer we labour in discussion over them, the more mischievous they will become."

Robin looked far from convinced. "How many 'children' can track a man as silently as this one," he asked wryly, "yet still remain hidden from view?"

Philip felt his cheeks burn. Was Robin mocking him? He swallowed hard. It was all Holger's fault he decided. Had the Norseman given them proper directions, they'd have located the settlement and rescued Marian by now. Moreover, they'd have his errant brother locked in chains and been busily storing provisions for the journey home. Instead of which, they were no closer to finding Eustace or any of the others than they had been nine days ago when the ship's keel had first touched sand and Philip had vaulted ashore with the steersman's assurances still ringing in his ears.

Of course, a less hasty man might have noted the so called 'unique' assemblages of rock and bay Holger accounted 'familiar landmarks' were in fact replicated many times over along the heavily wooded coastline. But Philip had spent his entire life being patient. Now for the first time he sensed the prize was within his grasp. And kneeling in the shingle, praying for the repose of Gilbert's soul, with the frothy tide lapping restlessly at his heels, he'd been unable to suppress a little shudder of delight each time he'd imagined the surprise on his younger brother's face when they finally caught up with him. It was only later, as he joined Robin atop a small hillock and saw a frown develop in the bowman's expression as he cast a careful eye over the landscape below, that Philip suffered his first real flutters of concern.

"How well do you suppose Holger knows these lands?" Robin asked him at length, contemplatively rolling the silver coin between his fingers. There was an inferred irony to the question, suggesting Robin had already drawn his own conclusions on the matter.

Philip tensed, his jaw tightening. "As well as any man who has been here," he rejoined defensively, more rattled by the insinuation than the enquiry itself. Adding quickly that Holger had not only 'been here' on two previous occasions, but had also returned both times to tell the tale.

"I have also *been* to places and *returned to tell the tale*." Robin stated flatly. "It does not follow that I *know* them."

Philip smiled thinly, adopting the tone of a weary parent, whose tolerance has been pushed to its limits. "We are but one moment on dry land," he sighed, "and already you find fault. Very well Robert, name your grievance, and I will do my best to rectify it."

Robin shook his head. "It is no *grievance*," he said, "we are safely arrived, and I thank God for that." He paused and reflected on the misty slopes of mountain and the endless canopy of woodland beneath. The furrow on his brow returned. "But there's a magnitude to this place," he mused. "And like Jonah perceiving the whale, I have no wish to find myself devoured by it."

Philip shrugged off his doubts and gave Robin a good natured slap on the back, confidently assuring him that the only one in danger of being 'devoured' was Eustace, and the quicker they got about it the sooner Robin would see that Holger's steering skills were beyond all contestation.

What wild delusions are borne on the hope of success! At the time Philip had no reason to doubt the grey-eyed Norseman. Indeed, so confident was he in Holger's abilities, that he'd even started making plans for the future, particularly with regard to Marian.

Up until that point he'd only concerned himself with the business of rescuing her. But with this almost achieved, he began to think about what he might do next. He realised it would be foolish of him to suppose things could simply revert to the way they'd been before. For one thing, he had no way of knowing how much she'd suffered at the hands of his younger brother. There would need to be a period of reflection he told himself. Some time spent in a nunnery perhaps. Not France, where people might talk, but England, where it rained all day, and penitence was said to be much harsher. Somewhere remote, yet not inaccessible, a place he could visit without arousing too much suspicion. Kirklees maybe, where the sisters were reputedly discreet and the world kept its distance. And then, after a suitable period of adjustment, he could summon her, and there would be a joyful reconciliation, followed by marriage and a new life together. By that time he would have secured a royal posting and they could put all this behind them. As to what he told their children? It would depend upon Eustace, and whether or not Philip decided to let him live. But either way their future would be assured. After all, his family were in good favour with the King.

Alas, all Philip's plans were in vain. As he quickly discovered, Eustace and his settlement were not to be found where Holger had assured him they'd be. Nor were they to be found anywhere in the immediate vicinity. And though the following days saw him significantly widen the area of search, one full week later there was still no sign of them.

Faced with the sudden possibility of failure, Philip had been forced to improvise. A new stratagem was hastily devised, and ignoring the advice of those around him, particularly Robin who counselled caution, he set off again at a relentless pace, this time in a direction of his own choosing.

To begin with he led them south, their thick boots crunching along shores salted with tiny fragments of shell, as they followed the winding coastline. Initially they made good progress, but gradually the terrain started to worsen and before long they found themselves wading blindly through acres of soggy grasslands. With no end in sight, Philip turned west, clambering up over a series of muddy ridges, before forging a narrow brown rivulet and heading further inland, where they quickly encountered the woods.

And it was here, several days later, stumbling amidst the endless columns of pine that Philip finally came face to face with reality. Tripping on a bony root, he dropped to his knees and, just as Robin had predicted, found himself suddenly looking up from the belly of Jonah's whale, to discover the men around him weary-eyed and jumping like rabbits at the crunch and snap of every twig.

Though he'd swiftly tried to rectify things, blithely promising each of them more money, not to mention a week's rest once they'd found Eustace and the others, it was already too late. By now most were already convinced the woods were conspiring to lead them astray, with secret pathways opening and closing and silent eyes watching their every move. Even Gisbourne had become infected by the idea, twitching awkwardly and pausing every few moments to indulge his compulsion for touching or checking things. He'd even started to emit the occasional *yelping* sound, which drew reproachful looks from the others, who by this stage had taken to continuing their journey in almost total silence.

As for *the one who would betray them*, he worked tirelessly to exploit these feelings of anxiety, whispering that Gisbourne was 'possessed by a demon', and suggesting the little *yelping* sounds were a signal to other demons already hiding in the woods. And as each afternoon drew to a close, he was quick to remind them of Holger's warning not to *'tarry too long in the woods, once the light is done'*.

At the same time he was constantly on the lookout for an opportunity to catch Philip alone. A few brief seconds was all he'd need. And afterwards, he'd simply blame the skraelings. Or better still, he'd start talking about the traitor again. Either way, he doubted he'd encounter too many problems. In such a febrile atmosphere, men as edgy as these were liable to believe anything.

All of which left him with just one small problem. What to do about Rosamond's maid? And he was still pondering this when Gisbourne suddenly stopped and discarded his long triangular shield, and without a word of explanation began unbuckling his sword, and removing the chain tunic and thickly padded aketon[21] he wore underneath. Philip immediately rushed over and demanded to know what was going on.

"If we are to travel in ever greater circles, with no map to guide us, and no plan for getting there, I will at least do so in comfort," Gisbourne returned sourly. And hearing this, Roger of Doncaster and one or two of the others, including the so-called 'mute' Crispin of Lincoln, began removing their armour too.

Philip fastened Gisbourne with a look. "We have been here but nine days," he reminded him. "Our search is only just begun."

"*Nine days* or nine hundred," Gisbourne replied, "if we have no idea where to look, and no strategy for looking, how are we to know if our search is *begun* or ended. Would you have us walk on blindly forever?"

It was a reasonable question. And one Philip had yet to fully answer. Moreover, Gisbourne wasn't the only one complaining. Just that morning, Rosamond had accused him of 'holding her prisoner'.

---

[21] ***Padded garment worn underneath mail armour.***

A typically gratuitous charge given that he'd only confined her to the relative safely of the ship for her own protection. But even Philip couldn't have imagined as he marched off with the rest of his small force that first morning that nine days later she and the other three women would still be languishing there.

At the same time, he knew it would be irresponsible to risk bringing them ashore too soon. So far there'd been no actual sighting of the indigenous population, but Robin had felt their presence everywhere. He was continuously stopping to examine some broken piece of leaf or barely discernible depression in the soil, his expression growing more pensive with every find. And when they paused to rest he would often sit apart, buried in his own troubled thoughts. After several days, when Philip had finally enquired, somewhat testily, if it was really necessary for him to stop and study every single item of foliage he came across, especially as it was beginning to unnerve the others, Robin had looked him quietly in the eye and replied: "If we wish to prosper in these undertakings, we cannot rely on what we know. We must learn the skraeling methods, and we must learn them quickly. For already I see much here that is mysterious to me."

Of course, had Philip stopped to think for a moment, he would have realised that marching men for days on end in heavy armour, with no particular destination in mind, was bound to wear on the resolve of even the hardiest amongst them. Let alone those like Ralph of Shrewsbury and Oswald of Norwich, who within a short time of setting out were already complaining about sore shoulders and blistered feet, and how the surrounding woodlands seemed to 'watch them'. But Philip had been in a hurry, and each subsequent day's disappointment had simply increased his sense of urgency.

Now, as he watched them discarding their shields and helmets into the dirt like so many pieces of unwanted baggage, he recognised it as a disaster of his own making. Even worse, he realised one foolish word out of place and the whole thing might quickly develop into a full scale insurrection. Nevertheless it was still his expedition, and he wasn't about to let it simply fall apart without a fight. And so he reminded them of the one detail he knew they couldn't ignore. Namely those 'invisible' skraelings he had hitherto dismissed as 'fevered imaginings'. What would happen he asked, if the savages fell upon them now with their heathen cries and blunt war instruments. Without armour, how would they protect themselves?

It was Gisbourne who replied, stating with customary hauteur, that it was his understanding Philip accounted all such 'savages' no more dangerous than 'harmless children', and that anyway in an environment such as this, it would be far easier to fight without the restriction of heavy garments.

Maybe it was the disappointment of not finding Eustace. Or maybe it was simply because he had grown to dislike Gisbourne even more than he disliked Brother Geoffrey. But whatever the reason, Philip momentarily forgot himself and angrily countered that wearing no armour might well make it 'easier' for them to fight, but it would also make it much 'easier' for them to turn tail and run away too!

There was an abrupt hush. Anxious eyes suddenly forgot about the surrounding trees and their disconcerting shadows and focused instead on the two men now stood facing each other. Gisbourne frowned, as if he hadn't quite heard, and for a brief moment Philip wondered if he might be able to retrieve the situation. But then he saw the spark of anger in Gisbourne's eyes as he registered the charge, and realised it was already too late. Having spoken the words, he would now have to stand by them, or beg forgiveness. Philip gritted his teeth and prepared for the worst.

"I am a Knight of Christ," Gisbourne said at length, unable to quite master the little twitch at play on his shoulder. "And I *run away* from no man."

Philip gestured toward the armour abandoned at his feet. "Yet I am persuaded to the contrary?" he replied calmly. "And I feel no requirement to set the gloss of religion upon it." Strangely enough, the starkness of the situation had filled him with a sudden and powerful sense of equanimity, and he spoke the words with the quiet assurance of man who is no longer afraid.

This strange calmness appeared to briefly wrong foot Gisbourne. He searched Philip's face intently for some sign of weakness, but found instead only steely resolve. He twitched slightly. Was it possible he'd underestimated the man now stood opposite him? And Gisbourne wasn't alone in wondering this. Even *the one who would betray them* was no longer sure.

He glanced around nervously to see if anyone was going to intervene. But he needn't have worried. Gisbourne's reputation had cast its own spell. And with Brother Geoffrey back on the ship, no one was about to risk their life attempting to save someone who'd spent the last nine days marching them around in circles, whilst continuously berating them for their supposed idleness.

Except that is, for Robin. The man from Locksley clearly hadn't forgotten the pledge he'd made to protect Philip, nor the strong bond he'd felt when the two of them had embraced on the ship. And the traitor noticed how he surreptitiously slipped an arrow from his belt and laid it on his bowstring in readiness.

"Your foolish words have put a new face on this business," Gisbourne told Philip at last. "But I hear the weariness in them too. So I give you this one opportunity, crave pardon now and no more shall be said of it."

A slow smile grew in Philip's eyes. It seemed his life had taken many strange turns since he'd left the monastery of Sainte-Genevieve. And he'd found little happiness in any of them. But here in this strange land, confronted by perhaps the most formidable young knight in England, he finally felt at peace with himself. "I would crave pardon for a great many things Gisbourne," he replied honestly. "And if I listed each one, we should be stood here until the end of time. But for slighting you?" He shook his head adamantly. "I would not offer one single word of regret."

The young knight nodded gracefully, almost in approval, for he greatly admired the courage in Philip's response. "Then by the holy rood, I must set my mark upon you," he said respectfully, picking up his sword and standing ready.

And there it might all have ended, the entire expedition over before it began, struck down in one fatal moment. For Gisbourne undoubtedly intended to use his sword. And without a doubt Robin would have moved to stop him. And as he did so, the traitor would have responded, plunging his poniard[22] deep into Robin's heart, in turn provoking a reaction from one of the others, and thus affording Roger of Doncaster the opportunity to make his name by launching a bolt from his crossbow deep into Gisbourne's back. Thereafter all would have turned on all, as is the wont on such occasions, and the world would have ended the day a very different place indeed.

But then something quite extraordinary happened. And though neither Robin nor Philip realised it at the time, it was about to change their lives forever.

---

[22] ***A small dagger with a slim blade that is triangular or square in its cross section.***

FOURTEEN

Twenty Five Years Earlier...

North East Vinland, 'The Great Eastern Woodlands Region'
Veneration of the Thorn
4th May, 1157.

To begin with she'd thought about killing him with her bare hands. Smothering him maybe, or dashing his small head against a rock. And sometimes, whilst he was sleeping, she watched him and imagined a great fire. The entire longhouse ablaze and everyone running, with him still trapped inside, screaming out for her *"Mama, Mama"*, as he struggled helplessly to free himself from the fastenings she'd tied to his wrist and ankles.

She would have liked that, pelts and baskets burning, thick black smoke everywhere, orange flames dancing brightly in her eyes, the whole night on fire. But what if someone saw him? Worse still, what if they went to his aid? Even after four years there were still those who refused to believe her. They might even point to the bindings and say she was the evil one. And then what would she do? No, a fire wasn't the answer. She would have to think of something else, something far less obvious, and much more permanent.

In those days the Five Nations of the Iroquois held dominion over the entire known world. Mohawk,

Oneida, Onondaga, Cayuga, and Seneca, all lived side by side in a vast band of territory that ran from the Finger Lakes region in the north, down through the valleys and forests of the Great Eastern Woodlands to the more arable lands in the south.

Fierce warriors, the Iroquois were taught from an early age how to fight. In combat they gave and expected no quarter, believing only courage in death would guarantee them a happy afterlife. Their mortal enemies were the Algonquian, whose lands they continued to appropriate, and with whom they were now locked in a vicious cycle of raid and counter raid. Indeed, such was the warlike nature of both societies that no young man, be they Iroquois or Algonquian could expect to become husband or lover without having first acquired distinction on the field of battle.

Unlike the Europeans, they were an egalitarian society, preferring to live together in large communities of extended families, rather than separately according to religion or birth. As well as hunting and fishing, they excelled in the cultivation of sunflower, squash and maize. And though their reputation for savagery preceded them, their art was both considerable and accomplished.

By 1157, when the boy was barely four years old, and his mother still only in her teens, they'd been established in the region for over three hundred years. Despite their constant feuds with the Algonquian, it was a golden age for the Five Nations, a time when everything was in perfect harmony and the future seemed assured. Unfortunately the young boy would never get a chance to share in that future. His own mother would see to that. And on May 4th, with the weather still unseasonably cold, she took him to the cave, and his short life among the Iroquois came to an end.

* * *

They left the village early that morning, tip-toeing quietly through the sleeping longhouse, their breath puffing mistily in the cold dawn air as they made their way down to the river. It had to be a secret she told him as they pushed the small canoe out into the water. If any of the others found out, they'd want to come too. And that would spoil everything.

Leaving the slumbering village behind, they travelled with the current for a while, gently stroking the water on either side with their paddles, gradually picking up the pace, until soon the trees on both sides were rushing by. With the first glittering hint of sunlight, she dug sharply into the river and steered the canoe over to the far bank. He watched as she carefully concealed the small vessel under a canopy of fern. There was always the danger of an Algonquian raiding party she told him. And everyone knew what despicable thieves the Algonquian were. Better to keep it hidden from view, just in case.

With the canoe safely secured, they headed off into the woods proper. He skipped along happily at her side. He didn't ask any questions. They were going on a journey she said, and that's all he needed to know. Besides, she seemed different today, almost in high spirits. And that put him in high spirits too. He couldn't remember the last time she'd smiled at him or let him hold her hand. And yet he continued to live for these moments, when the fog of madness would briefly clear, and she'd look at him with genuine love in her eyes, and maybe even do him some small act of kindness.

The pity of the mistreated child is that they continue to hope, long after all reason for hoping is gone. And the boy was no different. Just being with her now, when she was like this, to feel his hand resting gently in hers, was all he needed.

But as the day wore on, and they travelled deeper into the woods, he began to discern a change in her. She spoke less often now, and when she did, it was always in a nervous whisper, as though she suspected someone might be listening.

At first he wondered if it was all part of some elaborate game they were supposed to be playing. "Shall I hide Mama? I see a tree over there. It would be a perfect place." But then he saw the fear in her eyes, and he knew it wasn't a game at all, and he gripped hold of her hand, suddenly afraid too. "Let's go back now Mama. It's dark out here. I don't like it. Let's go back. Please."

She glanced down at his small face looking up into hers. "We can't go back," she told him flatly. "We're almost there."

The boy frowned. "Almost *where* Mama, where are we going?"

She smiled, but this time it wasn't a good smile. It was one of her *other* smiles. The kind he'd grown to fear. "We're going where we should have gone a long time ago," she declared curtly. "We're going to see your father."

His frown grew deeper. He didn't understand. She'd always told him that he had no father. "Mama…" he began tentatively, but she slapped him smartly across the face. "Be quiet," she hissed, "and don't ask questions. Just do as I tell you!"

He flinched slightly, as though expecting her to strike him again. She snarled in contempt. How dare this pathetic creature claim to be a son of hers! Just look at him, the puny armed imbecile, cringing in fear, forever spilling or dropping things, and with that awkward way of talking that always drew jeers from the other children. If ever she'd doubted herself, here surely was the proof. This charlatan had caused her more than enough shame. It was time to put things right.

* * *

They didn't bother to look for the young girl or her child until late in the afternoon, and only then at the behest of her mother. Over the years they'd grown weary of her irrational behaviour and many were secretly pleased to see the back of her. Not only did she fight incessantly with the other women, she paraded immodestly in front of their husbands, inviting all kinds of trouble, yet always complaining afterwards that it was she who'd been taken advantage of. And if that wasn't bad enough, it was rumoured she disappeared into the woods at night to cast enchantments and copulate with a powerful false face.[23]

Most Iroquois warriors, especially the younger ones, were usually prepared to forgive any number of failings in a young girl, provided she was well shaped and happy to share her affections, but even their generosity of spirit foundered when it came to this one.

"Leave her be," they dismissively told her mother. "Let her wander as she will. When hunger starts to bite, she'll come back soon enough."

But the old woman shook her head. The boy was in danger she insisted. She'd seen the way her daughter had looked at him, and knew only too well the dark designs she harboured. She remembered the morning of his birth. The wretched girl had taken one peek at his tiny face and screamed at them to 'take it away'. Later she alleged a woodland spirit had defiled her while she slept, causing the boy to take root in her stomach. It was an outrageous claim even for someone with a reputation for saying outrageous things, especially as her mother already knew the truth. The girl had been so reckless with her charms, that any number of young men in the village could have been the boy's real father.

And yet in the days that followed, she stuck doggedly to her story, embroidering it with a wealth of detail, including a re-enactment of the alleged 'corruption' itself, performed with such gusto for the tribe elders, that she very quickly convinced not just the gullible and superstitious, of whom there were always many amongst the Five Nations, but also a

---

[23] ***Evil spirits which lived in the forest and caused sickness.***

great number of those who might otherwise have considered themselves above such fare. Even those who didn't believe her blamed the boy for putting the wild glint in his mother's eye. It was his fault they said. He'd swollen up to such a size inside her, that in passing him she'd passed not just the progeny of her ills, but also the spirit of her sanity too.

Had the holy man not dreamt about a limping deer being hunted by two wolves, and interpreted it as an instruction from the sacred forces to spare the child's life, it's doubtful the boy would have survived beyond his first few weeks. Even so, his stay of execution proved a mixed blessing, with many in the village completely shunning him, and those who did show any kindness, doing so out of superstition rather than genuine affection. Only his grandmother continued to provide him with the unconditional love he craved.

As for the girl herself, she made no secret of her feelings, punishing him harshly whenever he erred and regularly joining in with the other children when they mocked him. In a society where the veneration of killing and war had become a natural propensity, cruelty was often considered a virtue, and eventually the boy's eyes ran dry of tears, but the hurt in them was ever present, as was the tiny flicker of hope.

* * *

It was starting to rain outside the cave. That was good she thought. It would help wash away their tracks. She gave him the last of the water and made him promise to wait there until she returned. As she peered further into the murky cavern behind him, a troubling thought suddenly occurred. She picked up a small rock and threw it into the darkness. It travelled some distance before landing with a faint *crump*. Clearly the cave was much deeper than she thought. She waited for a moment but nothing stirred in the silence.

"Is he there mama?" The small boy asked anxiously. "Is my father there?"

She shook her head. "But he will be soon," she told him. "So we must be ready."

Instinctively he clutched hold of her arm, gripping it with such intensity that she stopped moving for a moment and looked down at him with an expression so strange, he thought she was about to strike him again.

"I know you're angry with me mama," he said, "but I'm frightened. Is my father going to hurt me?"

Something briefly flickered in her eyes, but the anticipated blow never came. Instead she gathered him in her arms and suddenly hugged him to her. She held him close, as if all the fleeting moments of clarity in her life were finally coming together in one last perfect embrace. "Close your eyes," she whispered as she nuzzled her face next to his. "Close your eyes my darling and wait. He'll be here soon."

But the boy no longer cared about his father, or what would happen when he arrived. For the first time in his life he was completely happy and all he wanted to do now was hold onto that feeling for as long as possible.

"Please," she implored him, "please little one, you must let go. There isn't much time."

He gave her one last powerful squeeze, then reluctantly closed his eyes and relaxed his grip. In the same instant, she pulled away. "Mama!" He called out desperately, his eyes still shut. But *mama* was already gone, hurrying back out into the woods, rushing to put as much distance between her and the cave as possible.

He sat there for a long time after that, waiting for her to come back and thinking about the way her arms had felt around him. When he did finally open his eyes again, the light outside was already beginning to fade. He wondered if something had happened to her. Perhaps she'd fallen over and hurt herself. Or maybe she was lost in the woods somewhere. It never occurred to the boy that his mother had simply abandoned him there. That even now she was carefully laying a false trail and convincing herself it was all for the best, and that the fault was all his for not being more like the other children.

He chewed nervously on his lip and found the bloody scab where she'd hit him earlier. He sucked on it for a while, unsure what to do. He thought of the warm longhouses and the crackling fires. "Mama", he said softly. But now there was only the cave. *And father.* He hugged onto himself and waited, a tiny hum of misery rising in his throat. For the first time in his life, Tomakin was alone.

FIFTEEN

North East Vinland, the 'Great Eastern Woodlands Region'
The Purification of the Virgin
2nd February 1183.

Twenty five years later, Robin sat in the smoky longhouse and listened in silence as Chepi told him the story. He pictured the small boy, all alone in the cave, waiting for his mother to return. And he thought about his own mother, the bloom in her cheek already faded, her frail fingers trembling as she took his hand. *When our dear Lord was dying on the cross, the Robin flew to his side.*

He reached for the clay pipe again and sucked heavily on the stem, choking back the memory, asphyxiating it in a thick cloud of uppowoc smoke. *Pick at the thorns Robert. No matter how many you find. Pick at every single one.*

His thoughts swam dizzily as his lungs filled with the powerful fog. *The child who receives always gives. And the child who gives always receives.* He closed his eyes and waited for the painful recollection to pass. "Is there no mercy?" he mumbled softly, the words escaping his lips in a slow misty plume.

Chepi frowned. Of all the salt water people, Robin was the one who intrigued her the most. There was a boldness of thought and movement about him which set him apart from the others. He smiled more easily too, an ability which seemed to elude the rest, especially Gisbourne who spent most of his time looking as if he'd just been bitten by a snake. Most impressive of all, Robin was quick to learn, displaying an endless fascination for the Iroquois and their way of life. And in a very short time, with her help, he'd become as proficient in Chepi's language as she was in his.

And yet there remained a part of him, always lurking, that was exactly like the rest of them. Less endearing, it would surface occasionally, as it did now, heavy with regret and wallowing in a melancholy so distinctively 'Christian' in flavour that even a people as prone to sentiment as the Iroquois struggled to understand it.

Cloud Man had called this gloomy interloper his 'conscience'. In the *rain lands* he explained, far beyond the *great salt waters*, the swannuken lived false and unhappy lives, feigning fondness for those they hated whilst neglecting those they loved. A 'conscience' he claimed, was a kind of wisdom; it called a man to account and at the same time prevented him from slitting his brother's throat.

But Cloud Man was a coward, and cowards were always full of excuses and self-pity. What baffled the young Iroquois girl was how a great warrior like Robin came to be afflicted with the same malaise.

"Why do you grieve, Robin Who Wears the Hood?" she asked him in puzzlement. "The storm is passed. The branch is broken. It can never be returned to its place on the tree. These are Tomakin's woes, not yours. Do you share his shadow that you must also share his tears?"

Robin smiled. In a very short time, he'd come to love the young Iroquois girl as though she were his own dear sister.

"I *grieve*," he told her quietly, "because the storm is never passed, and because Tomakin's shadow is now crossed with mine. I grieve because mercy is a weaker instinct than revenge. And so we must spill our blood, in perpetuity, not just for our sins, but for the sins of our forefathers too."

"Then you grieve in vain," she advised him sharply, irritated by all this feeble 'conscience' talk. "Because the boy who was Tomakin is gone, and the *mercy* you speak of is gone with him. Now there is just the wendigo. And if you chance upon him he will kill you and devour your *conscience* just as readily as your heart."

And because she was wise beyond her years, Robin wondered if she might be right. Ever since arriving in Vinland he'd heard many strange stories about the shaman. Some said he could render himself invisible. Others that he could manifest illusions so powerful, men acted upon them without hesitation, usually to their own doom. Most shocking of all however was the act to which she now referred, namely his reputed fondness for human flesh, particularly fingers, which he apparently bit off, nails and all, with his own teeth.

To the Iroquois this was sure proof, if any was needed, that Tomakin had fallen prey to a powerful wendigo. These malevolent spirits were believed to roam the Great Eastern Woodlands, posing as animals or dreams, taking possession of the weak and feeble minded whom they then forced to commit acts of unspeakable horror. Once possessed by a wendigo, it was said, the unfortunate host was lost to his friends and family forever. And only death could provide a release.

Robin had no reason to doubt such creatures existed. The devil's hand was always busy, and his acolytes were known to perform feats of astonishing transformation, turning themselves into whatever shape or size best suited their purpose. As a young boy in Locksley Robin had received regular warnings about the 'trickery of demons', and in Barnsdale he'd even witnessed one being pulled from the backside of a frightened young monk. Small and furry, it had appeared not unlike a small grey rodent.

It would have been easy for him therefore to assume, as the Iroquois did, that Tomakin's murderous rampages were all the result of an evil wendigo. But something in Robin's gut told him this wasn't true. The shaman's ruin had little to do with supernatural forces. And the more he thought about the small boy, who'd sat alone in the cave and waited in vain for his mother to return, the more convinced of this he became.

"What need of a wendigo", he mused at length "when the devil's work is already done?"

He put down the pipe and listened to the wind brawling in the trees outside. *The storm is never passed,* he told himself. And he knew if he ever wanted to see England again, he would have to find that small boy and kill him.

SIXTEEN

North East Vinland, the 'Great Eastern Woodlands Region'
The Purification of the Virgin
2nd February 1183 (a few moments later).

Even as Robin reflected on this, just a short distance from where he was sat *the one who would betray them* squatted in front of the longhouse fire, and pondered silently on his next move. The tarry darkness of the longhouse and the intermittent *clicking* of the fire put him in mind of a tavern he'd frequented back in England. And when one of the lolling savages offered him the pipe, he took it without hesitation, sucking greedily on the stem and filling his entire body with the powerful medicine.

It had been over five weeks now since he'd attended to the matter of Rosamond's handmaiden. Five whole weeks and he still couldn't get the thought out of his head. It wasn't the blood either. Blood was his business, and spilling it in the past had never bothered him. It wasn't even the look of disappointment in her eyes as he'd passed the knife across her throat. No, this was something else entirely. Something he'd never experienced before. A growing feeling he could only describe as... *shame.*

Why her death should affect him so adversely, he had no idea. If anything, he should have been pleased. She'd posed a threat and now that threat was removed. He was safe again. Yet as he sat in the dark longhouse, lost in a thick fog of uppowoc smoke, his grief was so great he could barely contain it.

The squalor of the crossing with its endless petty squabbles, together with the relentless strain of maintaining his false identity, not to mention the unsatisfactory turn of events since arriving in Vinland, had left him in a deep fugue-like state. He no longer attended Mass each morning or practiced his sword skills along with the others. Nor did he eagerly anticipate the large sum of money he'd been promised on his return to England. Instead, he began to steal off during the day and visit the place in the woods where he'd buried her body. Sometimes he would lay flowers. Sometimes he would kneel in the dirt and pray.

He'd been a true knight once, not the make-believe one he was now, a man who carried God in his heart as well as on his shield. The girl had reawakened that memory in him. With her he hadn't needed to pretend. After all, she had come to him. In good faith or bad it hardly mattered now. She had come to him willingly, knowing full well who he was and what he was capable of doing. Yet she'd still chosen to place her trust in him, to press her lips against his. And now she was dead. The traitor felt the knot tighten in his throat again.

He exhaled mistily, a long ribbon of smoke curling up from his nostrils. Once again his bleary eyes fell on Robin and Chepi. Why does the skraeling child keep looking across at me he wondered? And what is she telling Huntingdon that he appears to find so interesting? They were always together these days he thought, always talking and laughing, always trading secrets.

Despite beginning to feel dizzy, he reached for the pipe again. All he wanted now was total oblivion. But the more he sucked on the pipe, the more vivid his imaginings grew, swirling around him until the whole longhouse had become a misty haze of conspiracy and paranoia. He looked again at Robin and Chepi. She knows who I am he thought, as the young Iroquois girl caught his eye. *She knows who I am!*

SEVENTEEN

North East Vinland, the 'Great Eastern Woodlands Region'
The feast of Saint Crispina of Tagora
5th December 1182.

Just eight weeks earlier, on the feast of Saint Crispina of Tagora, the last place on earth Robin would have expected to find himself was sat inside a skraeling long house, imbibing uppowoc smoke whilst conversing with an Iroquois child in her native tongue.

That fateful day in the woods, as he'd watched Gisbourne and Philip square shoulders and prepare to do battle, Robin had feared the entire expedition was about to come to grief. Even as *the one who would betray them* furtively drew something from his belt – a poniard Robin guessed from his slight shift in balance – the man from Locksley was readying himself to respond in kind. But at such close quarters, he knew it was unlikely any of them would survive the day, let alone emerge unscathed to continue the search. And then what would happen?

With no decent 'finder of trails' to guide them, and nothing apart from sea-fatigue to keep them in Vinland, how long would it be before the survivors set sail for England again? No doubt Alyne would find employment with some other noble, and his songs might still resound down the ages. But who would sing of 'great deeds done beyond the seas'? All in all, things would be very different indeed. Fortunately, at that precise moment fate had chosen to intervene.

* * *

It was Robin who spotted him first, just a shiver of movement on the very fringes of his vision but with enough substance to send his arm shooting out and raise a single cry in his throat. "Skraelings!"

In an instant Gisbourne and Philip had forgotten all about spilling each other's blood and turned as one with the rest of the expedition, to follow Robin's pointed finger towards a spot in the nearby tree line, where a muscular young man was now emerging from the undergrowth. The knights stared in collective wonder. Here at last was their first genuine sighting of a Vinland native.

"A venturesome bunny, if ever I saw one," Gisbourne observed dryly, his manner suggesting he was already weighing the man's considerable physical qualities against his own.

Mindful of the knight's previously stated intention of pitting himself against the 'biggest skraeling he could find', Robin wondered if the day might yet end in catastrophic bloodshed. "Rest easy upon that thought Gisbourne," he whispered anxiously, "we have him outmanned by fifteen to one." And when Harold of Leicester notched an arrow Robin immediately threw out a hand to stop him. "Stand off", he hissed. "The fellow presents himself unarmed. We must do likewise." And leading by example, he slowly lowered his bow and carefully placed it on the grass by his feet. After a moment, the others followed suit, even Gisbourne, though not before he'd completed the requisite number of yelps and twitches.

"God spare our blushes if this miscreant has two dozen more like him hiding close-by," he opined with a smile. "I shall have to use you as a shield Huntingdon."

The 'miscreant' in question was none other than Chepi's older brother Kocoum. The same fearless warrior who'd once stood with Eustace outside Tomakin's cave. His experience that day had clearly left its mark on him. And though the European Knights weren't to know it, for almost a year now he'd lived alone in the woods, preferring frosty stars and the company of nature to a warm longhouse and his fellow Iroquois.

Watching them lay down their weapons, he walked the short distance to where they stood, and with a curious grin presented himself in front of Philip. He wore no armour or padding, and apart from a pair of deerskin moccasins, a breechclout which barely preserved his dignity and a necklace not unlike the one Philip had recently given to Elizabeth, he was completely naked.

Philip felt a chill of reality as he surveyed the powerfully built savage. For the sake of expediency he'd described the skraelings as being like 'mischievous children'. But what if he'd been wrong? This one had several deep scars which could only have been incurred in battle. But battle with whom, he wondered, and in what numbers? Summoning all the reserves of bravura he could muster, Philip smiled confidently and announced to the others: "See how easily he gives himself to us. It's as I told you. A knight of good faith has nothing to fear from these people."

Kocoum responded with something in his own tongue. A greeting as it transpired, though as none of them were able to understand, it served only to further their astonishment. Up until that moment, despite Holger's assurances, many of them had privately doubted the skraelings possessed the capacity for anything as sophisticated as language. Now they were forced to think again.

"Call me fool," Gisbourne opined with customary sarcasm, "but that sounded remarkably like speech."

Kocoum said something else, and this time accompanied it with the up-and-down motion of hand and arm he half-remembered learning from Cloud Man.

"He crosses himself like a Christian," Ralph of Shrewsbury breathed in wonder. And all around him they crossed themselves in return at the manifestation of this miracle.

For a second no one moved a muscle, and then all at once curiosity got the better of them and they quickly surrounded him, busily examining every aspect of his appearance and filling the air with a cacophony of questions and speculation. *How many sharpened teeth did he have? Where was his tail? Could he see in the dark with those eyes?* Everything about the Iroquois was fascinating. From the strange feathers he wore in his hair, to the flatness of his face, which Gisbourne reckoned the Almighty must have fashioned from some mysterious red clay.

While the others crowded around him, eagerly prodding and passing comment, Robin kept a watchful distance. Something was wrong, he told himself. The rest of them hadn't noticed it yet, but Kocoum's eyes exhibited all the signs of a man struggling to maintain his grip on reality. The 'busy glint of confusion' his father had called it. Something Robin had witnessed regularly in the restive stares of wild men and religious hermits as they roamed the woods of Sherwood and Barnsdale, forever at odds with themselves and the world around them. Now he saw it clearly in the young Iroquois too. This one has a powerful *daze* in him, he thought grimly. The only question was whether he'd been cursed with it from birth, or whether something had happened along the way to put it there?

All of which brought him to the second most troubling aspect of the young warrior's appearance. Namely his two missing fingers! Robin had spotted it the instant he'd emerged from the undergrowth, but now, with the others milling excitedly, he had a chance to examine the stubby wound in more detail.

"What do you suppose happened?" Philip asked a few moments later when Robin brought it to his attention. "Could such an injury be the result of a hunting accident perhaps?"

"Only if he went hunting for nipples on a dragon's chest," Roger of Doncaster ventured crudely.

"Perhaps he got hungry", Ralph of Shrewsbury interposed, attempting to instil a little of his own famous 'humour' into proceedings. But neither Robin nor Philip was much in a mood for laughing now.

"A man with the daze in him is either born that way or brought to it later in life," Robin observed bluntly. "But even lacking full wits this skraeling was able to move around us undetected for almost three days. More reason if any were needed for us to proceed from here with even greater caution."

Whilst Robin and the others were discussing the young warrior, Kocoum was conducting a similar assessment of them. As fighting men he decided, they lacked even the basic abilities. They had no eye or ear for the world around them. They moved noisily through the woods, leaving a heavy print wherever they trod and reacted sluggishly to any signs of danger. When they paused to relieve themselves they rarely bothered to conceal the evidence afterwards. Worse still, they squabbled incessantly, grumbling and casting blame like small children. And like small children they appeared to have little sense of direction, travelling first one way and then the other without ever seeming to arrive at a destination. If, as he suspected, they were looking for Cloud Man, why hadn't they started at the settlement? And if they were searching for the settlement, what were they doing out here in the woods? It was completely baffling.

And yet the young Iroquois felt himself inexorably drawn to whatever idiotic caprice they were pursuing. Perhaps it was because they reminded him of Cloud Man. Or maybe he'd simply grown lonely out here in the woods. Either way, he desperately wanted to make contact with them, and strained his memory to remember the right words.

A year ago he'd been almost as proficient in the swannuken tongue as he was in his own. But the wendigo had robbed him of that gift, along with two of his fingers and most of his reasoning. Now he lived alone in the wilds, feeding on berries and roots whilst attempting to make sense of his scrambled thoughts. He paused in his deliberations as he realised one of the knights was attempting to communicate with him.

"My name is Philip Mark", Philip was saying slowly, enunciating each word with almost comical exactitude. "I have crossed the seas in search of one who was stolen from me. I carry as proof the seals of many esteemed personages, including the Bishop of Hereford..."

Gisbourne guffawed offensively. "Why not tell the unfortunate brute how much 'good favour' your family is in with the King?" He suggested mockingly. "Or better still; show him the hole in your arse. Either way I'll wager the return on it will be just the same."

Philip turned on him angrily, and for a moment Robin feared the feud between them was about to break out all over again.

"We are Christian Knights," Philip rejoined sharply. "Here to perform an office of justice. Find such humour in it as you will Gisbourne, but I'm resolved to perform that office to the best of my ability."

"Then put a sword to his throat and have done with it," Gisbourne replied irritably. "Even a savage will understand that."

"Not everything can be done with a sword Gisbourne," Robin reminded him with growing frustration. "This skraeling has the daze in him. Good judgment is required."

"If 'good judgement' is required," Gisbourne asked with typical bluntness, "why is this oaf talking to him?"

Robin braced himself for Philip's response and the inevitable escalation that would surely follow. But fortunately Philip had spotted something on Kocoum's necklace and was no longer listening to them.

"What is it?" Robin asked, grateful for an opportunity to amend the temper of things.

"Marian's ring", Philip said softly, his eyes widening at the sight of it.

Robin followed his gaze to Kocoum's necklace. To begin with he saw only the same bones and trinkets he'd detected the first time. But as he brought his eyes to a much sharper focus he suddenly perceived the delicate curve of a small bronze band nestled neatly between the scraggly feathers and yellowing teeth. "Are you certain it's hers?" He asked.

Philip nodded solemnly. "I gave it to her myself," he said, "when she took my pledge."

Robin glanced at Philip and saw there was an alarming change in his expression.

"I would advise caution", the young bowman counselled seriously. "It would be imprudent to make a display of this without first establishing the facts."

Philip huffed in exasperation. "We're stood at the end of the world Robert, ready to murder one another, and your only advice is *caution*? I'll show you *caution.*" And before Robin could stop him, he reached out and violently tore the necklace from around the young warrior's neck.

Not unsurprisingly, Kocoum reacted angrily to this 'theft' and immediately attempted to snatch it back again, causing both men to grapple for a moment in a manner which might have been comical had the consequences for everyone not been so grave.

Robin and several of the others struggled gainfully to pull them apart, but it was Gisbourne who decisively resolved the dispute, stepping forward and with a sickening *clunk,* employing the flat handle of his sword to render Kocoum unconscious.

No sooner was the young Iroquois felled, than Philip was calling for a length of rope with which to 'bind the savage', announcing to all and sundry, that the discovery of Marian's ring was 'sure proof' that they'd finally 'captured' one of Eustace's 'fellow conspirators'.

Robin knew this was highly unlikely. But he also knew that after so many weeks at sea, followed by nine fruitless days searching, and a near-insurrection, Philip desperately needed something he could herald a 'success', however fleeting that 'success' might eventually prove. And so the 'finder of trails' kept whatever concerns he had to himself. The important thing now, he decided, was to ensure no additional harm came to the young warrior.

"Guilt or otherwise can be established later," he told them, anxious to avoid further disagreement. "For the moment I suggest we return him to the ship.

With some proper food in his belly who knows what knowledge we may be able to wrest from him."

"God be praised," Roger of Doncaster breathed with mock piety. "Nine days chasing our tails and now we return to the coffin that brought us there."

"The ship at least has ale," Oswald of Norwich reminded him. "Not to mention a number of other, far prettier attractions."

And picking up the theme, Ralph of Shrewsbury added with characteristic lustre: "All of them with better nipples than you'll find on a dragon's chest."

Thus it was decided. They'd return to the ship and take Kocoum with them. Between Brother Geoffrey's praying and Holger's few words of 'skraeling' they were sure to discover the whereabouts of Eustace and the settlement. As he knelt down beside the young warrior to check his injury, Robin caught Gisbourne's eye.

"Speak on it as you will," the knight warned him, "but know also that I could just as easily have split his skull in two."

Once again, Robin made no comment. To communicate any additional alarm to an already alarming situation would have been pointless. He shouldered his bow and helped the so-called 'mute' Crispin of Lincoln bind Kocoum's arms and legs. It had been a bad end to a bad day, and unbeknownst to any of them, it was about to get much worse.

EIGHTEEN

North East Vinland, the 'Great Eastern Woodlands Region' (Somewhere inland from what is now the New York/Connecticut coastline)
The feast of Saint Ambrose of Milan
7th December, 1182.

Marian tried hard to pray, but the words were barely a tremble on her lips. *I thank Thee Lord that Thou hast kept me from nightfall to the hour of the morning.* What sorcery was he planning now she wondered? *I pray that by eventide I may again give thanks, praise and blessing unto Thee my Lord and Saviour.* Maybe I'm still asleep, she thought. Perhaps this is all just a dream, another one of his clever 'tricks'.

She opened her eyes and stared at the cave entrance. Craggy and black, it was sunk into the rock face like a deep wound. If it *was* a 'trick', she decided, it was certainly a strange one. She tried to calculate how long it had been since he'd first disappeared inside? Judging by the sun it was already past noon. Marian thought briefly about running away. But where would she go? Vinland spilt like milk in all directions. To navigate its vast canopy of woodlands without the aid of a chart, one would need to take wing and soar above it like a bird. Besides, she'd run away in the past and where had it got her. Each time they'd brought her back again, and each time he'd been waiting with another pipe. And it was the pipe she'd come to fear more than anything else. Fear…*and love*.

Marian took a sip of water from a small clay pot she carried. Trying to escape was a mistake she concluded. It was what *he* wanted her to do. Eve cast out for the sake of an apple, with only the serpent willing to help. But what if little Eve had a plan of her own? How would the serpent fare then? A surprise attack she told herself. First destroy him and *then* escape. That was the only answer.

A surprise attack! She took another sip of water and let her mind drift back to that terrible night, almost nineteen months before. The settlement she and Eustace had founded shortly after arriving in Vinland had taken weeks to construct. Men had worked tirelessly, digging ditches, erecting wooden palisades, often going days without sleep to get it finished. Yet in a few short moments all had lain in ruin, its young inhabitant's butchered beyond recognition and Marian herself taken captive.

At the time she'd sought consolation in the thought that whatever happened next, death would find her with God in mind. Instead of which the grinning savages had dragged her from the burning settlement and tied her to a tree, from whence she'd witnessed the final horror, as all around their hatchets and scalping knives went to work on her dying friends with renewed vigour. She'd called out, but her pleas for mercy had been ignored. They'd chopped and tore at everything they could find until the surrounding grasslands had glistened with their endeavour.

More than sixty strong, their black eyes glittering in the dark, these were the feral band of misfits Tomakin liked to describe as his 'family'. Painted and grotesque they moved through the Great Eastern Woodlands like a plague of rats, slaughtering, and devouring everything in their path. Iroquois or Algonquian, it made no difference. They weren't warriors like the other skraelings, they were killers, and they set about it with a twisted glee. Most had been abandoned or cast out by their own tribes long ago and consequently bore neither love nor allegiance for anyone apart from the charismatic shaman who now led them. And it was thanks to him that Marian had been spared.

Tomakin, it transpired, had known all about the Europeans and their settlement from the very start. His scouts had spotted the strange ship with its distinctive square sail and long oars, and had made daily reports until eventually the shaman had come to see for himself. Crouching in the undergrowth, he'd watched perplexed from the fringes of the wood as the pale skinned interlopers celebrated Mass, repeatedly drawing their fingers upwards and crosswise over their bodies as if to form the shape of an invisible tree. And then later, as the sun went down, he'd crept closer for a better look, and that's when he'd first spotted her. Marian had left the others and was wandering alone through the deep banks of waist-high grassland that surrounded the tiny settlement. Eustace had originally intended to clear this area for fear of the cover it might provide an approaching enemy. But with Vinland being hailed as a 'second Eden' such precautions were quickly deemed unnecessary, and he'd put his mind to work on a grand feasting hall instead. All of which meant Tomakin had been free to gaze unhindered as Marian passed within a hairsbreadth of where he was hidden.

Apart from his mother, the shaman had never really cared about women. The wendigo inside him had made certain of that. But watching her now, arms raised as if gathering in the dusk, her voice floating sweetly above the billowing grasses, *o pastor animarum*,[24] Tomakin had suddenly dared to hope again. Here was a beauty unlike any he'd ever seen before. Dark skinned and mysterious, yet so perfectly shaped she near stopped the breath in his throat.

Marian discovered later that he'd wanted to seize her right there and then and that only the sudden tolling of the angelus bell in the settlement behind had prevented him from doing so. Nevertheless, he returned the following day and every day thereafter in the hopes of seeing her again. And by the time Eustace reduced the night watch to a single sentry, her fate, along with that of every other European in the settlement had been decided.

With regards to Eustace, Marian knew only that his one attempt to rescue her had ended in disaster, leading to the capture or death of virtually everyone with him. According to some of the skraelings present at the rout, Eustace himself had fled into the woods, eyes bulging and screaming like a man no longer in possession of his wits. Perhaps unsurprisingly,

---

[24] ***O Shepherd of Souls***

Marian had chosen not to believe this. Yet as to his current whereabouts or state of mind, she had no knowledge. Most days she simply refused to think about it. And when she did, she always pictured him as he had been. Not as he might be now.

It would have greatly surprised her therefore to learn that by an extraordinary twist of fate, she was at that very moment stood precisely where her young lover had stood almost twelve months before as he contemplated his ill-fated rescue attempt. But whereas Eustace had looked on the gaping cave entrance and despaired, Marian saw only a miserly black hole. If this was another fabrication of Tomakin's mind, she told herself, it was a wholly unimpressive one. Had the shaman really wanted to prove his worth, why not place her in feathery grasses by some great blue lake? No, she decided firmly, this was real. And the journey here had been real too, which meant the means of her escape would have to be every bit as real. All she needed now was the strength to do it.

Deep inside the cave, Tomakin waited with growing impatience for *father* to answer him. He took a heavy breath, smoothing his long black hair with both hands and stared at the figure in the shadows. Last night he'd again dreamt about the two hungry wolves and *the old woman who knew how to heal*, and the pain behind his eyes, which had been slowly building all day, was quite intense now. "Father", he began again, though it sounded more like a plea this time. "Father, please. I'm asking for your help."

The wendigo inside him sneered mockingly. *Father please*, it trilled in cruel imitation. *I have sworn myself to ruin. I cry like a baby and bleed like a girl. Mama says I was cursed in her womb. When I screamed for the teat, she gave me her hand. And now I am without joy in the world, excepting that which I take for myself, and even this brings me sorrow.*

Tomakin shut his eyes. With every passing moment the pain in his head grew more excruciating. "If you would die but once," he whispered to the wendigo. "I would take that part of you and bury it in a place from which there is no return."

The wendigo laughed. *I will always return Tomakin. And you will always welcome me. We are as one, and nothing can separate us, not even death.*

Deep down, Tomakin knew the evil spirit was right. Fear had sealed them into the same body a long time ago, and no amount of denial would ever change that. Yet even now he refused to accept it. "No", he insisted stubbornly, "I have the song of her in my head. It plays sweetly. Soon it will be the only thing I hear. And then you will be gone forever."

The wendigo scowled. *Her song is not for you. Her song will never be for you. You will kill her. I will make you. And together we shall feast.*

Tomakin covered his ears, desperately trying to shut out the scornful voice. The pain behind his eyes was almost unbearable now. "Father," he cried out in distress. "Father, why won't you answer me?"

He swayed dizzily on his feet for a moment. The shadows in the cave around him suddenly seemed to take on new shape. The last thing he heard as oblivion beckoned was the sound of the wendigo laughing at him.

At the cave entrance Marian was remembering her first evening in Vinland. She and Eustace had stood together on a cliff top and looked out over the ocean, both of them drunk on the prospect of infinite horizons. If she closed her eyes she could still hear the rushing sigh of the shingle below as the waves tumbled and retreated blindly in the night. How far away was Eustace from her now she wondered? And why hadn't he tried to rescue her again? She sighed unhappily. It was best not to speculate on such things.

Glancing down, Marian picked up one of the painted stones that lay in a pattern across the cave entrance. She tried to discern how many times she would need to dash it against Tomakin's head in order to kill him? Fell him with the first blow and surely all the others need only connect with sufficient purpose to see the job done. And hadn't she killed him once already inside her own head. Why should this be any different?

And yet somehow it *was* different. Plunging down with an imaginary knife was one thing. But cracking open a man's skull, blooding your hands with his life, that was something else altogether. She cast the stone aside. Am I taking root in his mind, she wondered, or is he taking root in mine?

She looked at the cave entrance again. Was this the place he'd told her about?

She tried to imagine what it must have been like all those years ago. How had he survived, that small boy with sloping shoulders? Abandoned by his own mother, cast out by his tribe, what terrible evils had been done, what appalling cruelties inflicted that had brought him to such a bitter resolve?

Marian took another sip of water and quickly spat it out again, suddenly angry with herself. Was this sympathy she was feeling? *Sympathy* for Tomakin! Was such a thing even possible? And before she could remind herself that as a Christian not only was it 'possible', but sometimes also necessary, she'd swept the image of the hapless boy aside and replaced it with another. This time of the celebrated Benedictine, Reynald of Clairvaux, who apart from Eustace and Marian, had been the only other survivor of the initial attack on the settlement that night. *Remember Reynald,* she told herself bitterly, remember what happened to him and then decide who deserves your sympathy.

The young monk had been a late addition to the band of friends and vagabonds Eustace had amassed for his journey to Vinland. He'd previously taught at the famous Sainte-Genevieve, and was one of the original 'free thinkers', his classes attracting hundreds of adoring students, amongst them Philip Mark, erstwhile son of 'Bloody' John and, as luck would have it, older brother to Eustace. Philip had often squeezed into crowded rooms at the monastery to hear Reynald condemn the church authorities and loudly proclaim it better to *"shovel manure on a pig farm, than besmirch the teachings of Christ with false piety."*

Unfortunately, radical theology wasn't the only use Reynald had found for his 'fiery tongue'. And when it was brought to the Bishop of Burgundy's attention that his favourite niece was a regular beneficiary of its 'persuasive qualities', paid ruffians were hired to put an end to the young firebrand and his 'teachings' once and for all.

Reynald subsequently survived three attempts on his life before hearing a rumour about Philip Mark's younger brother and the mysterious trip he was planning. Abandoned by church and disowned by his friends, the young monk had no choice but to reluctantly jump aboard as the ship set sail from Portsmouth. In spite of this, Reynald had swiftly established himself as one of the more valuable crew members, keeping a calm head when the seas roared, and winning over the first skraelings they encountered with his impressive juggling skills.

Now, with the settlement ablaze and virtually everyone around them dead, he once again rose to the occasion. Unlimbering a huge sword and standing ready, Reynald attempted to barter both for his and Marian's life by challenging the masked shaman to prove his worth in a duel of arms. Issued with the kind of aplomb only those who've taught adoring students can ever truly master, Reynald's challenge immediately drew sharp intakes of breath from the savages around him. This was quickly followed by wild hoots of derision, which even at the time had filled Marian with a terrible sense of dread. All heads now turned towards Tomakin, and a sudden hush fell as they waited to see how he'd respond.

Without a word, the shaman raised his powerful arms and slowly removed the all-encompassing headdress he'd worn since the attack's inception. Looking back, Marian wasn't sure what she'd found most disturbing about that moment, the terrifying headdress itself, or the young man now emerging from beneath it. Given the horror of the attack, she'd fully expected the person responsible to prove equally as grotesque. Instead, she'd found herself looking into a face of almost startling beauty. Unlike the other skraelings whose features were covered in garish swirls of paint, the young shaman's skin was flawlessly smooth, its reddish hue finding perfect definition in firm upper cheekbones, deep-set, almost luminous eyes, and just the barest accentuation of a lip line. In many respects it was the face of an angel, in particular his eyes, which contained a quality that was almost otherworldly.

And yet at the same time there was something very unsettling about it. As though it wasn't really a face at all, but rather some approximation of a face its bearer thought you might wish to see, an exquisite mask worn to disguise its owner's true intentions. *I know who you are,* Marian thought in a sudden rush of panic. And no sooner had the idea formed in her head than she heard Reynald utter it aloud. *Satan!*

The Benedictine had gambled his life on a physical duel. But as Marian would quickly come to understand, it was in the darker recesses of the human mind that Tomakin preferred to fight his battles. And this one would be no different. He fixed Reynald with those big luminous eyes, at the same time conjuring a stick-like rattle, apparently from nowhere, which he shook about him in a series of strangely insistent *scratch, scratch, scratch* rhythms.

To begin with the young monk appeared unaffected. And then all at once Marian saw him stiffen sharply and suddenly drop his sword, a look of utter bemusement on his face. Although she had no way of knowing it, Reynald's confusion had been brought about by the advent of another *voice*, apparently emanating from inside his own head. No more than a whisper, this new *voice* grew steadily louder with each *scratching* flick of the shaman's rattle, until eventually it had blocked out all other thoughts and noises and replaced them with one unequivocal demand, *submit!*

To his credit the young monk attempted to resist. His face twisted painfully as he strove to drive the *voice* out. But the more he fought, the more insistent it became. For several moments the former firebrand from Sainte-Genevieve, who in his time had helped shape so many young minds, struggled desperately to save his own. But all to no avail. The shaman had him now, and before Reynald could recover, those luminous eyes had melted his resolve and bent it to a new purpose.

What followed was so appalling; Marian had spent her first weeks in captivity trying to convince herself it had all been a bad dream. She'd even fashioned a different version of events in which Reynald of Clairvaux had met his death in the same way he'd met life, condemning hypocrisy, praising God and pledging his love for the Bishop of

Burgundy's favourite niece. So preferable was this second 'version' that for a while at least she'd even allowed herself to believe it.

But believing something and knowing it were two very different things, especially in Vinland, which was why Marian now paused again and looked across at the cave entrance. *Sympathy?* Never, she told herself. She would burn in hell before she felt sorry for the shaman again. She thought about Reynald of Clairvaux, and pictured him stood amongst the whooping savages. And this time she forced herself to remember the way it had *really* happened.

Tomakin came to, in the cave, a short while later. The unbearable pain behind his eyes had gone now. He sat up slowly and looked around. Apparently the wendigo had gone too. But for how long he wondered? He sniffed involuntarily, his senses prickling in apprehension. Something was different. He peered into the cave, waiting for its familiar shapes to appear out of the gloom. And then all at once he understood. Everything will be put right now he told himself happily. Everything will finally be settled. *Father* was here.

After so much time spent trying to convince herself it had never really happened, Marian was surprised how quickly it all came flooding back. And not just the horrors either. This time it was the inconsequential things. The smell of the cooking pots, the sight of a savage happily defecating amidst the mayhem, even the appearance of a cherub-faced moon playing peek-a-boo through the choking black smoke. Each tiny element adding to a sense of a world in which reason could no longer be taken for granted. As for Reynald of Clairvaux, he was stood in the middle of it all, his arms hanging limply at his side, his body swaying gently back and forth, as if keeping time with the *scratch, scratch, scratch,* of the shaman's rattle. Around him a huge circle of jostling savages had formed, all pushing and shoving like children at a fair, each one desperate for a better view. Nearby the settlement continued to burn but no one seemed interested anymore. They were all watching Tomakin, waiting to see what he would do next.

Once again he fixed Reynald with those luminous eyes. "Thou hast a large worm burrowed deep inside thee," he announced gravely, in what Marian afterwards reasoned must have been Iroquois but at the time sounded like perfect French. "It grows fat in the slop of thy belly." He unsheathed his hunting knife and handed it to the young monk. "Cut it out!'

As if willed by some external force, Reynald saw his trembling hand reach out and take the knife. Marian gasped in disbelief. She instinctively knew the shaman was lying yet there was something about the persistent *scratching* of his rattle, together with those luminous eyes that made the image of the monstrous worm almost impossible to resist. For Reynald, things were even more desperate. He could actually *feel* it wriggling around inside him. And when he looked down he saw that his stomach was grotesquely distended, like the belly of a heavily pregnant girl.

Tomakin moved closer. "It grows," he purred softly, his voice prevailing upon Reynald. "Feel it twist and turn."

Reynald's grip tightened around the hunting knife. He was sweating profusely now, struggling frantically against the terrible proposition in his head. He looked at Marian, but there was nothing she could do. He was trapped inside a nightmare of demonic proportions. The other *voice* inside his head was simply too strong. He could no longer refuse. He *had* to submit.

With a cry of despair, he turned the knife on himself, and with both hands plunged it into his own stomach. Though his face registered horror, his hands worked with an apparent frenzy of their own, and within a matter of seconds he had completely disembowelled himself. He stood there for a moment, gaping in incredulity at his handiwork. And then with one enormous cry the surrounding skraelings converged en-masse and proceeded to hack him to pieces with their hatchets and war clubs.

In the year that followed, Marian had witnessed a great many terrible things. She'd seen fingers bitten off, hearts torn out, and countless unsuspecting warriors go meekly to their deaths, all of it willed by the shaman's luminous eyes. But nothing compared to the image of Reynald of Clairvaux, staring down in astonishment as the contents of his stomach spilt out onto the ground at his feet.

"Open your mind to me and I will happily expunge its sorrows," Tomakin had whispered many months later as she lay in a daze of pipe smoke, silently grieving for the young monk.

But Marian, even though heavily numbed by the sacred herb, had wiped away her tears and replied. "If I open my mind I will be enslaved twice over. I already serve this pipe. I have no wish to serve you also."

And so she continued to resist him. Not just for herself, but for Reynald and Eustace and Chepi's brother Kocoum, who'd accompanied Eustace on the raid to free her, and for everyone else in Vinland who had reason to loathe the name *Tomakin.* It was a resistance that had often incurred his wrath, as when he'd seized her one day in the woods, his patience apparently at an end. Though even as they'd grappled she'd shown him her boldest face, shouting, "If you wish it done by brute force, then take what pleasure you can. But know that in my mind I am cutting your throat again and again while you do so!"

The shaman had slowly relaxed his grip, the slump in him almost palpable. "What is death but a kindness", he'd asked as he turned away. "Cut it twice over. I shall not complain." His words had been imbued with such a melancholy that it had left her momentarily mystified. What was it that he wanted from her? Did he really imagine that by affording her freedoms and privileges not enjoyed by the other women in his 'family', he would earn her gratitude? Or that by fostering her need for a pipe that robbed its user of all energy she would come to forget she was his prisoner? Let him toil from now until the crack of doom, she told herself. She would never become slave to such an impious savage.

Yet as Marian stood outside the cave entrance and pondered this, a new and troubling thought occurred. What if he wanted none of these things? What if Tomakin had kept her alive not out of spite or curiosity, as she'd always imagined, but out of some desperate hope that one day she might actually look on him with favour? Was it possible this *hope* had been obvious in him right from the very start and that she'd deliberately chosen to misconstrue it for fear of confronting the unthinkable? And if *hope* was the thing that sustained him, might not that same *hope* also be fashioned into a weapon and used against him. Marian immediately felt ashamed for contemplating such a cruel deception. Yet at the same time she was conscious of a tiny flutter of excitement too. After all, why bludgeon a man to death or brandish a knife, when there were other means just as deadly?

Inside the cave, Tomakin listened as *father* spoke. The two hungry wolves were searching for Marian he said. Soon they would transform into men with hair on their faces, just as Tomakin had dreamt. If he wanted to stop them, he would have to put an end to *the old woman who knew how to heal*, or she would lead them straight to him.

As for Marian herself, *father* advised, Tomakin would need to make a decision. Was she so necessary to him that he was prepared to risk not just his own life, but the lives of his entire 'family' too? If the answer was yes, then he would have to find another way to her heart, one that didn't involve fear or deception. She must be convinced, *father* explained, *persuaded* not *made* to love. This was a venture of the heart and its outcome could not be forced.

Tomakin told *father* he was worried about the wendigo. What would it do when it found out? For weeks now it had been making threats, promising harm if Tomakin didn't do as it commanded. But *father* said he was not to think about the wendigo, or concern himself with its threats. The woman's love would drive it out he promised. And then, at last Tomakin would finally be free.

When Tomakin emerged from the cave a short while later, Marian was astonished at the apparent change in him. Only that morning, he'd led her from the village with barely a word. Now he stood before her in such good humour she could scarcely believe it was the same person.

Had something happened inside the cave, she wondered, to alter his mood so dramatically? She enquired with a lightness of tone that kept the mood merry between them and played well to her new stratagem. Tomakin beamed, barely able to contain his joy. *Father* was waiting, he told her happily. Marian was astonished to see there were actually tears welling in his eyes. She briefly considered finding some of her own, but just as quickly decided against it. Whatever else he might be, the shaman was no fool.

Unfortunately, when she followed him into the cave a few moments later and saw the abomination he called *father*, the tears came anyway. And this time there was no need for her to pretend.

NINETEEN

North East Vinland, the 'Great Eastern Woodlands Region'
The feast of Saint Agatha of England
12th December, 1182.

By the time Robin realised they were in danger it was already too late. He barely had time to hold up a warning hand and urge them into defensive positions before the first salvo of arrows and whooping savages were upon them. The fight itself proved brief, vicious and, Gisbourne's swordplay notwithstanding, was lost almost as soon as it was begun. Robin remained at Philip's side, fending off blows as best he could, but the enemy's numerical advantage was irresistible, and after a few moments he knew they were done for. As howling Iroquois warriors converged from all sides, Robin pictured his mother, her tremulous finger beckoning to him. *Say the prayer* he told himself. *Say the prayer she taught you.* But in the end there wasn't even time for that.

* * *

To his credit, Robin had been trying to save them. With Kocoum unconscious at his feet and Philip calling excitedly for a 'length of rope', he'd feared a repeat of the situation that had led to his own ordeal at the hands of Gilbert and the others six weeks before. Fortunately no one had suggested putting the rope around Kocoum's neck, but Robin knew enough about his fellow knights to realise it was only a matter of time before one of them posited something equally as foolish. And so he'd set about persuading Philip that he had a stratagem for turning the situation to their advantage, though in truth this 'stratagem' was nothing more than a ruse. Its real purpose was to prevent the unnecessary spilling of any more blood. That had been five days ago, and like all plans conceived in haste, it hadn't taken long before this one had started to unravel.

It began almost immediately with a dispute between Philip and Ralph of Shrewsbury over how best to proceed once they'd got Kocoum back to the ship. Unsurprisingly, Philip was determined to force the young Iroquois, by means of torture if necessary, to lead them to Marian and the others. Ralph of Shrewsbury on the other hand favoured a less belligerent approach. Mindful of Robin's words about the savage having the 'daze in him', and sensing that however curious they might be about those two missing fingers, it would almost certainly prove disadvantageous to investigate the matter too thoroughly, he argued that instead of threats they should attempt to barter for the information.

Philip responded angrily that they were 'men of action' not 'commerce', and suggested that trying to arrange such a transaction would be tantamount to a 'beggar crying out for alms or broken meat!'

Far from being dissuaded however, Ralph of Shrewsbury was quick to remind him that they'd brought all manner of baubles and garments with them for precisely such an eventuality, and that even a ‘lowly beggar’ knew the wisdom of ‘first finding favour’ with his potential benefactor.

Realising this was getting them nowhere; Robin quickly interjected with an idea which sought to reconcile both suggestions. “First ply him with honey,” he proposed. “And if that fails, then turn to the whip.”

The ‘honey’, he said, would be administered in the shape of warm food, a soft mattress and some of those ‘gifts’ they’d brought for the purpose. The ‘whip’ would only need to be introduced if all this failed. “In the meantime, Holger has a better understanding of these people,” he advised calmly. “I say we let the Norseman reason on it for a day or so.”

In actual fact Robin had no confidence whatsoever in Holger’s ability to ‘reason’ on anything. Nine days of aimless wandering up and down the Vinland coastline had seen to that. But he knew Philip was in no mood to let the young savage go free, and at least the ship would afford them better protection than the woods. In addition, Brother Geoffrey would be on hand to ensure any recourse to the ‘whip’ didn’t get out of control.

However, on this occasion Robin would be proven wrong, and the ship would quickly reveal itself a far more hazardous place than any of them had expected. So much so that it would provide the setting for one of the most objectionable incidents of the entire expedition.

When they finally reached it later that night, the ship was already shrouded in darkness and they had to wade out into the black waters, swords held high above their heads as the tide lapped restlessly about their waists. Having regained consciousness only to discover he was bound and gagged, Kocoum had accompanied them without further protest, partly out of curiosity, and partly because he realised any additional dissent would only result in another blow to the head.

However, if Robin was hoping the ship might provide them with a brief interlude of respite, he was in for a nasty shock. As they got within hailing distance he was surprised to find no one stood watch on the elevated deck, ready to challenge them or return the password he called out. And by the time they'd clambered aboard and begun the process of warming themselves at the brazier it was evident that all was not well. Clothing and food were strewn everywhere, part of the canvas sail was torn, and someone had amused themselves by carving a succession of graphic illustrations into the mainmast.

Philip shook his head in disgust. "Must I be in all places at one time," he muttered bitterly as they took it in.

Prodding a slumbering Holger with the toe of his boot, Gisbourne declared the steersman to be 'taken with ale'. And he wasn't the only one. Alyne was discovered slouched at the bow, vomit still dribbling from his lips, whilst others were sprawled in drunken heaps at various points along the main deck. As for Rosamond; she was found, by *the one who would betray them*, passed out in her cabin with three naked members of Holger's crew in attendance and the comely handmaiden draped insentient across their feet. The traitor thought briefly about slitting her throat right there and placing the blade in the hand of another, but in the same instance he was joined by Roger of Doncaster and the opportunity was lost.

"A mighty feast," Roger reflected glumly as he surveyed the comatose bodies, "and not a single one of us here to enjoy it."

"It was the witch from Navarre," Brother Geoffrey informed them a short while later, explaining that the drinking had started shortly after dawn and lasted all day. "She broke out the ale and told them to make merry. She made great sport of it, promising a kiss to the man who drank his measure, and then a gold coin to the one who supped more. And when all were full to the brim, she sent out her two harlots to seek what lewd entertainment they could."

He and Elizabeth were the only ones who'd refused to take part in the revelry, he announced grandly. Both of them remaining at the bow where they'd spent their time in prayer and reflection. Philip listened quietly. He knew there was little love lost between Elizabeth and Brother Geoffrey. Furthermore, he knew their enmity was only exceeded by a mutual hatred of Rosamond. So he had no reason to doubt the monk's version of events. All the same, it didn't prevent him from trying to assign him some of the blame when he'd finally stopped talking.

"Prayer and reflection are all very well," he observed dryly. "But sometimes strong words are required too."

Brother Geoffrey sniffed at this, a shrewd glint in his eye. He knew exactly what Philip was trying to do and he was having none of it. "Oh, my words had strength in them," he assured the future High Sheriff. "Be in no doubt of that. But when a child is left alone to serve no useful purpose, and when that same child has been taught to scorn prayer and truth, what wonder she finds pleasure in devilment and revelry."

He was right too. If anyone was to blame, it was Philip himself. Having confined Rosamond and the others to the safety of the ship, he'd failed to appreciate how difficult a second period of incarceration might prove after so many weeks at sea.

Having funded the entire trip, the last thing Rosamond expected was to find herself held prisoner once they'd reached their destination. Under such circumstances it was hardly surprising the young 'Messalina' from Navarre had rebelled in the only way she knew how, with gleeful disobedience and equally gleeful spite.

Nevertheless, Philip remained impervious to the charge, and sensing Brother Geoffrey bristle with indignation, Robin again moved swiftly to intercede. "Whatever the reason, it's lost on us now," he opined tactfully. "In the morning those responsible can make amends. Until then I suggest we turn our attention to more pressing concerns." He was talking about their young Iroquois prisoner, whom everyone seemed to have forgotten about since returning to the ship. "If he has knowledge regarding the whereabouts of Eustace and the others, we need to find some way of communicating with him."

Brother Geoffrey's eyes turned towards the dark huddle of men stood directly behind Robin and Philip. He gave a small gasp of astonishment as he noticed Kocoum for the first time. "And behold, a leper came to him," he uttered softly after a moment or two. And then noticing the warrior was bound and gagged added indignantly, "Is this how you would treat a brother in Christ?"

"He is no *brother* of mine," Philip replied tersely. "According to Robert he had the track on us for three days. When we finally took him we discovered this." He thrust the small bronze ring at Brother Geoffrey, as though the monk himself bore some responsibility for the circumstances in which it was found. "This is the ring I gave to Marian. It is testimony of my pledge to her. What further proof could you or any other man require that this rogue is in league with my brother and his fellow villains?"

Sensing that Philip already had the matter tried and sentenced in his own head, Brother Geoffrey turned hopefully to Robin. "Be he in league with the devil himself, I see no gain in treating him like an animal," he said reasonably. "Loosen these bonds at least. How is he to regard us if we behave thus?"

Robin shook his head, aware of the monk's concerns, but unprepared to further undermine Philip by siding against him. "We have come here for a single purpose", he stated flatly. "And that purpose is better served when we act and think as one." He pointed at Kocoum. "This poor wretch has the daze in him. Any man with the daze in him has to be secured, both for his own protection, and the protection of those around him. These are the rules of any expedition."

Brother Geoffrey glanced from one to the other, clearly unconvinced, but he took the hint in Robin's tone nonetheless and even helped him tie Kocoum to the mast, muttering a prayer of absolution as he did so.

Much as Robin had suspected, when finally roused from his stupor, Holger could offer little by way of illumination, though he did suggest the young warrior 'looked hungry' which provided them all with an excuse to eat. A short while later, as the others sat in a circle at the brazier, eating the seabird stew Elizabeth had prepared for them; Robin quietly drew the girl to one side. He asked if she'd had a chance yet to study the skraeling prisoner, particularly his hand with its two missing fingers. She told him that she had.

"And how do you suppose he came by such a wound?" He asked evenly, taking care not to pose the question in a way as to illicit any particular response.

"Not by a blade," she informed him assuredly. "The fingers have been torn not cut. Maybe his hand was trapped and he had no choice but to wrench it free. Or perhaps some wild animal seized hold of him in a great frenzy."

They were both quiet for a moment and then Robin asked: "Could a man have inflicted such a wound?"

Elizabeth thought of Holger's story about the young skraeling girl who'd spoken of a powerful warrior priest who could 'bend shadows to his will' and tear fingers from the bone with his bare teeth. It was an unnerving thought that a man made in God's image could commit such an unspeakable act. Yet privately it was a conclusion both she and Robin had already reached. She gave a barely perceptible nod of her head. "Yes", she murmured, "a man *could* have inflicted such a wound."

The following morning, despite Robin's recommendation that he let the matter rest, Philip assembled everyone on the main deck and after Brother Geoffrey had led the prayers, addressed them all in what would ultimately prove a futile attempt to reassert his authority. This expedition was not an 'adventure' he told them pointedly, men should not find themselves so 'taken with ale' they could barely stand. This was a crusade for justice, backed by the Bishop of Hereford and the Holy Father in Rome. He reminded them that Marian was a woman of 'gentle origins', whilst Eustace knew only the 'cruel desires of his own heart'. At which point Rosamond mischievously whispered to Walter of Malmesbury *"Would that he were here now."*

Philip ignored their sniggering and pressed on. "We are of one brotherhood", he told them grandly. "If every one of us is to meet death on this quest, what better way to welcome it than with honour and dignity?"

Needless to say this invocation to duty come-what-may was greeted with scant enthusiasm by the likes of Roger of Doncaster and Ralph of Shrewsbury, both of whom had little intention of 'welcoming' death with either honour, dignity or in any other guise he cared to mention. Despite this, Philip finished with a rousing flourish, charging them all to "shoulder their responsibilities like true Knights of Christ and ride bravely upon the challenge, however daunting it may prove."

It wasn't a bad speech, and one or two of them even gave it a half-hearted cheer, but there was a strong breeze which not only carried away most of his words but also caused the ship to rock unpleasantly, prompting several of the previous days more prominent revellers to suddenly throw up. With the waves slapping up against the side of the hull, Philip rhapsodising interminably and a third of the crew bent double and retching, the morning quickly became a cacophony of competing sounds.

In the meantime those who could hear him weren't listening anyway. Their attention was already focused on the young Iroquois warrior bound to the mainmast.

Rosamond in particular was extremely smitten with their new 'guest'. She confided her enthusiasm to Walter of Malmesbury as soon as they were back in her cabin. The savage was not only of 'good stature'; she declared excitedly, he was 'more finely bodied' and 'handsome in the face' than any man she had ever seen. Adding offensively that Ralph of Shrewsbury was practically a leper by comparison.

And that wasn't all. With a shiver of delight she went on to explain that 'poor little Eve' would need to be 'on guard' against this 'savage Adam'. Whilst at the same time proclaiming that 'just the thought of him' filled her with 'exquisite complications'. As if to demonstrate this, she spent the rest of the day parading back and forth in front of the mainmast where Philip, Robin and Brother Geoffrey – who'd now declared himself Kocoum's 'spiritual guardian' – were all attempting without success to initiate some form of communication with the young warrior. She paused every now and then directly in front of them on the pretext of adjusting some small piece of jewellery or item of clothing, glancing up as she did so, to give the Iroquois a knowing smile.

Eventually Robin grew tired of these constant distractions and shooed her away by threatening to put his boot on her rear. This immediately brought Walter of Malmesbury running to Philip. "My Lady deserves to be treated with honour and respect," he complained haughtily. "If you can't make this bird sing, don't look for blame elsewhere. My Lady has wiles beyond the understanding of any man. Put her to work on him and she'll coax all the songs you need."

It was complete nonsense of course. Rosamond could no more 'coax a song' from Kocoum than she could walk on water. But just the mere suggestion that she was again being excluded from their 'great adventure' put Philip in an extremely difficult position. Things had changed irrevocably in the last few days. Rosamond's gold now circulated freely amongst the crew, with the promise of more to come once they'd all returned safely to England. Under such circumstances, the question of who actually held command was suddenly moot.

Philip took a deep breath. "Tell your Lady…" he began slowly and then paused, caught between what he *wanted* to say and what he knew he *had* to say. "Tell your lady if she has the time to spare, we would greatly appreciate her assistance."

And so Rosamond joined them at the mainmast, where she flashed her eyes a great deal and tossed her hair, before dissolving into a fit of giggles at the increasingly absurd hand gestures Philip was forced to employ in an attempt to communicate with his captive.

As for Kocoum, he was more confused than ever. Although still shackled to the main mast – ostensibly for his 'own protection' – he was extremely well-attended by the majority of swannuken, many of whom appeared to regard him with a curious kind of reverence. Some however seemed less well disposed towards him. They were apt to shout and gesture threateningly whenever they became frustrated, which in Philip's case was all the time. And after a day or so he began to discern a deepening menace in their approach.

On top of which, his head still throbbed from the blow Gisbourne had delivered it back in the woods. He tried his best to concentrate on what they were saying but it was no use. In his current state it was like listening to a pack of wild dogs, all barking and yelping at once. The sound was clear enough, but its shades and cadences were virtually impossible to discern. He knew they were looking for Cloud Man, that much at least had been obvious from their blunderings in the wood. But had they come to rescue him or kill him?

With regards to Rosamond, Kocoum knew only that she was the strangest creature he had ever set eyes upon. Up until this point, Swannuken women had remained a pleasant mystery to him. Marian had always cut an extremely lonely figure, even though it was for the love of her that Cloud Man had purportedly crossed the great salt waters. The others had seemed to divide their time between praying to their strange god and squabbling with each other, neither of which pursuit appeared to bring them much happiness. None however had looked quite as extraordinary as the young woman sat opposite him now. Constantly preening and pouting, with those big black lashes and flushing red cheeks, not to mention the long piece of garment which she dragged behind her as though it were a tail, the Iroquois warrior had presumed she was there simply to provide some spectacle. Yet the more he watched them together, the more he came to understand it was Philip who considered himself on display and Rosamond who actually held power.

Kocoum shut his eyes and tried to clear his mind of all these conflicting sights and sounds. But it was impossible. Tomakin had placed a tiny insect inside his head, and every time he attempted to focus his thoughts he could hear it scratching restlessly against the inside of his skull.

Rosamond pressed a damp cloth gently against his forehead and held it there, almost as though she were conscious of his pain. Kocoum opened his eyes again and looked at her. Rosamond smiled, her eyes playfully lingering on his. "Health and plenty attend you," she whispered pleasantly, but the young warrior winced as he felt the tiny insect bite into the gristle behind his eyes. Kocoum didn't know it yet, but he was already dying.

TWENTY

Twenty Nine Years Later...

Kirklees Nunnery, England.
The Feast of Adam and Eve
24th December 1211.

Elizabeth decided she had no reason to be afraid. They were still on holy ground after all. And on holy ground the Prioress of Kirklees held sway. Let him rage and bluster as much as he liked. In this place *she* would have the final word. The frown on her face eased, and for the first time in years as she watched Philip warm his hands at the small library fire, Elizabeth took comfort in the rigid bindings of coif and wimple.

It had been some time now since either one of them had spoken and she was beginning to grow irritable. Why such an air of melancholy, she wondered, when the whole world was getting ready to celebrate? Hadn't he always envisioned an ending like this? After all, who was left to oppose him now the greatest one of all was gone?

Outside, a sudden gust of wind collected up what remained of the dead autumn leaves and drove them in a great swirling wreath across the open cloister, throwing wide one of the window shutters and guttering several of the candles in the process. With an airy swish, Elizabeth moved quickly to fasten it shut again. *By His hand,* she reminded herself as she wrestled with the rusty lock. *And by my own hand too. I have done what you and no other man alive could do. I have killed Robin Hood!* But just thinking it no longer gave her any satisfaction. And saying it aloud was apparently out of the question given his strange reaction to its expression the first time.

Why is he trying to ruin this, she wondered? For twenty nine years she'd craved nothing but poetry and adventure. And now she'd finally found them at the tip of her bloodstained fingers, he seemed intent on spoiling it. Was it jealousy? Would he prefer it if the blood were on his own hands rather than hers? In all the time that had passed since they'd parted on the beach at Portsmouth, Elizabeth had never known one man so intent upon the ruin of another. Yet now it was finally achieved, he seemed almost morose. It was beyond passing strange, she decided tetchily. Worse still, it was perverse, and she'd had enough of it.

"God keep you sir," she ventured pointedly, "but you grieve most sorely for this man's death that I cannot but wonder, was he by chance a good friend?"

Philip ignored the mischievous sarcasm in her voice and continued to stare down into the fire, apparently absorbed in his own thoughts. She'd told him many things since his arrival. Yet she'd still not answered his original question. *Where?* And he was beginning to grow impatient.

"I grieve not for his death," he replied after a moment, "but for its manner." He paused, a pained expression on his face, as though merely saying it aloud could do him some injury. "For it was not a godly death. And I am not a 'godly' man. And I fear that where the two meet, there shall be the association."

Elizabeth smiled thinly. So that was it. He was thinking of his reputation. "My Lord High Sheriff," she reminded him piously, "you entrusted me with a sum of money and in return I was to ask but one simple question. Yet see how much further I have gone on your behalf, and in the process served you twice over. Mark my word, any 'association' made will be one of courage tempered by justice, and we shall both be celebrated for it." She fairly beamed at the prospect, though Phillip continued to look miserably into the fire, his right hand anxiously massaging the place on his left where he was missing a finger.

"Does it give you much pain?" she asked, eyeing the small bony stump.

He shook his head, quickly removing the hand from view. "Some slight irritation. But I've become accustomed to it." His face grew graver still and he stared into the fire with renewed intensity. "When Marian was here," he began uneasily, "did she ever talk to you about Vinland?"

Elizabeth was silent for a moment. There was a sudden vulnerability in his voice, and for the first time since his arrival she had no wish to scorn it. "Sometimes," she replied delicately. "Though I'd venture she never told me more than she wished me to know."

Philip picked up a stick and poked unhappily at the hearth. "For many years I could not speak of it at all," he confessed candidly, his eyes lost in the reawakened flames. He opened his mouth, as though to say something else then hesitated, silently working the fire with the stick again.

"Do you wish to speak of it now?" Elizabeth enquired, with an uncharacteristic sensitivity that put him briefly in mind of the young girl he'd helped rescue on the Great North Road twenty nine years before.

Phillip nodded keenly, though his eyes never once left the fire. Even as she spoke he was thinking about the last time he and Marian had seen each other and how wretchedly it had gone between them. The meeting had been brokered through the religious offices of Brother Lucius and the Benedictines at Barnsdale, though the setting had been a small wooden chapel on the fringes of Sherwood Forest, presided over by a stout scoundrel named Tuck, whom Lucius had described as a 'sturdy fellow, both in faith and appetite.'

It had been almost a year since they'd last stood together like this, and just the sight of Marian had filled him with renewed hope. Perhaps there was a way to reconcile their differences after all, he'd thought. And to begin with, everything had gone well. They'd talked happily, reminiscing about their younger days in France, as the plump friar discreetly busied himself in a corner, out of earshot but within hailing distance should he be needed. But things had quickly turned sour when discussion turned to their own relationship. Marian had refused his pleas to return with him to Nottingham, making it clear she no longer considered herself in his debt.

"Whatever arrangements were made between us on the ship back to England, I have endeavoured both in gold and prayer to see them fully honoured." She told him flatly. "All I ask now is that we be allowed to go our separate ways in peace."

Having spent two years at Kirklees, submitting herself to the 'discipline' of the sisters there in order to atone for her 'transgressions', whilst at the same time permitting Philip to trade her mother's collection of Saracen jewellery for a lowly position with the crown, Marian considered she'd met any obligations she had to him. Unfortunately Philip felt differently, and angrily told her so.

"I released you from your oath because I sought nothing from you," he declared irately. "Had I looked for the bonds of marriage, or demanded a large dowry, do you think it likely we'd be stood in this dismal place, talking to each other as we are now?"

Seeing his determination to belie the facts, Marian had reminded him that he'd been quick enough to withdraw his own pledge once they'd arrived safely back in England, citing an 'association' with his brother Eustace, as well as her apparent 'love for a savage', as his main reasons for doing so. This had thrown Philip into a mindless fury. Rescuing her had cost not just his time and money, he'd raged, but also the life of his closest friend Gilbert of York, and no amount of gold or prayer would ever release her from that debt. At which point the meeting had come to an abrupt end, with Marian fleeing in tears and the friar moving swiftly to block Philip's path when he sought to follow her.

That had been almost twenty seven years ago, and thereafter Philip Mark had been a noticeably changed man. He rarely attended Mass or left Nottingham's walled citadel without good reason. At the same time he pursued a king's posting with renewed – many said 'ruthless' – vigour. When not soliciting support from some minor noble or spying for Bernat of Navarre, he took to brooding for days on end, drinking more than was good for him, and wearing a face that kept everyone at a distance. He'd even released Alyne from his service, forcing him to abandon the history of 'great deeds done beyond the seas', and advising him instead to 'go on crusade' and 'seek his fortune' in the land of the infidel.

As the years passed, and his behaviour grew steadily worse, a number of troubadours began to chronicle his misdemeanours, most of them bemoaning his cruel and devious nature, though one or two bawdily speculated on his missing finger and where it had been lost. Perhaps unsurprisingly, given Philip's reputation, his own backside was most often cited as the answer to this baffling mystery.

Although harmless in themselves, these songs were dispiriting stuff should you happen to find yourself in a meadow by the River Trent, playing host to Prince John – as Philip did in the spring of 1189 during the Nottingham Goose Fair – only for a barge of drunken peddlers to go gliding by, each bawling voice raised in praise of Philip's 'small brown arrow'. Moreover, they caught on very rapidly, further reinforcing the general impression of him as a mean and degenerate upstart whilst simultaneously compounding his own sense of paranoia and isolation.

"My name is dirt", he complained bitterly to Elizabeth. "When not coupling with my horse or cavorting with a toothless imp, I'm apparently to be found seeking solace from the oracle by way of my own back passage!"

As she listened to him grouse, the Prioress of Kirklees began to discern a trait in Philip she'd hitherto failed to recognise. He wanted people to think well of him. More than wanted, he *needed* them to think well of him. Unfortunately his contradictory nature had made it all but impossible. The strain of trying to reconcile what he'd once described to Robin as the 'two hungry wolves that grappled daily for his attention', had led those around him to conclude he was two-faced and not to be trusted. Indeed, it was said he could speak both 'ill and good' of any person and still hide his true feelings. Nowhere was this more apparent than in the way he spoke about Marian. One moment yearning after her, the next castigating her as someone whose 'notoriously bad reputation' had almost ruined him.

"I would have bent my knee to her even then," he told Elizabeth, still reflecting upon their last encounter. "Had she wished it, I would have set about the stars themselves to see us joined as man and wife." And then, in one of those abrupt turnabout moments that had garnered him such a bad reputation, he added gruffly, "Had I prevailed however I feel most certain she would have eventually coerced me into prayers and candles for the savage. Such was her fondness for him." He gave a humorous snort, though his eyes were devoid of all mirth.

Elizabeth fingered the bear tooth, her eyes agleam with new understanding. "Some have a great wish to be accounted wise or strong," she opined seriously. "They take careful measure of every word, bending it back and forth in their mind, making certain of its purpose before speaking it aloud. Others simply conduct themselves from the heart. Words are spread freely, regardless of their consequence. Who's to say which is best?"

Philip looked at her sharply, aware that his character was being called into question. "I would find more merit in such an opinion if it served some purpose and was not shaped like a rebuke," he warned her tardily.

She gave him a flicker of a smile and pressed on regardless. "You call him a savage", she ventured with careful insight. "And speak as if he had nothing but the base instincts of an animal. Yet you don't believe it. Robin himself numbered Tomakin amongst the most formidable foes he had ever encountered."

He dismissed this with an airy wave of his hand. "He loved the skraelings. By the end of it he was practically a savage himself."

"And what of Marian," she enquired boldly, "by the end of it was she also *practically a savage* too?"

He laughed offensively and answered: "Madam, your imagination is a thing of wonder. Do you really believe I'd have journeyed to this joyless place if that were true?"

"I believe you would have journeyed to the very crack of doom," she rejoined with equal offence, "such is your desire to see her again."

Her sudden self-assurance took him by surprise. He'd grown accustomed to people treating him with deference, and hearing her answer back like this briefly flummoxed him. Picking up the stick he stirred the fire again and tried his best to look suitably noble.

Elizabeth fixed him with a knowing eye. "I have heard tell of a small child abandoned by his mother at the entrance of a cave," she told him, her voice soft and probing. "They say this child was corrupted by the miseries of his life."

"All children are corrupted by misery," he returned curtly, thinking of his own wretched childhood. "Misery *is* the business of life. It makes us who we are."

She nodded sagely, allowing him to make the point for her. "But some wither by it," she suggested candidly, "whilst others survive and even prosper." And here she looked at him directly again. "Perhaps it's to reconcile yourself with these two paths that you've chosen to journey to such a 'joyless place' on this holy feast day of Adam and Eve."

Philip stared at her, his eyes blazing. "You talk as though I share some common ground with the savage," he snarled, barely able to keep outrage from his voice.

Elizabeth remained unperturbed. "Strange to imagine is it not," she prefaced evenly, "that the same God, who fashioned us in His image and provides so ably for our needs, also provides for the needs of the savage, half a world away?"

On another day Philip might have rebuked her for blasphemy. He might have cuffed her smartly across the cheek and shouted that such an assertion was from the devil himself. But this wasn't *another* day. This was the day he'd travelled fifty one years to reach. It was journey's end. So he swallowed heavily and squared his shoulders, just as his father had taught him, and prepared himself.

"I've done hurt enough in my time for ten men," he began awkwardly. "I've set my mind to scheming in the same way a hermit sets his mind to prayer. With rope and mangle I've made my way and never once glanced back. I've sworn good men to ruin and seen whole families put out, all for the sake of a few measly acres. I say this not to excuse or explain, but simply to show I know my own nature. I do what is well by me and worse still, I take pleasure in doing it."

He smiled faintly, more in shame than amusement. If this Cistercian with her blood stained habit and glimmering eye, was to prove his only confessor then so be it. If truth be told, even this small mercy was more than he deserved.

"My father would jeer to see me stood before you like this," he informed her candidly. "I'll warrant it was to prevent precisely such occurrences that he first raised his hand to me." He paused, and even at this great distance Philip could still hear the old tyrant's voice summoning him to judgement. *No piss*, it bawled. *No piss at all!*

"I have heard him called 'great'" he mused bitterly. "Though 'bloody' is the title more often assigned to his deeds. I'll grant he had rage enough in him for a hundred knights, the spite to find reason in it too, but I would not credit either attribute as 'great'. 'Speak it false or speak it true but never make a blend of it'. That was his conviction. But I say sometimes the two *are* blended. That is *my* conviction."

He took the small silver coin she'd given him earlier and rolled it carefully through his fingers. As he watched it crest and fall his expression grew ever more ponderous. "I would tell you something of my time in Vinland," he said at length, his eyes still riveted on the coin. "Perhaps you are acquainted with the details. I cannot say. But each man's story is his own, and for what small balance it may bring, I would have you hear mine."

Like unhappy men everywhere, Philip collected memories in order to facilitate his misery. Remembering certain events with a particular keenness allowed him to nurture a specific grudge or indulge some private anguish he might otherwise have dismissed as self-pity. This time however his memory served a far greater purpose. It allowed him to tell the truth. And with barely a pause he launched into a full and honest account of his time in Vinland. Much of it she already knew. But that didn't matter. Confession was his purpose. And because of that, she listened attentively.

He began by speaking about Eustace and Gilbert and the 'catastrophe' which had befallen Rosamond, before moving on to describe in grisly detail the horrifying discovery he'd made in Tomakin's cave, and the moment when the shaman's teeth had closed around his finger. He reflected on his 'thorny friendship' with Robin whom he claimed to admire 'more than any man living', despite having issued a dozen warrants for his arrest in the past year alone. And finally, he confirmed the demise of *the one who would betray them* in Jerusalem five years later.

Most of all however, he talked about Marian, his voice cracking with emotion every time he recalled her wonderful 'brown-eyed face', beautiful 'beyond all imagining'. He cursed his obsession with 'reputation' and the opinion of others, which he claimed had caused him to lose her in the first place, and damned Eustace for 'putting him to the test' when he must have known what the likely outcome would be. If Elizabeth had been in any doubt at all about his true feelings for Marian, by the time he'd finished there was no question at all. He loved her to the point of distraction.

When he'd finally finished, they stood in silence for a moment, and he fell to examining the back of his hand, the sudden awkwardness between them almost palpable. Looking up again he was surprised to find her eyes were reddened from crying, and even more surprised to discover his own cheeks were wet with tears too. In fact the sudden change in both of them was startling. She positively glowed with feminine empathy now, whilst he'd shed the air of remoteness he'd toiled so hard all these years to cultivate.

And so, before either of them could speak, he did the only thing he could think of, the thing he'd wanted to do ever since he first got here, the thing he should have done twenty nine years before on the ship. He took her in his arms and kissed her.

"Please Elizabeth," he pleaded when they finally broke. "I must know. Tell me where she is or by the faith I swear I'll not have sound sleep again."

She held onto him for a moment, taking pleasure in the firmness of his body against hers. "I will take you to her," she said at last.

TWENTY ONE

North East Vinland, the 'Great Eastern Woodlands Region'
The feast of Saint Olympias
17th December, 1182.

Ten days after her extraordinary encounter with *father*, Marian woke to a new and even more immediate danger. It arrived early one morning in the form of a deadly fever and by sunset of the second day it had swept clean through the entire village, killing a dozen outright and leaving many others – Tomakin included – fighting for their lives.

With the shaman seemingly unable to protect them, most of his 'family' simply packed their belongings and fled into the surrounding woods. Those who remained gathered around the fires at night, chanting and singing and muttering darkly about Marian. All of their current misfortunes, including the fever, had begun with the advent of the swannuken settlement and her arrival amongst them.

In addition, many of them resented the way Tomakin had favoured her over all the other women in his 'family'. In particular, they resented the *wifely* status he'd conferred upon her, even though she clearly reviled him and appeared to perform no 'wifely' duties whatsoever, apart from rendering him constantly unhappy.

Now, with the shaman unable to intercede on her behalf, this under-swell of resentment turned to open hostility. Food was no longer provided, and when she approached one of the cooking pots she was angrily chased away. Such was the sense of malevolence towards her; Marian took to sleeping with a knife by her side, just in case.

One or two of the more docile ‘family’ members eventually took pity on her. But even they only offered her scraps. The rest simply ignored her or turned their backs, and before long Marian was praying for Tomakin’s swift recovery as keenly as she’d once wished for his demise.

Tomakin meanwhile, unaware of all that was happening around him, floated effortlessly between oblivion and life. Loosed by the fever from all bodily restrictions, he drifted up freely through the cloudy ether of memory and dreams, away from the two hungry wolves and *the old woman who knew how to heal*, away from *father* and the wendigo, and into a glittering new world of perception. And the more he lingered in this feverish state, the more he began to discern his life, picturing it, as if from a great height.

Though initially disorientating, this quickly proved an enlightening experience, especially as his celestial self was able to comprehend what the earthly part of him had never fully understood, namely that he was neither insane nor possessed by a wendigo. He was just a boy who’d continued to look at the world through the unhappy mist of his mother’s eyes. Deprived of the pipe and the potent mix of sacred herb which had kept him enslaved, he began to take a proper account of things. And with the past flowing through him in a great rush of clarity, he suddenly found himself at the moment just ten days before, when Marian had first run sobbing from the cave. Only this time *he understood.*

"That monstrous *thing*", she was shouting at him, and at the word 'thing' she threw an accusing finger back towards the cave. "That *disgusting abomination* is not your father! Nor is it any other part of your repellent 'family'. That *outrage* is a wickedness raised up by Satan, and you do ill to even look upon it."

Ten days ago he'd presumed this was all just a misunderstanding, a momentary delirium brought on by her first encounter with *father.* Now he saw clearly it was something else altogether. When he'd moved closer to pacify her she'd angrily pummelled him away with her fists, screaming, "No, no, I will not be hushed into silence. How can you behave as though this were natural? Is your head so foggy with uppowoc smoke that you've lost all reason? Do you not see it with your own eyes?" And before he could say anything she'd fallen to her knees, repeating the refrain *Jesu Miserere*[25] over and over to herself.

Feverish, Tomakin looked down as his bodily-self stared at her in bewilderment. "Aren't you happy?" he heard himself asking innocently. "Aren't you pleased that he likes you?"

But instead of answering his question Marian was slapping her hand against the ground in frustration, shouting, "*Father* cannot possibly like me because *father* cannot possibly like anything. Father

---

[25] ***Jesus have mercy.***

is an illusion. He is something you have fashioned from your own wounded imagination". And for the first time he noted there was something that sounded almost like pity in her voice. "I had once counted you a great master of deception", she was telling him miserably, "but now I can see you are more *deceived* than *deceiving.*"

This had originally thrown him into a mindless fury. It was a lie, he'd told her. Something she was saying in order to confuse him. *Father* wasn't an 'illusion'; he was as real as anything else in the world. To imply otherwise would be the same as comparing Tomakin to a small child who stared at the clouds and perceived in them shapes and faces that simply weren't there. A man would have to be deranged even to imagine such a thing. More than deranged, he would have to be…but no, he wouldn't say it. Not even to her. Marian was attempting to trick him. That was the beginning and the end of it. The wendigo had been right all along. Swannuken women couldn't be trusted. Only blood would suffice.

Only blood! The instant he'd thought it, a shiver of pleasure had run the length of his body. And with that shiver he'd felt the wendigo inside him begin to uncoil itself. *We are as one*, it had purred soothingly. *Nothing can separate us. Nothing can soften our bite. Let me loose on her so I can avenge thee.*

Yet despite a terrible compulsion to obey, Tomakin had braced himself. "I still have the song of her in my head," he'd protested weakly. "It is a song I cannot refuse, even though it fills me with doubt."

The wendigo had snorted in derision. *It is a melancholy song,* it had hissed. *And soon we will bring it to an end. Say the word and I will sing thee a song of my own.*

Now, as he floated between life and death, the shaman realised it wasn't Marian's dash from the cave that had disturbed him. It was what she'd told him afterwards. And now he'd had time to reflect on it, not just *what* she'd told him, but *how* she'd told him, the sense of despair in her voice. A sense of *despair* not even the pipe had been able to subdue.

"I am cast down into hell", she'd wept wretchedly. "Cast down into hell and here surely is the final proof!"

"But *father* has chosen you," he'd reminded her weakly. "He spoke to you."

She'd shaken her head vigorously at this. And from the clarity of his fever, he saw that when she'd looked at him again there had been a new and terrible understanding in her eyes. "No", she'd informed him sadly. "Father didn't speak to me. He cannot speak. You hear his voice but he does not speak."

"But *father* has promised," he heard himself insisting. "He wants us to be happy together. He told me so himself." He'd said it like a small child, so hopeful and full of innocence that Marian had hung her head and sobbed. And he realised now that in her desperation she'd clutched at the only thing she had left.

"Do you love me?" The words had been so direct and unexpected they'd momentarily caught him off guard. And he remembered now that even at the time they'd sounded more like a challenge than a question. Tomakin had hesitated, immediately cautious. Of course he loved her. He loved her to obsession. Not like Eustace and the other boys back in rural France, who saw only the beauty and none of the grace. He loved her in the way Philip loved her, the way Robin would eventually come to love her. He loved her regardless of everything and everyone. And he would have shouted it too if she'd asked him. Yet he'd sensed this wasn't the purpose of her enquiry.

"Do you invite me to answer for the sake of amusement," he'd enquired cagily, wary of her attempts to trick him in the past. "Or do you have some deeper curiosity?"

"I invite you to answer as a man to a woman," she'd rejoined purposefully. And here was the challenge again. "I invite you to answer in truth."

"Have you ever doubted it?" he heard himself reply. And from his fever he saw for the first time how touched Marian had been by this simple response. He also saw that her real purpose hadn't been to manipulate him as he'd supposed, but rather to bring about a genuine transformation in his understanding.

"I will not lie," she'd told him flatly. "I had first thought to play upon these feelings, in the hope they might bring me some advantage in our future dealings." She'd hesitated briefly at this point, perhaps realising what she was about to say would have grave consequences for both of them. "The truth is I cannot love you." She'd told him squarely, her fists bunching tightly into white knuckles of resolution. "And I *will not* love you. But if you do me this one service I promise to remain at your side for as long as you desire it."

Somewhere between the reality of the longhouse and the memory of that moment outside the cave, Tomakin struggled desperately to break the fever's grip. Something was happening he told himself. It was something important and he needed to return to his body in order to make certain he was ready for it.

"What would you have me do?" he heard himself asking her.

"Close your eyes and return to the moment your mother left you," she'd instructed him evenly. "See *'father'* as you saw him that very first time. Before fear and pipe smoke put a fog in your soul." And she'd taken a firm grip on both his arms, her voice exhorting. "See him clearly Tomakin. See him as he really is. Not as you imagine or wish him to be. See him as I see you now."

And even from this great distance Tomakin felt himself respond. Outside the cave he'd resisted her, pulling away angrily and cursing her for trying to deceive him. But now, as he shivered in the longhouse, he knew he had to go back. He had to see what she had seen. He had to know the truth.

Twenty five years before, he'd woken to the sounds of a new day and the dawning realisation that his mother was never coming back for him. Summoned by the light, he'd walked cautiously to the cave entrance. The sun outside had dazzled his eyes. And as he raised a hand to shield himself, he'd seen *father* for the very first time. He could still picture the moment, even after all the years. The slow roll of *his* enormous shoulders, the ponderous nature of each heavy footfall, the terror Tomakin as a small boy had felt as he'd watched this immense figure come crunching through the undergrowth towards him.

And suddenly he was conscious and in the longhouse again, and Marian was sat over him and the fever was finally abating and everything around him was returning to normal. Except for the shaman himself, who'd returned to the world in a new rush of comprehension. "Why did she say it?" he asked desperately, as Marian reached over to soothe his brow. "Why did she tell me he was my father?" And it was the small child in him asking now as much as the grown man.

Marian's hand came to rest gently upon his arm. Despite everything he'd done, despite everything he might yet do, she didn't want him to hear any more lies. So she told him the truth. His mother had been touched by a terrible malady she explained, and in time that malady had made her behave in a way that was neither rational nor kind. It was a sickness of thought she told him, not of body. And because Tomakin the child had sought refuge from her malice, he too had eventually fallen victim to it. Picture the woods, she said. See how a healthy tree will grow in harmony with itself. Yet a tree that sickens will begin to spread branches it does not require or recognise. In time its trunk and branches might even start to believe they are not from the same root. In confusion, one part may even imagine itself *possessed* by the other. A tree in such an unhappy condition can spread many branches she said, each one stranger and more jagged than the last.

Tomakin listened quietly as she described the symptoms. He understood perfectly now. Watching from his celestial vantage point he'd quickly come to realise all was not well. Yet even as he told himself the wendigo was not real but merely a deceit of his imagination, he felt it struggle suddenly to raise itself and heard its rasping voice whisper in his ear. *I will always return Tomakin. And you will always welcome me. We are as one, and nothing can separate us, not even death!*

Six days after its arrival the fever had finally left him completely, and by the seventh day he was up and walking around again. In taking him to the brink of death, the infection had performed Tomakin a great service. In addition to weakening the power of the wendigo, it had also ended his craving for the pipe, leaving him more conscious of his own condition. Perhaps for the first time in his life the shaman now understood *what* he was as well as *why*.

As usual he sought out Marian. They talked a lot that day. And as they talked a new feeling gradually came upon him. Not hope exactly, much quieter than hope, but a kind of peace nonetheless.

He reached out and let his fingers slowly tighten around hers. "I am fully recovered," he assured her quietly. "I have dreamt the long dream, but now I am awake again."

That night he disappeared into the woods. When he returned again, two days later, he brought news that would have ramifications for Marian far beyond the Great Eastern Woodlands.

TWENTY TWO

North East Vinland, the 'Great Eastern Woodlands Region' (Somewhere along what is now the New York/Connecticut coastline)
The feast of Saint Ethelgiva of Shaftesbury
9th December, 1182.

The day of what Brother Geoffrey would quickly come to describe as 'the great shame' began much as any other. The ship rocked gently to and fro, the sky above was a mottled grey, yet not oppressively so and the slight breeze which ruffled the sea around them, brought a pleasing freshness to the main deck. The night watch had reported no movement on the mainland and Oswald of Norwich was stoking the brazier with his customary zeal.

Brother Geoffrey himself led the morning worship, and Rosamond knelt alongside the others, head dipped as if in prayer. But she did not pray. For the young heiress from Navarre, religious observance had become something of an obligation rather than an act of faith. In large measure she no longer believed in anything other than her own good fortune, and of late even that had seemed in much shorter supply than usual.

The previous afternoon, following two fruitless days spent waving his arms at the skraeling captive and shouting the name *'Marian'* over and over again, Philip had finally agreed to take her ashore. But having raised Rosamond's expectations he'd then abruptly dashed them again by insisting she remain within sight of the ship, limiting her explorations to nothing more than a short paddle in the shingle. Meanwhile Robin and the others had been permitted to hunt freely in the woods beyond, ‘replenishing’ the ship’s supplies according to Philip, but partaking in ‘a great adventure’ as far as Rosamond was concerned.

“Madam, I think only of your safety,” Philip had told her tetchily when she’d complained about this latest restriction.

“Sir, you *think* only of my purse,” she rejoined sharply, unwilling to be browbeaten any longer by this familiar edict. Whereupon Philip’s patience had appeared to finally snap, and he’d angrily suggested that if she felt this way she should ‘run to the woods immediately and leave the rest of them in peace’. Adding that if in the course of doing so some ‘terrible danger’ was to present itself, he would ‘greatly appreciate’ it if she refrained from calling out as he no longer wished to concern himself with her absurd wittering.

Rosamond had felt the spite in his words and though she’d said nothing at the time, the more she’d thought about it afterwards, the more she’d wanted to repay it in kind. More than just repay it, she wanted to defy it. To do something so bold, so utterly shocking, it would leave Philip and the rest of them with no recourse other than to gasp in wonder and whisper amongst themselves ‘only Rosamond of Navarre would dare do something like that’.

As usual with Rosamond, there was no plan, just a general air of recklessness waiting for the right moment. Thus, at the tinkling of the Sanctus bell the following morning she rose suddenly to her feet. All night she'd lain sleepless on her mattress, thinking about the savage. Here was a real man she told herself, instinctive and free, roaming like Adam in his own private Eden, unencumbered by all the rigours and morality of religion. She longed to reach out and touch him, to sink her nails into his thick arms and feel his weight bear down on her. As Brother Geoffrey elevated the sacred host high above his head an impulse suddenly took her and she turned towards the mainmast. Seeing the devilment in her eyes, Philip immediately stood and followed her.

She arrived in front of Kocoum a second or two before him – Ralph of Shrewsbury would later claim that she'd bared her breasts at the young warrior, but this was largely wishful thinking on the excitable knight's part. Nevertheless, the way she shaped herself, the arch in her back, the provocative swing of her hips as she circled him, and the trailing finger she ran lightly along the young Iroquois's shackled arm, suggested she had come here to do more than just flutter her eyelashes.

As Philip approached, she inclined her head in mock courtesy. "A peaceful day," she chirruped innocently, though she couldn't quite keep the mischief from her voice. She wore her hair in looped braids, with a jewelled fillet crowning the small veil upon her head. Unlike her two handmaidens she'd forgone a heavy cloak in favour of a thin shawl which barely covered her shoulders let alone her dress, which was fashioned from expensive silk, tapering in at the waist so it was less wide in the skirt than usual, and far more closely fitting. Her cheeks were heavily rouged and her arms were adorned with the customary profusion of ringlets and wrist bangles. Even though he loathed her, Philip had to admit she still presented a rousing sight.

"By the grace of God," he answered cautiously, aware of the wicked glint in her eyes.

She extended a languorous hand towards Kocoum, sat dolefully with his back against the mainmast, shackled at both wrist and ankles, and pulled him slowly to his feet. "This poor creature needs exercise," she declared lightly. "Release him from these fetters and I will walk him around the deck a time or two."

Philip ignored this request, reminding her instead that morning Mass was 'not yet finished' and prayers 'half said' were worse than 'prayers not said at all.'

Rosamond smiled privately, her pretty little elfin face with its pointed chin and sparkling eyes playing over him with a look of quiet disdain. "Are you my priest now, as well as my jailor?" she enquired derisively. "And if so, by whose authority do you proclaim yourself such?" As she said this she moved closer to Kocoum, petting him like a tethered horse and making small cooing noises in her throat.

Philip was determined not to let her provoke him in front of the others. "My Lady", he warned her calmly, "I pray you keep a guard upon your thoughts, less you should find they lead you astray."

She snorted in contempt. "Do not seek to catechise me sir," she warned icily. "I was made promise of a great adventure. Instead of which I find myself held prisoner on board this stinking barge."

"You lack for patience madam", he informed her with all the equanimity he could muster. "I have told you many times, when all is safe, you shall have as much 'adventure' as you desire."

She slapped the mast in frustration with the flat of her hand. "Have you not heard me?" she demanded. "Am I speaking in a foreign tongue that you so wilfully ignore what I repeatedly say to you!"

Her voice was raised now, and Philip didn't need to glance over his shoulder to know that everyone was staring at them. Even Brother Geoffrey had stopped saying Mass in order to watch.

"I will not trade insults with you," he told her firmly. "I have spoken my last. Now retire to your cabin and remain there until you have regained your composure."

But Rosamond wasn't about to 'retire' anywhere. Nor was she going to let Philip speak to her as if she were a disobedient child. After all, it was nearly eleven weeks since they'd first set sail from Portsmouth and what did she have to show for it? One night of carousing with Ralph of Shrewsbury, which had barely proved adequate, a decidedly prickly encounter with Huntingdon and the loss of her only true love Lycomedes. Added to which most of her clothes were ruined, whilst the other knights no longer appeared to regard her with anything like the same appetite they'd shown at the journey's outset, and this despite her continued efforts to persuade them otherwise. It was beyond all reasoning. Was she

Job's wife that she had to endure misfortune after misfortune without a single moment's recompense? No, she decided, Philip Mark had burdened them long enough with his fusty rules. Now she finally had everyone's attention, it was time to make some new rules of her own.

"I hear you count yourself a man of learning," she opined airily, though the edge in her voice was unmistakable. "Well I have some teachings of my own to perform. So take heed, you may wish to be a beneficiary of them yourself one day." And in a deliberate act of defiance she moved herself even closer to Kocoum, nuzzling against him in a manner which was barely decent.

Philip's heart sank. She was making her challenge, and he was powerless to stop her. Ever since returning to find the ship in disarray and Rosamond's gold common currency amongst the crew, the balance of power had shifted markedly in her favour. Any attempt now to retaliate would only divide the ship in a way not seen since Gilbert of York succumbed to the sweating sickness.

"My Lady," he began softly, but it sounded more like a plea than a command. "I swear you do yourself no good by acting this way."

She laughed in his face, her dark eyes gleaming like sloes. "But I detect I do a great deal of *good* somewhere else," she returned. And before Philip could respond, she dropped her hand suddenly, and with a squeal of delight whipped away the flimsy breechclout which preserved Kocoum's modesty, leaving his naked genitalia exposed for all to see.

The gasps of astonishment which greeted this, where as much reserved for the shocking act itself as for what it had actually revealed. Here was wanton behaviour on an unprecedented scale. Surely only an incorrigible harlot would conduct herself in such a bold and shameless manner. Even boisterous old rogues like Harold of Leicester and Roger of Doncaster were temporarily rendered speechless, whilst the so-called 'mute' Crispin of Lincoln was heard to utter his first 'ooh' sound.

It wasn't so much the sight of the savage's reproductive organ, or even its size. It was the unambiguous *condition* in which it now presented itself. As Gisbourne had observed on more than one occasion, Rosamond was clearly no stranger to the 'society of men', and judging from the effect her close proximity had coaxed in the young Iroquois, they were equally enthusiastic about her.

Ralph of Shrewsbury, as ever the eager fool, was first to break the stunned silence. He called out jokingly that having 'summoned the devil' it was surely Rosamond's duty to 'attend to him' in a manner befitting his 'proud appearance'. Like all stupid things it was said largely for effect. But Rosamond was not someone you readily put to the test, even in mirth. And no sooner were the words spoken than she had her hand on Kocoum's penis, and was working it purposefully back and forth.

It's a curious fact of life, but there are certain moments when time appears to both hurry and stand still simultaneously. Thus, whilst unfolding, a particular incident will appear to last forever, yet in retrospect be shown not to have lasted any length of time at all. In this manner, unpleasant acts are often said to have occurred in the 'blink of an eye'. What now transpired between Rosamond and the young Iroquois would prove no exception to this unhappy rule.

When she'd originally torn away the breechclout, the flighty young heiress had no plans beyond simply shocking them. However, with Ralph of Shrewsbury daring her to go further, and everyone else gawping in horror as though she were from the devil himself, she'd suddenly felt emboldened and sensed an opportunity to set her mark upon the expedition once and for all. As a result she was now going at Kocoum with a genuine purpose, like Messalina disporting with a slave at some Roman bacchanalia.

There were a several murmurs of 'shame' and 'harlot' as well as one or two half-hearted cheers – mostly from Ralph of Shrewsbury, who didn't really approve at all, but having unwisely voiced his encouragement now felt obliged to see it through come what may. By and large however, apart from the gentle 'tingling' sound of Rosamond's wrist bangles, and the odd spontaneous 'yelp' from Gisbourne, the entire sordid spectacle proceeded in awkward silence. Indeed there was even an air of complicity. After all, they'd watched her parade on deck each day. They'd heard all the rumours. Now they wanted to see if any of it was true. Like mourners at an open grave, it was a mixture of curiosity and detachment that kept them watching.

That and the little thrill that came with finally discovering just how far she really would go!

Brother Geoffrey would later attempt to extricate himself from any blame by claiming to have confused Rosamond's initial ministrations with an attempt to 'coax information' from the savage, or even to place a 'restraint' on him. But even if that had been true, which of course it wasn't, it still didn't explain the peculiar state of paralysis which now gripped not just him, but Philip and Robin too.

To understand that, one would first need to recognize that young women like Rosamond of Navarre did not spring fully formed into a world of their own making. They were carefully fashioned in the fears and desires of men by a clergy fixated on 'fleshly sins', and then routinely chastised when they attempted to make good on those fears and desires. It was a world in which women were portrayed as horses, fit only to be mounted. Where female 'wickedness' was accounted 'greater than all the other wickedness of the world put together,' and where even a young boy's own mother was liable to warn that the 'poisons of asps and dragons' was 'more curable' and 'less dangerous' than the 'familiarity of women.'

Yet at the same time the cult of the Virgin had swept through Europe, raising shrines in every village and filling its churches and cathedrals with freshly cut flowers and images of motherhood and 'courtly love' quite at odds with the prevailing depictions of women. It was even claimed the girl from Palestine could mediate directly with God. In such a febrile atmosphere it was hardly surprising that while some like Philip sought refuge in old 'certainties', others like Rosamond occasionally ran to excess.

Not that Kocoum minded. As a young man he'd regularly visited *the old woman who could heal*, and happily allowed her to perform a similar service on him, quite often while his friends stood watching. And that was the difference between them. Unlike their European counterparts, the indigenous peoples of Vinland openly celebrated the union between men and women. And despite the frozen expressions on the faces of those watching, he was finding the whole experience rather pleasurable. Little of what he'd seen or heard thus far had made any sense to him. But here was something he *did* understand. Added to which, the woman's touch was soft and her technique surprisingly accomplished. It even occurred to him that she was offering her proficiency as a gift and that he shouldn't cause offence by refusing it.

Surprisingly, Rosamond was feeling nowhere near as comfortable or indeed self-assured as her demeanour suggested. Now she'd finally got their attention, she was no longer sure she actually wanted it. Her throat was bone dry and her heart was hammering frantically against the wall of her chest. At the same time, she feared if she stopped now, the jeering and catcalls would prove even more damaging than the gasps of horror. All which left her with no alternative other than to smile confidently and see it through.

Philip meanwhile had visibly crimsoned with shame. He'd not felt such a conflict of emotions since secretly following Elizabeth down to the brook on the

Great North Road to watch her bathe. As Rosamond draped herself around the savage, Philip wanted to reach out and stop her. Yet there was something so hypnotic about that rhythmic 'tingling' and the languid movement of her elbow, that he felt his arms lock into position at his side and his feet take root where he stood. Yes it was abhorrent and sinful, and yes his cheeks could already feel the flames of hell. But as much as he was repelled and disgusted by it, there was also a part of him that wanted to see it done now. Properly done, the way he knew only she would do it.

Nearby, Robin felt himself stirred by a similar impulse. He adjusted his hood so that his face was hidden from view, like a monk disappearing into his dark cowl. As for Brother Geoffrey, the sight filled him with such a mixture of anger and desire that for a brief moment he felt as if he might faint. He wanted to look away but like Philip and the others, found he was incapable of doing so. Next to him, Harold of Leicester was staring open mouthed, a look of besotted fascination etched on his face. It was so brazen, and the savage so uninhibited in his desire, that they might have been witnessing the 'magic hour' of any May festival back in England when young revellers took to the woods in search of the green man, and nature was set loose to roam and ravage as it willed.

Rosamond caught the roguish look in his eye and gave him a flicker of a smile, but there was an eager, almost desperate motion in her now that matched the quickening pace of her hand. "I am Eve."

She whispered in Kocoum's ear. "I run naked through the soft grasses of Eden. Release yourself to me." She sensed the movement in his body and hastened her hand accordingly. "Let go my darling", she murmured, "show them all how Eve brings forth life!"

She'd practically forgotten about the others watching her now. Who cared what any of them thought? She was Rosamond of Navarre. She could do as she pleased. She suddenly felt light-headed. The fear and uncertainty of just a few moments ago was cast off, and for the first time in weeks she was completely free. No longer would she let them restrict her or tell her what to do, she decided. From this point forward, she would be in control.

As Philip and the others continued to watch, a soft rain began to patter gently on the deck around them. It was one of those steady mizzles and despite the slight breeze it felt sticky and uncomfortable. Moreover the continual beads of water that dripped from their eyelashes and bearded chins did nothing to improve their self-esteem. In addition, Gisbourne's 'yelping', accompanied by the compulsive tap of his foot, had bizarrely established a kind of rhythm with Rosamond's hand, creating the impression of a squeaky water pump being worked with ever increasing gusto.

Perhaps surprisingly, of all those present, only Walter of Malmesbury found it within himself to finally break the trance-like hush and raise a voice in protest. "Rosamond", he pleaded fretfully. "Rosamond, I beg of you, enough now." He stepped forward in a belated attempt to intervene, but it was already too late. With a final victorious little jerk she completed the task and in the same moment pulled away just as the Iroquois released his seed, which splattered unpleasantly against Walter's chest. This provoked a ripple of cruel guffaws, and served to break the strange spell which had thus far rendered them all transfixed.

"There's pith in her arm, and no mistake!" Roger of Doncaster observed dryly to *the one who would betray them* in what might have passed for admiration had the circumstances not been so grim.

Rosamond looked at Philip for the first time and smiled, as if daring him to rebuke her. "You seem angry my lord," she remarked with mischievous smirk. "Has something happened to rouse your blood?"

Philip shook his head. "Not angry My Lady," he answered quietly; "it is disgust I feel."

She raised an amused eyebrow. "Disgust you say. And I am not even half finished yet. Take care sir, or you will run out of disapproving words long before I run out of deeds requiring your disapproval." She removed the shawl from around her shoulders and used it to carefully wipe the mess from Walter of Malmesbury's chest.

"You misunderstand me My Lady," Philip informed her evenly. "The 'disgust' I feel is entirely for myself, as is the shame."

Rosamond was taken aback. She'd expected him to be furious. Instead of which he seemed to be blaming himself. Or was he? Even as she listened the young heiress detected that all too familiar note of censure in his voice. Was it possible, she wondered, that Philip Mark had found a way to both insult her and appear to apologise at the same time? The instant the thought struck her she was certain of it. Yet like Gisbourne before her, she realised the words were so masterfully weighted that to challenge them would only invite further opprobrium.

"It is curious is it not," she opined wryly, determined not to be outfaced, "that the longer we spend together on this ship, the less pleasure we appear to take in each other's company."

Philip exhaled sadly, as though in sympathy. "It is curious indeed My Lady," he rejoined solemnly. "But I fear we have laboured hard to make it thus."

Rosamond's expression changed. They'd played this game long enough. It was time for her to remind him who was in charge. "Make good on your promises Philip Mark, whose family are in such good favour with the King," she told him firmly. "Give me an adventure or I will turn this ship around and sail it back to England. And if you doubt I have the will to do so, think upon what you've just seen and remember whose gold funded this expedition in the first place."

Despite the elfin chin and painted cheeks, there was an unmistakable grit to Rosamond's words, suggesting the matter was already past debate. Philip guessed this came from the knowledge that seven of his knights had formerly pledged their swords to her, with a further three on the brink of doing so. Faced with such ruinous odds, the future High Sheriff of Nottingham, Derbyshire and the Royal Forests had no option other than to gracefully acquiesce.

"I am willing to do whatever My Lady commands," he assured her courteously, dipping his head in reverence.

Satisfied they'd reached an understanding; Rosamond drew a deep breath and then flounced off triumphantly towards her cabin. "By my own hand," she boasted as she passed Elizabeth on the way, depositing the soiled shawl at her feet.

The rest of them stood on deck for a moment, their heads bowed in the soggy gloom. There wasn't a man among them who hadn't found himself momentarily aroused by Rosamond's 'tryst' with Kocoum. And there wasn't a man among them who didn't now regret those shameful stirrings. Even Kocoum, whose innocence Rosamond had exploited, found himself infected by the sombre atmosphere.

"A new verse is added to your history of great deeds done beyond the sea," Brother Geoffrey advised Philip derisively as they eventually drifted back to their posts. "Inscribe it well my lord, for I shall make sure men sing upon it for many years to come!"

That night, abandoning his post as night watch, Robin crept quietly over the sleeping bodies and, taking care not to wake anyone, unlocked Kocoum's chains. He gestured silently with his hands towards the mainland and even with the daze in him the young warrior didn't need telling twice. Slipping off his shackles he climbed quietly over the side of the ship, and wading the short distance to the shore, promptly disappeared into the woods. The moment he was gone an anxious looking Philip appeared at Robin's side.

The two men spoke softly so as not to alert any of the others. There would be time enough in the morning to explain the plan to them.

"Do you think it'll work?" Philip enquired nervously, his eyes peering blindly into the dark.

Robin shrugged, after the past few weeks he was no longer sure of anything. "We shall know in the morning," he replied. "But even if we find a trail, there's no telling where it might lead. This one has the daze in him, and the daze will cause a man to wander without reason. We could track him for days and still not see an end to it."

This seemed to bother Philip much less than the possibility of losing Kocoum altogether, and far from being dismayed, he actually appeared buoyed by the prospect. "Have no fear" he assured Robin. "His trail will lead us directly to Marian. And where Marian is, there also shall we find Eustace." He said it with such a reviving confidence of success that for the first time in days the ghost of a smile actually appeared on Robin's weary face. Seeing it, Philip smiled too, and they stood in the uncertain moonlight for a moment, grey faces on a shady backdrop, neither one quite sure how the other now felt about him.

"We must not let this place change us Robert," Philip opined suddenly, in what Robin assumed was a reference to the earlier 'incident' with Rosamond. "Even when we lose our way we must never forget the Holy Virgin is still our guide. She goes before us in all things. She is our protector. As long as we remain true to her, no harm will come to us. I feel most certain of that." He caught the glint in Robin's eye and anticipated what was coming next. "*Friends call you 'Robin'*, yes I know. But friends will also twist their words and hide their true faces. A family will do neither. And that's what we are Robert, a family. A family with all its faults and feuds I grant you, but a family nonetheless."

Philip turned his face towards the moon, and Robin saw that the arches and hollows around his eyes and cheeks had grown much darker and more pronounced than they'd been the last time they'd stood together under moonlight like this. It was almost as if his features were beginning to mirror the lunar landscape far above. Is that what I look like, Robin wondered? Has the madness of Vinland turned us all into shadowy faced spectres?

Unaware of Robin's disquiet, Philip was rhapsodising in earnest on the theme of 'family'. Conveniently forgetting all about his own brother, he declared Robin to be his 'brother' instead. And the more he spoke the more convinced of it he seemed to become. Far from barren, he insisted, the future was seeded with opportunity. Once they'd rescued Marian, and settled his affairs with Eustace, they could all return to England where the King would find him a posting and the two of them would see out their days together in everlasting friendship. Things might seem a little difficult now, he avowed, but rest assured, the life that awaited them would yield a truly wonderful harvest.

Three days later as the savages drove in on them from all sides, Robin wondered if Philip might have been a little hasty in assuming the Virgin's unequivocal support for their expedition. How else to explain the catastrophe which now threatened to overwhelm them? *Say the prayer*, he told himself. *Say the prayer she taught you.* But in the end there wasn't even time for that. As he notched an arrow, one of the skraelings fetched him a vicious blow across the head. For an instant the world swam around him and he felt his legs begin to buckle. The last thing he saw as darkness rushed in was the face of the devil, complete with horns, looking down at him.

TWENTY THREE

North East Vinland, the 'Great Eastern Woodlands Region'
The Feast of Saint Drostan
15th December 1182.

They tortured the so-called 'mute' Crispin of Lincoln for almost two days. At times he screamed so loudly that even Brother Geoffrey covered his ears and prayed for it to end. At night, the burning torches in the village outside gave off a light which permeated every crack and fissure in the wooden longhouse; illuminating its dark alcoves and making their bruised and battered faces flicker with a savage red glow.

Of the eighteen who'd followed the second trail into the woods, only nine now remained, one of whom (Crispin) was currently being put to death somewhere close by in a manner too grisly to contemplate. Indeed, *the one who would betray them* wept openly when he thought about the paltry sum of money he'd accepted in return for journeying into this living hell. And even Ralph of Shrewsbury, who in turning to Brother Geoffrey two days before as they'd been led captive through the skraeling village, had joked "I doubt you shall be able to plead 'benefit of clergy' here Brother" appeared to have finally run out of funny quips. Only Gisbourne, sitting apart from the others, virtually motionless except for the occasional twitch on his shoulder, seemed impervious to the sound of his fellow knight's suffering.

"For a man of relatively few words, he makes enough noise now," he complained bitterly. "Would that I could stuff his mouth with something and end this miserable squealing once and for all."

"Have you no pity," Roger of Doncaster enquired with incredulity. "Our brother is being murdered and you talk as though he were a pig at slaughter."

"He is not *my* brother," Gisbourne rejoined stonily. "Nor is he yours. As for 'pigs at slaughter', we are paid men come to do a job. And that job is not best served when one of us is made to prevail upon the fear of others."

"You speak as though he were complicit in some way." Philip interjected angrily. "Do you imagine these savages caress him with anything less than the devil's own hands? We are Christian Knights. And our purpose is 'best served' by maintaining faith in each other. If you have reason to think otherwise I charge you now, keep it to yourself!"

"You make false play of my words," Gisbourne countered huffily. "I offer no accusation. I merely speculate on why the savages have chosen to keep us imprisoned in this filthy pen whilst inflicting their cruelties elsewhere?"

Philip snorted in contempt. "If I were perverse enough to reason on such an abstract thing," he answered with about as much scorn as he could muster in the circumstances. "I would suggest it was to prevent us from making riot. Though I'm minded to guess you're about to provide us all with a more illuminating explanation."

Such was the increasing absurdity of their debate that Alyne, who until this moment had sat quietly in a corner, found himself beset by a fit of nervous giggles. He tried to master it by sucking in his cheeks. But this only rendered his conduct even more unbecoming, which in turn stoked the force of his mirth. As usual when hysteria couples with laughter, the inappropriate results quickly proved highly contagious, and within seconds several of those around him were also struggling to contain their sniggers.

Gisbourne meanwhile ignored the sarcasm in Philip's voice, as he ignored Alyne's heaving shoulders, and got unsteadily to his feet. "I would venture our capacity to *riot* is considerably hindered both by our lack of weaponry and the large number of savages now gathered outside our door," he opined gravely. "Therefore the purpose of these cruelties cannot simply be to inflict pain. Crispin of Lincoln, God grant him mercy, is purely an instrument. It is we who are being tormented." He jabbed a finger at his temple. "In here," he declared bluntly.

"By the faith Gisbourne," Brother Geoffrey exclaimed in exasperation. "Can you not let the matter rest! For a man who yelps and gives sound without the slightest justification, you are a poor one indeed to pass judgement on the *noises* of others."

By now, there was barely a soul left in the longhouse, with the notable exceptions of Gisbourne, Brother Geoffrey and Philip himself, who wasn't laughing or trying to suppress laughter. Even Robin, who liked to think of himself as above such revels, had finally succumbed to this pointless but infectious hilarity.

Gisbourne looked hurt. “It is not my intention to pass judgement,” he replied solemnly. “I merely point out that if we are to be murdered one by one, then surely the more we cry out, the more encouraged the savages will be to make us cry out, thus our sufferings will prove both more painful *and* more protracted.” He paused and looked directly at Philip, though this time his tone was almost contrite. “Therefore it is precisely for the sake of *pity* that I speak as I do,” he declared truthfully. “Even though it appears my lack of delicacy in voicing that *pity* has led you to believe otherwise.”

His final words were lost amidst a wave of wild and completely nonsensical laughter. But Gisbourne didn’t really mind. Despite everything he felt closer to these men and their quest than he’d ever felt to anyone or anything before in his life. They would probably never know it, but the young knight was actually proud of them, even Ralph of Shrewsbury, whom he’d long considered a hopeless fool. When their time had finally come, they’d acquitted themselves with distinction. And despite the unfavourable odds, not a single man had fled or begged parley. And yet, he supposed, the logic of asking them to silently endure their final moments in order to ensure they were just *moments* and not days was perhaps a little too macabre, even for these brave knights to grasp. Maybe a surge of foolish laughter was a better remedy.

He caught Robin's eye and a silent concurrence seemed to pass between them. Huntingdon understands he told himself. And sensing Philip about to take issue with the laughers, he rested a counselling hand on his shoulder and quietly confided: "It is *grave* humour I grant you, and it affords them little comfort. But it is humour just the same. And I say we thank God for it."

Perhaps surprisingly, Philip didn't take offence at the young knight's latest intervention. Perhaps even more surprisingly, given their recent enmity, when he turned his face towards Gisbourne's, he was actually smiling.

"You have me wrong Gisbourne," Philip advised him affably. "It is precisely *for* humour that I intend to speak. Five nights past," he explained, "after what I believe our dear Brother Geoffrey called 'the great shame', I prayed God the maid from Navarre would not prove the death of us. And lo…" he raised his arms in mock wonder at their current predicament. "…My prayers are answered."

"Then God is praised twice over," Gisbourne rejoined happily. And in another break with tradition he even sought to try a little humour himself. "For so grave is the hour, I'd foolishly come to fear He must have forsaken us completely. Yet now I see we are most gloriously saved."

Philip laughed quietly. The two would never be close. In the years that followed they would find common cause on many different occasions, but never real friendship. And yet something of this moment would remain with them forever.

The laughter was dying out around them now, leaving faces every bit as drawn and anxious as they'd been before. *The one who would betray them* hung his head and returned to his own wretched deliberations. Even at this final hour, his mind wriggled and twisted with serpent-thoughts. Surely there was some way, he told himself, something resourceful he could do, some accommodation he could reach with these savages that would still enable him to escape. He thought about the five gold coins he had hidden in his boot. But would the skraelings understand him? Did they even care about gold? He'd certainly seen no signs of it in the village outside. He could offer to lead them to Holger and the women who remained on board the ship. But again, how did he signal his captors without alerting the others?

Nearby, Brother Geoffrey mistook his tormented expression for something noble and Christian and by way of comfort advised him quietly: "We are all stood in Gethsemane. Yet even as our enemies gather, I can think of no better place to be."

The one who would betray them could think of many better places to be, most of them involving Rosamond, a girl he'd once known in Antioch, and that poisonous little creature Elizabeth. But he wisely kept these feelings to himself. At least the Benedictine believed in something. What did he believe in? Money had been his entire life, and now it was about to prove the death of him too. He thought about Rosamond's comely handmaiden, and the way her long hair had tickled his cheek. And in the same way Alyne had found himself overcome by an untimely urge to laugh, the traitor was suddenly overcome by an urge to tell the truth.

"I am a sinner..." he began to confess miserably.

But no sooner were the words out than Brother Geoffrey was interjecting sympathetically. "We are *all* sinners," he insisted. "That is our natural condition. But fear not, for the Father knows what's written in our hearts. And He will judge us accordingly."

The traitor shook his head. "You don't understand," he persisted. "I am not the man you believe me to be."

But the young monk was adamant. "None of us are the men we believe ourselves to be," he advised solemnly. "But faith will raise us up. And faith will ensure we shall all be delivered at the final hour, even though our sins are great."

He said it with such unwavering conviction that it lifted not just the traitor's spirits, but the spirits of every other man in the longhouse too. And as if by one common consent they began to recite the Pater Noster. Eight voices suddenly praying together in perfect unison. *Pater Noster, qui es in caelis, sanctificetur nomen tuum.*[26]

Robin shut his eyes and allowed the beauty of the words to wash to over him. Crispin's screams were noticeably fewer and more intermittently spaced now. Soon they would cease altogether. And then the

---

[26] ***Our Father, who art in heaven, hallowed by thy name.***

drums would start to beat again and the demon with the horns would return to select another victim.

TWENTY FOUR

North East Vinland, the 'Great Eastern Woodlands Region' (Somewhere just inland from what is now the New York/Connecticut coastline)
The Feast of Saint Ehulalia of Merida
10th December 1182.

The wretched turn of events which would lead to their eventual incarceration had begun five days earlier, on the Feast of Saint Ehulalia of Merida, the morning immediately after what Brother Geoffrey was already calling 'the great shame'.

As plans go it couldn't have been any simpler. Allow Kocoum to 'escape', wait a requisite amount of time, then pick up his trail and follow it all the way back to Marian. And if not to Marian, then hopefully to some point en-route that would eventually lead them to Marian. That at least was the theory. And compared to repeatedly shouting her name or waving their arms in frustration, it seemed to make good sense. Yet at the same time it was growing increasingly apparent to Robin that every new stratagem he devised was in part necessitated by the failings of a previous one. And though he said nothing, the irony of replacing his first plan, which had involved getting Kocoum from the woods onto the ship, with a second that required getting him from the ship back into the woods again, was not lost on the young bowman from Locksley.

Perhaps that was why Philip had been so nervous about the others finding out. 'Do it at night', he'd insisted anxiously. Let them think the savage had simply 'escaped'. Why bother to invite the opprobrium that would surely follow if things went wrong? Much better to wait until it had proved a success. After all, they both had reputations to protect.

Unfortunately, Philip's 'reputation' was as someone who barely slept, fussed over every detail, and drove everyone to distraction about the need for *vigilance.* Convincing them therefore that he'd fallen asleep at his post during Night Watch, and allowed the savage not only to extract the keys from his coat but also to release his chains and slip quietly over the side of the ship, was near on impossible.

"You do not speak truthfully," Brother Geoffrey sniffed suspiciously when informed of Kocoum's 'escape'. "Something is awry and I'm determined to find out what." The Benedictine was secretly convinced that Philip and Robin had inadvertently killed the young warrior during the night and deposited his body in the ocean. Philip laughed this off but it got the others thinking. And it was no surprise when, having discerned the true purpose of his small 'foraging party, Rosamond presented herself in front of Philip and demanded to go with them.

"I do not ask nor seek permission," she declared haughtily, in what, for Philip at least had become an annoyingly familiar refrain. "I will travel at your side and there it is. Now, tell me what I should wear and do not say 'heavy armour'. I have heard the talk, and I know Gisbourne and the others favour much lighter attire."

Philip smiled winsomely. “Rest assured My Lady, if I were to suggest ‘heavy armour’; it would only be for the pleasure of seeing you sink at the forging of our first river.”

She tossed her hair dismissively. They disliked each other with a resolve bordering on dedication now and there was little point in either one pretending otherwise. “You are a fine humourist,” she trilled facetiously. “We shall travel well together. And at the ‘forging of our first river’, I shall expect you to carry me.” She smiled unpleasantly. “And rest assured Philip Mark, whose family are in such good favour with the King, I am no *humourist* at all.”

Watching Rosamond skip off gleefully to gather up her things, Gisbourne turned to the so-called ‘mute’ Crispin of Lincoln and enquired wryly. “What say you now my silent companion? Are we still to claim God’s blessing or do we dance our way to hell with a merry grin on our faces?”

Despite not speaking, Crispin had made it abundantly clear on numerous occasions that he cared little for Gisbourne or his opinions. A feeling he again sought to demonstrate by pointedly turning his back on the young knight. Not that Gisbourne minded. He’d long suspected Crispin’s ‘silence’ to be an affectation of some sort, and secretly enjoyed baiting him. “Straight to hell you say and not a moment to be lost on the way.” He took a deep breath, as if in admiration. “My friend, I have misjudged you. At our outset I’d presumed you were simply a fool happy to wile-away his time in idle gloom. Now I see you’re as eager to die as I am.” He gave Crispin a reassuring pat on the back. "Fear not brave knight. With the Lords of Misrule now in command, I feel most certain our wishes will be granted soon."

Seeing Rosamond and her two handmaidens preparing to go ashore, Elizabeth had meanwhile approached Robin at the ship's prow. "I want to go too," she told him flatly. "I have knowledge of medicines. I can wield a dagger more proficiently than any man here." She paused and glanced tellingly back towards Gisbourne still stood with Crispin at the far end of the ship. "And I do not make curious or absurd noises when asked to be silent."

She had expected a long argument, but Robin simply nodded his head and told her to quickly collect everything she would need. He knew she was fearless enough and reasoned that whatever other faults she might have, stupidity certainly wasn't one of them. Besides, having her with them might prove useful should anyone succumb to illness or injure themselves along the way, a prospect now greatly exacerbated by the inclusion of Rosamond and her entourage.

And so, leaving Holger and a small crew behind to tend the ship, this strange procession – and by now that was exactly what it had come to resemble – set off, winding its way up from the beach into the ever thickening woodlands beyond.

With Alyne reciting verses from the 'Song of Troy', Oswald of Norwich supping ale, Rosamond wearing an outfit supposedly inspired by the fabled Amazon queen Penthesilea, and Walter of Malmesbury carrying a sword he looked incapable of wielding, the whole thing quickly took on the air of a jolly pageant. An impression further enhanced by Ralph of Shrewsbury and Harold of Leicester, who began to laugh and bluster as if the whole thing were one big joke. Apparently with four young women present it was necessary to make a great show of appearing completely fearless. Thus instead of the nervous silence that had accompanied their previous incursions ashore a mood of 'affected joviality' now prevailed.

It wasn't all completely bravado either. If truth be told, Rosamond's disgraceful behaviour the previous day, whilst shocking them with its wilful depravity, had also served to render the inhabitants of Vinland, through the personage of Kocoum, not just human but also rather likeable too. After all, what able-bodied man on board hadn't fleetingly wished he were stood exactly where the young Iroquois had stood whilst Rosamond 'attended' to him in similar fashion? Indeed, Ralph of Shrewsbury's assertion that the 'capability' in her arm might prove just as useful in their dealings with the skraelings as any bow or sword drew generous applause from everyone, including the young heiress herself. As did his subsequent claim that in the 'discharge of his seed' Kocoum had proved himself a most 'excellent marksman'.

This kind of good natured badinage continued all morning, with lewd riposte traded back and forth until virtually everyone, with the notable exceptions of Gisbourne and Brother Geoffrey, appeared to be thoroughly enjoying themselves. So much so that it wasn't long before the testy Benedictine was complaining to Philip about 'God's pure air' being 'tainted' by 'unseemly talk', leaving the future High Sheriff to wonder if perhaps allowing Rosamond to come ashore might not prove his finest decision to date.

Elizabeth meanwhile was staring about her in open wonder. In all the years she'd spent serving as a hearth girl to the odious Father Benedict, she'd never once imagined that someday she might experience something as remarkable or as magical as this. Standing on the elevated deck, she could only speculate about the mysterious land opposite. It was only now, as she passed under the colossal trees and, glancing up to where the branches arched at a great distance overhead, felt those first golden slats of sunlight fall across her face that she began to fully comprehend the true scale and magnificence of this beautiful land.

It was also Brother Geoffrey's first trip ashore, and when not admonishing the others for 'bald' conversation, the young monk was also pausing to consider the splendour of his surroundings.

"This place has been waiting for us since the world stood at morning," he opined to Walter of Malmesbury in one of those characteristic rhapsodies of praise and amazement the young knight had rather come to enjoy.

The trail itself had been easy enough for Robin to pick up. In his haste to escape, Kocoum had not bothered to cover his tracks. Nor had he taken time to lay false paths as was the Iroquois custom when attempting to evade an enemy. In fact, some of the imprints were so plainly made Robin had even started to suspect he might actually *want* them to follow him.

Nevertheless they kept doggedly to the task, and shortly after midday found themselves amidst swathes of tall grassland, finally wading towards the place they'd been searching for ever since first setting foot on Vinland.

Here at last was the small wooden settlement Eustace and the others had founded almost two years before. Or rather here was what remained of it. Because it was immediately apparent from a single glance that a frightful catastrophe had befallen both the settlement and its inhabitants. From the blackened palisade to the broken pieces of pottery they crunched underfoot, everything was in ruins. Moreover nature had already crept back in to reclaim the site, winding itself around the charred stumps, and burying the rest under a sea of billowing prairie.

They paused for a moment to take stock. *The one who would betray them* stared at the scene in dismay. If Eustace was already dead, as now seemed likely, where did it leave him?

"We are arrived at our journey's end," Brother Geoffrey pronounced solemnly. "And it seems we are arrived too late."

They fanned out slowly in a wide arc, silently sifting through the ruins to see what they could find. But it was an unpleasant task. Like a graveyard abandoned and overgrown, there was disquieting 'presence' to the place, and walking about it quickly began to feel uncomfortable, almost as though they were trespassing on someone else's misfortune.

Philip searched in increasing frustration. As a defensive site it had been well located. But why was there no raised mound on which to site a proper keep? And where was the surrounding moat? Had Eustace simply not bothered, or were the lack of these things a sign that his brother had considered himself safe here? Even more troubling, what had happened to all the bodies? If the encampment had been attacked and its inhabitants slaughtered, as all the evidence seemed to suggest, the entire area should be littered with their remains. And yet there was nothing.

It was a question that was also vexing Robin. From the insects and plant life, he could tell the settlement had lain in ruin for over a year. Yet apart from a few fingernails and the odd tooth there were none of the grisly items one might usually expect to find in such a place. The leathery pieces of skin alive with bugs, or the curious objects retrieved from the soil that would later reveal themselves as severed ear-lobes or rotting eyeballs. Even allowing for the activity of local predators, there should have been a fair scattering of large and indigestible bones.

However, the more he scrabbled in the earth, the more convinced Robin became that all was not as it appeared. For one thing, someone else had clearly been there before them. And as he went about the site, pausing here and there to scratch at some piece of blackened wood or prod a sprouting root with his finger, the more keenly he began to discern their purpose.

"Then they must surely be Christian," Philip enthused eagerly as Robin duly reported his discovery a few moments later. "Who but a Christian returns to bury their dead? By all the saints Robert, there are clearly survivors. What more proof do you need?"

"I make no guess as to their identity," Robin answered carefully, reluctant to be drawn any further. "There were many bodies and they have been moved. That's all I know. Whether they were moved for reasons too diabolical too contemplate or merely to afford them a proper Christian burial, I cannot say."

But Philip had already made up his mind. Just the mere possibility that someone might have survived and even now be hiding out in the woods nearby was simply too exciting to ignore. And before Robin could stop him, the future High Sheriff was cupping hands to his mouth and bellowing the name *Marian*, over and over at the surrounding trees, his desperate voice filling the skies above them with a flurry of startled birds.

Some distance away, *the one who would betray them* sat in the tall grass and miserably contemplated his next move. He glanced up as the comely young handmaiden approached. "This fool thinks he can conjure her by sheer force of will," he said dismissively of Philip, still shouting Marian's name at the top of his voice.

"Why do you call him fool?" she asked, genuinely perplexed by his disdain. "All he does is search for the one he loves. Why should that warrant your scorn?"

The question took him by surprise, as did her apparent reason for asking it. Ever since that night on the boat, when she'd sought his help in arranging the murder of her mistress, he'd considered her an 'associate' of sorts. Ready to do whatever was necessary in order to get what she wanted. Now suddenly, he saw she was just a young girl, enthralled by the prospect of 'love' and all its redeeming qualities.

Normally he'd have laughed at such naivety. But something about the bleak remains of the settlement coupled with the simple honesty of her question momentarily shamed him.

"I don't", he began awkwardly. "But I have known men who have trusted too much in love. And when that love is betrayed they can only seek solace in…" He paused. His voice had grown suddenly strained and introspective, as though he spoke only to himself. He thought about the girl he'd loved in Antioch nine summers before. She'd promised him her heart, only to desert him at the first opportunity for a nobleman's son. *Love is a tide,* she'd told him afterwards. *And when you stand at the water's edge, you will discover it retreats just as often as it advances.* Shortly after that he'd killed his first man. Split his head in two and called it 'God's work'. But it wasn't 'God's work' at all. Nothing he'd done from that day forth had been 'God's work'.

"When 'love is betrayed' they 'seek solace' in what exactly?" the young handmaiden was asking attentively, returning him to his initial thought.

He cleared his throat and focused his mind once more. "When love is betrayed," he told her with an air of despondency, "they seek solace in…*recompense*."

She sat down next to him, and placed her hand in his. "Then we shall seek solace in *recompense* together" she promised quietly. And for a moment the clouds parted and the sun shone, and the grass around them rippled back and forth with barely a sound.

"There is another course of action which is open to us," the traitor informed her discreetly, his gaze shifting from the general to the particular as his eyes locked on hers. "We can leave this place again with both our stones unturned. Leave it as it found us, nameless and without blame."

Her expression darkened. The idea clearly held little appeal for her. "But I have set my heart on justice," she reminded him pointedly. "Am I to be denied now, simply because your own journey is at an end?"

The one who would betray them smiled faintly. The threat in her voice was so risible it hardly warranted an answer, but he provided one just the same. "I had thought you more honey than poison," he mused resignedly. "Now I see it is the reverse. You are poison who merely pretends to be honey."

She leant forward and squeezed his hand a little more tightly than was absolutely necessary. "I am both," she assured him with a furtive smile, "to the man who would really know me."

The traitor nodded vaguely, preferring to keep whatever further thoughts on it he had to himself. Blood demands blood he told himself wearily. And the whole world wishes itself revenged on someone. Christian or Saracen, it made little difference. *Blood demands blood.* There was a stale predictability to it.

And judging by the ruins around them the skraelings were no better. Part of him wanted to despair. Yet at the same time he reminded himself he was a killer, and a killer serves only one purpose.

"I'm summoned to attend the demands of nature," he told her, getting to his feet. It wasn't true but he needed to be on his own for a while so he could think. Robin had warned them not to venture into the woods alone, but the traitor chose to ignore his advice and with all of them too busy to notice, he slipped quietly away into the trees.

He walked for a while in no particular direction, his thoughts abstracted from the world around him. Eventually he paused by a small deer path which ran down to a stream. Once again he was struck by Vinland's natural abundance of provisions. In these great wastes of forest a man need never go hungry he reflected. Better still, he might lose himself forever. It would be a risk of course, disappearing into a landscape as formidable as this. Yet for anyone wishing to start again, it also raised an infinite number of possibilities. Freed from the mistakes of his past, a man might begin again. He could write a new story of his life. He might even find his way back to God.

As he stood there, thinking about this, he suddenly became aware of something lying in the undergrowth nearby. At first he thought it was the carcass of a large animal, but walking over he discovered it was actually the body of a man. And not just any man. Here was the young Iroquois warrior Kocoum whom they'd been tracking since dawn. A quick examination confirmed he was no longer alive.

Yet both his body and the blood oozing from it were still relatively warm, indicating death had only taken him fairly recently. Of even more concern was the sharp rock still clutched in his hand. From the gory mess it appeared he'd used it to partially cave in one side of his head. Apparently applying it with such vigour that he'd succeeded in removing the top portion of his skull before death had taken him.

The traitor stood in silence, perspiration running down his nose. He told himself it was a mistake to tarry too long. Robin would find the body soon enough. And anyway, what did it matter if some savage with the daze in him had finally decided to put an end to things? He should simply ignore it and keep on walking.

Yet at the same time he knew there might never be a better opportunity to separate Philip from the others. And with Kocoum's body still warm he could even arrange it to look as if one had killed the other. Blood demands blood, he thought. And before he knew it, he was rehearsing the conversation in his head. *I have discovered something in the woods. It would be better if you came alone. We wouldn't wish to disturb the others.* He thought about the girl in Antioch. Death is everywhere he decided, and turned back towards the settlement.

TWENTY FIVE

North East Vinland, the 'Great Eastern Woodlands Region'
The Feast of Saint Stephen
26th December 1182.

Marian woke suddenly, as if in dread. It wasn't true, she told herself. I won't believe it. Philip Mark in Vinland! It simply wasn't possible. What sane man willingly undertakes such a journey? The cost alone would surely prove prohibitive. And even discounting finances, who in their right mind would agree to accompany him? At least Eustace had good friends, every single one of them filled to the brim with the spirit of adventure. Apart from Gilbert of York, who if anything was even more cautious than Philip himself, Marian couldn't think of another person likely to risk his reputation, let alone his life, on such an outlandish expedition.

She breathed a little easier. Tomakin had been mistaken she decided. There was no large ship at anchor. No young troubadour singing songs. And the European Knights he'd glimpsed were merely Iroquois warriors, wearing armour most probably plundered from the remnants of the settlement. Either that or he was deliberately lying to her again. Whichever it was, she refused to be alarmed. Shortly the sun would come up, the dogs would bark and everything in Vinland would be as it was.

She reached out in the dark for the comfort of the pipe, but found instead the scroll. Her heart sank.

As she'd lain half-wakeful in the longhouse, drifting in a haze of uppowoc smoke, she'd convinced herself it was all a bad dream. Now, as she ran her fingers over the scroll's waxy seal and felt the stiffness of its parchment, she knew that everything he'd told her on his return had been true. Philip Mark had come for her.

A short while later, with the day slowly waking in the sky around them, Marian and Tomakin stood on a small ridge and looked out over the misty woods below. Despite the extraordinary view, there was a dull greyness to the morning which perfectly encapsulated their mood.

"We were to be married," she told him after a moment. "He is Cloud Man's older brother. I believe he's travelled here to..." She hesitated, suddenly flummoxed for an explanation. *Travelled* here to do what exactly? Was it simple chivalry? Had he come all this way to rescue her? Or was some darker explanation required? How to explain the motives of a man who'd first brokered his pledge to her with the words, *'though you may be of mixed blood, my family are in good favour with the King'*? Marian doubted it was possible. "I believe he has travelled here to…to *find me*." She said at last, no clearer in her mind about it than she had been a moment before.

The shaman shifted his gaze from the distant horizon and looked at her directly. "You fear him," he said with an abrupt perspicacity that was typical. "He has travelled across the great salt waters because he wishes to…" and here he paused to repeat again the word she'd just used, though somehow in his mouth it sounded more like a reprimand. "…to *find* you. And in order to do this he will shed his blood if necessary and the blood of his warriors too. Yet you are afraid of him. I do not understand."

Marian felt her cheeks flush with discomfort. He was right. She was afraid. But as to why exactly, she had no idea. She wanted to tell him it was all to do with the unbearable shame she felt. After all, leaving a man for his younger brother wasn't something you boasted about, even in a savage place like Vinland. But she knew that wouldn't be true. The *shame* she felt was entirely transient. It came and went with her passing moods. And there were many days when she felt no shame at all.

As for Philip's temper, she wasn't even sure if he possessed one. Certainly in all the time they'd known each other, his conduct towards her had never been anything less than exemplary. And everyone in her village agreed that of the two brothers he was by far the calmest and most dependable. So why had the mere thought of his arrival in Vinland caused her to wake with such an icy dread?

"I don't fully understand it myself," she replied tentatively. "But I've done him a great wrong. And therefore he has every reason to be angry with me. Consequently it must follow that I have every reason to fear that anger." Yet even as she said it, she knew it wasn't true. Philip Mark hadn't come all this way to exact revenge. Not on her anyway. If anyone should be afraid, she thought, it should be Eustace. And for all Marian knew Eustace was dead already.

Tomakin listened pensively but made no reply. He seemed even more preoccupied than usual, and Marian discerned a reluctance in him that made her immediately suspicious. Was there something he hadn't told her yet?

"From the safety of the woods you watched him for a whole day," she ventured cagily. "Yet thus far you've made little report of what you saw. Am I to assume from this mystery that you've discovered some reason of your own to fear him?

Tomakin felt his jaw tighten. What point in telling her about the two hungry wolves or *the old woman who knew how to heal?* What comfort in knowing Philip had brought a warrior with him who could find trails like an Iroquois and launch arrows with unerring accuracy?

"Any man who demonstrates such persistence deserves to be feared," he acceded cheerlessly. "As to the rest, I saw very little, save what I've already told you." But that wasn't true. He'd seen someone else in the village. Someone he hadn't expected to see. And when she found out, he knew she would despise him for the rest of her days.

Tell her now, the wendigo urged maliciously. *She will hate you soon enough anyway. Tell her and see the wonderful pain fill her eyes. Even better, tell her as your hands fasten around her throat.* But Tomakin ignored the chiding voice. His priority now was to protect what was left of his 'family'.

Had he put an end to *the old woman who knew how to heal*, as he'd originally intended, none of this would be necessary. But instead of killing her, he'd hidden in the undergrowth, afraid to even show himself. And now it would only be a matter of time before she led them directly to him.

"I have to leave this place," he told her at length. "Cloud Man's brother has brought warriors with him. Good men with blood in their eyes. If we stay here, they're sure to find us."

He said it as one already decided on a course of action. Not that there were many 'family' members left to make the trip with him. Already decimated by the fever and increasingly riven by internal strife, his erratic behaviour – in particular his decision to banish all those who'd turned their backs on Marian during his illness – had reduced their number even further. Now there were fewer than thirty. And of these, almost half were young women.

In addition, the shaman's own extraordinary 'powers' were starting to falter. He'd developed a slight stoop, and his left hand now shook slightly, causing him to drop or spill things. At the same time, the fever had made it much harder for him to maintain the concentration needed to cast visions or mind-spells. If Philip and his knights came in force, he knew it was unlikely he'd be able to resist them for very long.

"Where will you go?" Marian asked at length, though she already knew the answer. He would lead them north, into the furthest reaches of the Great Eastern Woodlands, where the lakes were said to be full of salmon and there was no frost all winter. Here, they would rest until the following spring, when Tomakin would be much stronger, and they could begin the process of rebuilding again. Only one thing remained to be decided. What was to be done with her?

As if in answer, he pointed to a small deer path, barely visible from where they were stood. "That way leads to Cloud Man's brother," he told her. "Follow the trail until you reach the river and then turn south towards the sun. Walk straight for two days, always keeping the river at your side. By sunset of the second day you will find the village where Cloud Man's brother and his warriors are waiting."

Marian saw immediately how serious he was. He'd even brought food and water with him to ensure the journey wouldn't prove too arduous. She knew it could only mean one thing.

"You've made an arrangement with him," she said accusingly. "I'm to be traded like some wild animal so you and your 'family' might be left in peace."

The shaman shook his head, clearly offended by the allegation. "There is no 'arrangement'," he asserted stiffly. "I'm offering you the freedom you've long craved. But if you would go to him do so now, before any blood is spilt. For once blood is spilt this matter can never be resolved, not until one or all are dead."

Marian searched his face for some sign of treachery, but there was none. He was telling her the truth. After eighteen months of captivity, he was finally setting her free. All she had to do was turn and walk away. She stared at him in disbelief. She should have been thrilled. This after all was the moment she'd been praying for since the night of her capture. Yet instead of unbridled joy, she found herself experiencing something else all-together. Not numbness exactly. It was far too pertinent for numbness. If she'd been hard-pressed, the word she might have used was *disappointment*.

"It's true," she said after a moment, wondering at her sudden awkwardness. "I've long dreamt of the day when I would finally be free. Yet now it's here, I'm bound to wonder why, after spilling so much blood; you would happily abandon me without a fight?"

"I am not abandoning you," he assured her honestly. "I'm simply asking you to choose." He handed her the scroll. "I must go one way. Cloud Man's brother must go another. It is for you to decide."

Marian took the scroll from him as a prisoner might take the keys to their dungeon. In all the various scenarios in which she'd pictured herself attaining freedom, none had ever looked quite like this. Once again she quickly reproached herself for not feeling jubilant. And once again she couldn't quite shake off a deepening sense of unease. She gazed at the small deer path. If taken, she told herself, it would lead all the way back to her future life. The same future life she'd already run away from.

"I cannot keep my thoughts fixed," she confessed miserably. "Nor think rationally how best to proceed. Why must this be decided in such haste?"

"Because *haste* is all we have left." He declared flatly. "And the longer we delay the more cause we shall have to regret it." He turned his face to hers and she saw for the first time the tremendous turmoil in his eyes. "It is not without regret that I say these things," he acknowledged unhappily. "When I woke from the fever, there was a great clarity in me. I saw and heard the world around me as it really was, and not as I had imagined it to be. For the first time I found a freedom in myself. A freedom I'd not readily known before." He paused and his expression slowly darkened. "But that clarity in me is becoming clouded with doubt again. I still have the song of you in my head, but now there are other voices too, just as persistent. One in particular whispers to me with increasing conviction. It tells me things I don't want to hear. I've tried to silence it many times. But always it returns. And each time it returns it conspires to make me say and do things I know I will have cause to regret."

He paused for a moment and remembered how his mother had held him that last time in the cave. He briefly wondered how different his life might have been if she'd behaved more like the other mothers in the village. Perhaps he would have been happy too. He closed his eyes and saw himself as a small boy, dancing joyously in the embers of a long forgotten evening. That was the last time, he thought. The last time they'd been together before she'd led him to the cave. He heard the tiny tremble in her voice. *Close your eyes. Close your eyes my darling and wait. He'll be here soon.*

"I've long wished things could be different between us," he mused disconsolately, his words coming from a place so deep within him that Marian knew she would never be able to reach him there. "But everything I've touched. Everything I've…" He paused. Dare he use the word 'love'? "Everything I've hoped for, or tried to change, everything I've known…" He opened his eyes again, and she saw they were blurred with tears. "Everything in my life that I would take care of, I've ended up destroying." He turned away, almost in shame, and she understood perfectly now. He was trying to warn her. "If you stay here any longer," he informed her bleakly. "I fear I'll destroy you too."

Marian heard the despair in his voice and suddenly wished she'd never allowed herself to believe the miseries of a lifetime could be scrubbed away by a few kind words. There is only the process of existing she thought wretchedly; everything else is a construct, a vain futility of the heart.

She looked at the scroll in her hand, no longer certain if he was asking her to choose or telling her what to do. She slowly rolled it open and stared at the words. Tomakin's world might flow like a river, she told herself, but here by contrast was something permanent.

Like most women her age Marian couldn't read, but she understood the value of documentation. This was no swirl of pipe-smoke or trick of the mind. This was a declaration of intent, a physical testimony drawn up by men not governed or cowed by the natural flow of things. Here was verification if any was needed, that the will of law was far greater than the will of nature.

Yet even as she was telling herself all these things, Marian was besieged by another notion, even more powerful. What if she didn't want to spend the rest of her life with a man governed by 'the will of law'? Someone who entrusted his feelings to a sallow-faced monk sat in a flickering cloister somewhere inscribing cold words onto a dead sheet of vellum. What if she wanted something else? Something that was exhilarating and impulsive and completely incalculable? After all, wasn't that the reason why she'd fled to Vinland with Eustace in the first place?

And the more she stared at the scroll, the more the shape of the words began to speak to her. It didn't matter that she couldn't read. Their arrangement told her everything she needed to know. The narrow and obedient way they proceeded. The precise lines and exaggerated loops that announced themselves with a self-aggrandisement, the curved obsequiousness that seemed almost unnatural in a place like this.

How typical of Philip she thought. Where Eustace had swept her across the ocean with nothing but his passion to guide them, his older brother was pursuing her with a dry piece of parchment. That the Bishop of Hereford and various other minor emissaries' associated with the Holy Father had been persuaded to lend it their official seal came as no surprise. Marian knew Philip was incapable of seeking her as a prospective husband might seek his bride-to-be. He could never let simple emotion or heaven forbid something as spontaneous as…and here was that word again…*passion*, lead him. No, he had to invoke the law first. And having secured official approval he would need to seek out God too. Not for guidance. Marian doubted whether he'd actually ever stopped to pray on the matter. Knowing Philip as she did, she understood better than anyone it was the *appearance* of God that would concern him most. Kneeling in the royal chapel, being seen to kiss the Bishop's ring, having the weight of that high office inscribed in ink so he could show it to his friends. These were the really important things.

The wind picked up suddenly and she had to strengthen her grip on the corners of the scroll to prevent it from blowing away. How happy it must have made him to hold this in his hand, she reflected soberly. How important he must have felt. How *vindicated.* And yet even with the blessings of the church he'd waited for more than a year before finally setting sail!

She pictured the life awaiting her in England if she chose to return with him. The days spent kneeling in perpetual confession. The nights being bulled by a man she didn't love, without even the pipe to comfort her afterwards. She saw the hollow-eyed peasants toiling in the fields and the barefoot monks making their way in the rain. She felt her knuckles scrape against the cold stone walls, and heard the beggars crying out for alms. And the whispers! How would she survive the whispers? *See, there she goes. Look at that black hair. Saracen they say. Have you not heard? And with his younger brother too!* And all of it accompanied by the creak of the gallows and the cold slap of religion.

The wind tugged at the scroll again, and this time she let go. It immediately took flight, as if yanked suddenly by some invisible thread. She watched as it fluttered briefly in the air around her before hurrying away across the sky, flapping anxiously as it went. Within a few seconds it was lost from view completely. How apposite she thought. All that sycophancy and law-making swept away by a sudden gust of nature, with no more ability to save itself than an autumn leaf snatched by the breeze.

She looked at Tomakin. "I've made my decision," she told him.

TWENTY SIX

North East Vinland, the 'Great Eastern Woodlands Region' (Somewhere just inland from what is now the New York/Connecticut coastline)
The Feast of Saint Daniel the Stylite
11th December 1182.

They buried Kocoum where they found him, allowing Brother Geoffrey the opportunity to flavour the occasion with some meaty words of faith. Raising his arms to heaven, his voice booming, he prevailed upon the Holy Virgin to 'succour and present thy servant at this dread hour', and to 'see with thee the company of angels and the knighthood of paradise.'

For the young monk, and several others in attendance, it was a reaffirmation of eternal values after the bitter shock of finding the settlement in ruins and the sullying experience of 'the great shame'. Despite his rousing sermon however, the burial itself did not meet with universal approval. Robin for one had serious reservations.

"We blunder through these lands when we should go on tiptoe," he warned unhappily. "Instead of learning we hurry to teach. And our lessons are always the same. Even now Brother Geoffrey fills the woods with them."

"Our 'lessons' are handed down by Moses and the holy prophets," Philip reminded him tetchily. "They give us leave to behave as we do."

"That may well be so," Robin argued vehemently. "But we have no notion of how the dead are treated here. Suppose it's done by fire or some other method. How are we to explain our endeavours? What if this savage has friends or family who misconstrue our Christianity as proof that we've done murder and now seek to hide the evidence?"

But Philip had been in no mood to debate the issue. Since first approving his 'escape' from the ship, the future High Sheriff had come to regard the young Iroquois as a fellow traveller in his quest to find Marian. Now, in death, he'd almost become a friend.

"How then would you have us proceed?" he demanded irately. "Are we simply to abandon him body and soul? Have you not heard in whose likeness we are made?"

This notion of blithely forsaking something fashioned in God's image had been a bone of contention between them ever since Robin had persuaded him to leave the three dead brigands unburied on the Great North Road. Now, pointing to the wooden cross Walter of Malmesbury was still in the process of constructing, he asserted grandly. "We are here at Christ's behest. In His good name Robert I implore you, vex me no more with these endless protests. "

Robin knew better than to press Philip when he was in this sort of mood, and instead set about helping the so-called 'mute' Crispin of Lincoln dig the young warrior's grave.

Watching Robin dig, Alyne singing psalms of praise, and Brother Geoffrey leading them all in prayer, no one was happier than Walter of Malmesbury. Following 'the great shame', the foppish young knight appeared to have undergone a remarkable transformation. His flamboyant outfits were no longer accompanied by the same flamboyant attitudes. He'd grown quieter and more reflective. Each morning he practiced with his sword, and he'd ceased to hang on Rosamond's every word, or constantly attend her needs. Whether this was in response to the incident itself, or merely in reaction to her worsening behaviour, he didn't say. But something about the dizzying vastness of Vinland and its extraordinary colours had stirred him to fresh purpose. And whereas Rosamond had only been roused to excess, Walter found himself inspired to a new piety. So much so that he now actively sought-out the company and advice of his former nemesis Brother Geoffrey. And though Rosamond and her handmaidens mocked him mercilessly for it, the two men had become firm friends.

"See how everyone is changing," the comely handmaiden whispered to *the one who would betray them,* as Walter and the others gathered around Kocoum's grave to pray. "In this place, the entire world is stood on its head."

"On its head or on its arse, it's all as one to me," he answered tersely. He was already regretting his decision to return to the settlement. His plan to lure Philip away from the others had foundered almost immediately when Philip had insisted on summoning Robin to join them, causing the traitor to lose his composure and snap irritably: "Can you never be apart? The two of you have become indivisible, like form and shadow, though which is which, I can no longer tell!"

Philip had glanced at him curiously, his face momentarily colouring with what the traitor had presumed was embarrassment, before replying with equal irritation: "In certain things he is very necessary to me. If you have something of value to impart, speak plainly, or else be still and let us proceed with the business in hand."

Realising that he'd already said too much, *the one who would betray them* shook his head apologetically and quickly offered his mitigations. "There's much that is unseasonable about this place as a man may not easily think. My words ran in haste. If I've given offence, I most humbly beg forgiveness."

This seemed to satisfy Philip, and within moments, half a dozen of them were gathered around the young warrior's dead body, listening to Elizabeth explain that despite an apparently gruesome attempt to remove the top of his own head, Kocoum's death had not been the result of any self-inflicted injury but rather from a wound sustained several days earlier. In short, she attributed it to the blow on the back of the head he'd received from Gisbourne.

"That's impossible" snorted Roger of Doncaster. "He took his own life. Any fool can see that."

"Nay," she replied calmly. "His life was already taken. This was merely the final misery."

Gisbourne frowned unhappily. "What know you of such things?" he demanded with a characteristic little shoulder twitch.

“As hearth girl I accompanied Father Benedict on many woeful occasions,” she explained. “I’ve seen the different ways men and women choose to take their own lives. And I can tell you without equivocation that anyone wishing to die by their own hand, even someone with the ‘daze’ in them, does not do so in such an extraordinary fashion, particularly if there are less painful methods at hand.” She moved Kocoum’s head slightly, allowing more blood to leak into the undergrowth. “Furthermore,” she informed them, indicating the portion of his face that was most damaged, “this injury, whilst grotesque to the eye, is not in itself yet fatal.” Roger of Doncaster huffed contemptuously, but Elizabeth persisted undeterred. “There is another type of wound,” she explained keenly. “It remains unseen but is just as deadly. It bleeds slowly inside the head, gradually thickening like churned milk, until the flow of one or all canals are dammed. At which turn the body is no longer in accordance with itself. Thus a man might suffer a blow on Monday, yet not die from it for almost a week.”

She removed the rock from the young warrior’s hand and weighed it thoughtfully in her own palm. She had no way of knowing about the small insect inside his head, or of his ever increasing desperation to be free of it. But she knew the story of Zeus and the birth of Athena, and she understood better than most the extremes to which someone might go in order to escape incessant pain.

“I would say he was trying to release the suffering,” she said at length. “But the cause of it was already put there by something else.”

“Do you swear it,” Gisbourne challenged her angrily. “Do you swear it by the Holy Book and all who are spoken of in it?

“I swear it,” Elizabeth said, a tiny glimmer of spite in her eyes. “You’ve put an end to this savage just as surely as if you’d taken your sharpest blade to him.”

One or two of them shuffled uncomfortably to hear her speak so boldly. Only a witch with an intrinsic knowledge of poisons and a steady hand in matters of death would dare voice her opinions quite so fearlessly. And to Gisbourne of all people!

“No one attributes blame Gisbourne,” Philip reassured him, moving quickly to pacify the situation. “This poor creature was lost to the daze long before we arrived. What happened here was an accident.”

“Nor should they,” Gisbourne growled defensively. “I had no quarrel with the savage. And I take no pleasure in seeing him dead. Put him in the ground and have the Benedictine speak some words of solace. Afterwards I will stand vigil until the sun is down.”

True to his word, the moment they’d finished, Gisbourne drove his sword into the soft earth. And as the others began to wander off back towards the settlement, he knelt beside it and bowed his head in repentance.

“See how he pretends,” Rosamond whispered maliciously to Ralph of Shrewsbury as they went.

"Are we to be convinced by this great show of remorse? He must think us more easily deceived than children."

But the young heiress was wrong. Gisbourne wasn't 'deceiving' anyone. His remorse was genuine. And he was still knelt there several hours later when the moon took its place above the surrounding trees.

By now it was far too late to return to the ship, so they decided to make camp for the night. Water was gathered from a nearby stream and a large fire lit. Whatever could be salvaged from the wooden palisade was collected together to form a small defensive enclosure. And in order to dissuade any enemy from rushing their position, a number of encumbering trenches were dug, around which Robin and Harold of Leicester laid small animal traps, each one capable of ensnaring a man should he step upon it. With no natural vantage point from which to keep watch, Philip posted several lookouts, whilst Oswald of Norwich and the others took it in turns to constantly patrol the perimeter.

As night settled in, Robin joined Philip and the remaining knights sitting around the campfire and quickly fell to discussing the likely fates of Eustace and the settlement's other inhabitants.

"Here is an end to all your plans Philip," Brother Geoffrey opined morosely. "Be at one with it, and in the morning I will say a Mass for the hasty repose of their souls."

But something about the ruined settlement and its mystifying lack of bodies had seized Philip's imagination, and he refused to be downhearted. "Nay

Brother," he rejoined, almost heartily. "Save your prayers for another day. Make of it what you will, but something in my heart tells me our journey is not yet over."

Robin was less sanguine. Everywhere he looked he saw evidence of an overwhelming catastrophe. Moreover, there was an unmistakable air of wantonness to it that did little to reassure him. "If any survived, they did so by chance," he reflected at length. "I've seen blood spilt before, but never have I found the hand of the devil so plainly revealed as it is here."

"I would be revenged on these accursed savages," Ralph of Shrewsbury spat in response. "Would to God I could trade with them right now, bone for bone."

"Speak not of revenge," Brother Geoffrey reminded him sternly. "It is for justice and the glory of God that we fight. Anything less and we are no better than the savages who wrought this misery."

"Speak not of 'savages' at all," Robin ventured, plucking an Iroquois arrowhead from his pocket. "Heathen and Christian fell together in the defence of this site." And holding up the artefact he explained how he'd found it resting amongst 'beaded pendants' and 'strangely decorated carvings', indicating that both Europeans and natives had once shared the location, possibly even 'living together' in the settlement as 'one people'.

This idea seemed to please Brother Geoffrey no end and he immediately launched into a rhapsody about the Lord's 'good hands fashioning man from clay'.

Whilst he was still talking, Philip inclined his head slightly and whispered to Robin. "I understand the monk's delight. He thinks his work half done. But are you really suggesting Eustace made common cause with these savages? That despite their Christianity, he and his people entered into daily consort with them?" There was an intimation of outrage in his voice, as though the mere thought of it were an affront, not just to him, but to decent men everywhere.

Robin wondered if he'd forgotten that 'entering into daily consort' with the savages, especially their women, was half the reason why reprobates like Ralph of Shrewsbury had agreed to accompany him in the first place.

"I do more than just *suggest*," Robin assured him, with just a smidgen of relish. "I say it is a truth, established beyond all doubt. And any who disbelieve it need only look. They will find the fields around us littered with the debris of their union."

Philip eyed him sceptically for a moment before breaking into a broad smile and saying: "You think me a hypocrite Robert, because I love a woman with Saracen blood, yet cannot countenance the mingling of savage and Christian. It's a position that makes little sense, I grant. But as I warned you at our first meeting, I'm a man beset by contradictions. And they grapple with me daily, like two hungry wolves."

"All men are beset by contradictions," Robin avowed wisely. "I make no special mention of yours, and trust when the time comes you will return the courtesy."

His refusal to offer any further condemnation softened the mood. And by the time they'd supped a little ale and Brother Geoffrey had finished apostrophising, the feast of Saint Daniel the Stylite was already upon them and Philip was advising him to 'rest awhile' in preparation for widening the search as soon as light permitted. It was good advice, and they were all very tired. But as Robin closed his eyes, he did so in the certain knowledge that they were again being watched.

TWENTY SEVEN

Eight Months Later…

Andalusia, southern Spain
Estates belonging to Bernat of Navarre
The Transfiguration of the Lord
6th August 1183.

The traitor wondered if he should say something. It had been a long while now since either one of them had spoken and he was beginning to grow restless. On the table nearby a fly buzzed lazily around the olives and bread left there by the young maid. Whilst outside, everything drowsed in the thick heat of the afternoon sun.

The one who would betray them shifted uneasily in his chair. Lying to someone required a certain amount of complicity, he thought. You needed gasps of astonishment and eyes bulging with incredulity, not stony silence. He folded back the sleeves of his coarse woollen robe. Dressed as a monk, he'd travelled overland from England to Spain with barely a second glance. But sooner or later he knew word would slip out and he'd be forced to assume another new identity. I cannot spend the rest of my days living like this, he told himself miserably, being hunted from town to town, waking at the creak of every door, existing as one already dead to the world. I must be allowed to breathe again.

He remembered that fateful day in Vinland, and how wandering alone in the woods, he'd briefly contemplated starting a new life. Why hadn't he just kept on walking, he wondered? If a man knew something in his gut, he should act upon it immediately, not pause and weigh the odds. Doubt was a sin of un-intent, he reflected gloomily. It left you paralysed. And if you weren't careful it waited for you around the next corner with a scalping knife in its hand.

Yet for a relatively small amount of money he might yet still dispense with these tatty monk's robes and disappear forever. He watched the fly as it settled on a piece of bread. Why should he be shriven to beggary, he reasoned, when all around him the world grew fat on its own excess? The money was his by rights anyway, bought and paid for with the blood he'd shed in Vinland. He bit his lip unhappily. *Kill them all*, he thought, *kill them all, God will know His own.*

Nearby, Bernat of Navarre lay on his bed and stared listlessly at the wall. He looked pale and doomed, and everything about him, even the peculiar fragrance, seemed to linger. His fingernails had grown abnormally long, whilst his hair spread around his face, resting on the sheets alongside him like a tangled mane.

He looks like a dying hermit, the traitor thought disdainfully, the type of madmen the Cistercians sometimes recovered from the woods, dazed and emaciated and babbling incoherently about John the Baptist. Still, at least he wouldn't rot from the inside like his father. Not for him the bloated body of an ox or the ignominy of passing blood from every orifice. No, he thought, this fool would die quietly and without tears, gradually withering away until one day he would simply be gone, like a wispy cloud on a summer's day.

Somewhere in the distance a monastery bell chimed intermittently, infusing the warm air with a remote melancholia. "It was the child," he said at last, attempting to prompt Bernat into some kind of response. "I don't know how he knew, but Huntingdon insisted she'd been watching us the whole time."

Bernat turned watery eyes on him. "Child?" he asked feebly. "I don't remember you telling me about a child."

The traitor seized on the moment with renewed zeal. "The skraeling child," he replied keenly. "They called her Chepi. She was sister to Kocoum, the savage we found dead in the woods. When Huntingdon told the night watch, they swore they'd seen nothing, but at first light he went in search of evidence, and sure enough, there were fresh depressions in the soil all around our camp. What's more, they were clearly made by a child."

Something slowly began to register in Bernat's expression. "*Robin who wears the hood,*" he mumbled through cracked lips, his eyes sparking impishly.

The traitor was immediately encouraged. All this time he'd assumed Bernat hadn't been listening. Now it transpired he might have heard some of what he'd said after all. "It's true," he conceded happily. "It was in their childish nature to apply foolish, yet I'm bound to say surprisingly relevant, appellations to everyone they met." He explained how Huntingdon was named not for his father, but for the hooded garment he wore. Whilst Gisbourne became known as *Fidgets all the time*, on account of the peculiar movements he was always making.

Bernat gave a fey chuckle. "And by what 'relevant appellation' were you known?" he asked gleefully.

The traitor hesitated. Not for the first time he thought about Chepi. Why don't you want to say it, he asked himself? Bernat knows what kind of man you are. And anyway, they were only the words of a child. What did it matter who heard them now? He reached out to swat the fly and noticed the slight tremble in his hand.

"*The one who would betray them*," he answered softly.

Shortly after this, Bernat of Navarre raised himself onto an elbow and called for more wine. When it arrived, he sipped carefully and listened as the traitor described what had happened immediately after Robin's discovery of these new footprints.

It was Philip Mark, he explained, who'd appeared most taken aback. Despite constantly referring to the native inhabitants as being 'like children', he'd obviously never envisaged encountering any *actual* children themselves. And now, presented with the evidence, he seemed uncertain what to do.

Brother Geoffrey on the other hand, had no such doubts. Children meant families. And where there were 'families', there were almost certainly souls to be saved. "Here is our opportunity," he'd enthused happily. "At last we can begin our mission. Come, let's gather our belongings. We can afford to waste no time."

However, on this issue of a 'mission', the traitor reported, there'd been a sharp divergence of opinion. What if the villagers didn't want to have their souls saved, Robin had asked pertinently. Worse still, what if they turned out to be the same people who'd laid waste to the settlement? Brother Geoffrey had harrumphed irately at this, and accused Robin of having a 'distrustful nature', and a 'tendency to do nothing' that would 'vex even Jesus himself.' To which Robin had replied that his only 'tendency' was to 'stay alive'. And the debate might have raged on in its by now customary fashion, the traitor explained, had the second extraordinary 'find' of the day not been made.

Bernat of Navarre drew himself up a little further at the mention of this, his interest sharpening with every new detail. "The bodies?" he enquired attentively.

The traitor nodded, and paused for a moment, allowing Bernat's anticipation to build. It was Rosamond of all people who'd spotted it first, he said. Searching for some secluded spot in which to relieve herself, she'd found a small piece of what appeared to be clothing, and looking around had noticed the grass was much shorter here than elsewhere, suggesting the earth beneath it had recently been turned. At once she'd begun jumping up and down, waving her arms and excitedly calling for the others to join her.

It was immediately apparent, the traitor said, that Rosamond had stumbled upon something very significant indeed. And noting Robin's irritation not to have made the discovery himself, Philip had mischievously taunted him, "I had thought you a finder of trails Robert. Now I discover I must wait upon this girl and her need to filth before I am to make any progress."

The area itself had been relatively large, the traitor reported, and it appeared that a section of it had already been partially excavated by local predators. Dropping to their knees, Philip and Robin had started to dig frantically in the soil with their bare hands and within seconds Robin had unearthed a small piece of human skull. No words had been necessary to punctuate the look which had now passed between them. The truth was manifest. In her quest for privacy, Rosamond had stumbled upon a mass grave.

By this time Brother Geoffrey and several of the others, including the traitor himself, had gathered to see what was happening.

"All are finally joined together in death," the young Benedictine had espoused solemnly, "just as the Almighty would surely have wished it."

But, according to the traitor, Philip hadn't been willing to leave it there, and continuing to dig with his hands, had called out for Elizabeth to fetch them some shovels. Realising that he intended to excavate the entire site Brother Geoffrey had moved quickly to intervene. “What purpose in this Philip?” he’d demanded sharply. “Here they came and here they fell. In God’s name, let them rest in peace.”

But Philip had countered just as sharply, “Who can ‘rest in peace’ whilst a question still remains to be answered?” And he’d gone on to insist, “An exact figure must be established. How else are we to reason on the number of survivors?”

“There are no survivors,” Brother Geoffrey had rejoined bitterly, no longer able to contain his frustration. “Look around you. All are slaughtered!”

But Philip had ignored him, and seeing Elizabeth return with three shovels, had quickly grabbed one and set about digging as though his life depended on it, pausing only once, to suggest it would be ‘quicker done’ if the others helped him.

“I’ll wager not a single man scrambled to his aid,” Bernat of Navarre scoffed knowingly, as though it were in the preferred nature of people to constantly fail one another.

The traitor nodded sadly. It was true, he conceded. To begin with, not a single one had moved. Most were surprisingly superstitious when it came to death and wanted nothing to do with human bones. Even Robin, himself no stranger to bereavement, hesitated as though they were on the verge of committing an unforgivable trespass. And Walter of Malmesbury, turning to his new best friend Brother Geoffrey, had espoused loudly: “First he insists we bury the heathen, and I am at once minded to commend him. But then he demands we unearth good Christians, and I am again perplexed."

"It's beyond passing strange," Brother Geoffrey had agreed dolefully, and turning to Philip had again launched an impassioned appeal. "Must you take inventory in such precise fashion? Surely there is some other way it can be done."

"If there is, I would be most grateful to hear of it," Philip had replied irritably. "But while you ponder, be assured I've not travelled all this way to be left in any doubt. So, should the answer not be forthcoming, I would prevail upon you, either take a shovel or leave me in peace."

Hearing this, Gisbourne had unbuckled his sword, picked up a shovel and set about digging the earth alongside him.

"Do you trade in Christian bones now too Gisbourne?" Brother Geoffrey had enquired disparagingly.

"I trade in *all* bones," Gisbourne had responded cheerfully, apparently untroubled by the young monk's disapproval. "But I'm also availed of a rationale that is essentially fatalistic. God has already pronounced His judgement on this place. Therefore I see no harm in simply establishing the scale and severity of that judgement?"

As if persuaded by this exchange, Robin had also now cast aside his bow and joined the excavation. And in a short time, much to the disgust of Brother Geoffrey and Walter of Malmesbury, the three men had unearthed the remains of thirty five different bodies. Many of these had been badly mutilated, the traitor told Bernat. And seeing Rosamond sniff unhappily at the sight of it, Brother Geoffrey had turned on her angrily and proclaimed, "Here is your 'great adventure' Rosamond. Take such pleasure in it as you can. And when you've had your fill, pray God He forgives your unholy curiosity."

But Rosamond, true to form, had refused to be cowed by his rebuke, the traitor reported. And defiantly tossing her hair, had pronounced herself 'extremely pleased' that her 'unholy curiosity' had enabled them to bring an 'ending' to their quest. Whereas his 'constant praying' accompanied as it was by 'fearful warnings' and 'lamentations', had merely served to deepen their misery. At which point, the young Benedictine had shaken his head in open disgust and breathed "May Christ's mercy save us", before turning and walking off, still shaking his head in opprobrium as he went.

"She will not be put aside," Bernat chuckled proudly. "Even in death she remains as she was, impervious to all bar God Himself."

The traitor noticed how Bernat's eyes glazed tenderly at each mention of his younger sister. The bond between them was a curious one, he decided. In life, neither had been able to look at the other with anything less than contempt. Now she was dead, Bernat seemed to have bestowed upon her almost saint-like qualities. A fact he confirmed a few moments later when he informed the traitor of his intent to petition the Holy Father in Rome, so that he could begin the process of beatification.

I would sooner they beatify my own backside, the traitor thought dismissively, but managed to nod gravely at the same time and agree it was 'nothing less than she deserved', adding for good measure that Huntingdon would surely 'burn in hell for all eternity' after causing the death of one so 'brave' and 'kindly hearted'.

Bernat frowned, and the traitor momentarily feared his words may have been a little over ripe. But he needn't have worried; the frail young thing was merely deliberating on the exact amount of wood the devil would require in order to build a furnace proportionate to the offence.

"Even now I remain perplexed as to his motive," he reflected glumly. "Malice travels abroad on every breeze, I know. But what makes a man of some repute take his sword to such an innocent creature?"

"The devil finds reason enough," the traitor assured him, remembering one of Brother Geoffrey's more memorable sermons. "He makes his way in every wrong thought, and lurks at the elbow of every sinful opportunity. Huntingdon claimed afterwards that the skraeling sorcerer Tomakin had taken possession of his mind. But many of us were unwilling to believe him. We'd seen the way he looked at your sister. And we knew what black intentions he secretly harboured towards her."

He paused and did his best to look suitably anguished. Had evidence been uncovered proving beyond all doubt that Eustace and Marian were amongst the slaughtered, he said, they would most probably have begun their journey home much sooner, in which case Rosamond would almost certainly still be alive today. But proper identification had proved impossible, he explained. Bits of clothing had occasionally provided a clue. And Brother Geoffrey had even found a small crucifix belonging to his old friend Reynald of Clairvaux. But nothing could be established with any certainty. Furthermore, forty had made the original journey and only thirty five had thus far been recovered. Of those, several were apparently skraelings, which allowed Philip Mark to speculate wildly that his brother and bride-to-be had both somehow managed to escape the calamity.

"*It is our holy duty to remain in this place until every last Christian man and woman is accounted for*," the traitor declaimed piously, giving a faultless impression of the speech Philip had delivered shortly after the final body had been unearthed. "It was said with the astuteness of a saint," he observed wryly. "Many of us had already given up hope, but not Philip Mark. He would have parted company with Christ Himself, rather than leave those shores without knowing."

He began to explain how a plan of sorts had formulated around the idea of Robin tracking Chepi back to her village, but by this time Bernat had grown bored with the details and his thoughts were already turning to the future.

"All these things are as pebbles on a beach," he sighed, holding up a limp hand to indicate he'd heard enough. "My sister is long buried and I lie here weakened with grief. In the face of such evil, I ask only one thing, who will afford me the comfort of justice?"

"I wish to serve you in whatever way I can my lord," the traitor replied obsequiously. "But Huntingdon has sworn to put an end to me. And while this threat remains, I fear I shall be of little use to anyone."

"Then we must ensure his threat is removed," Bernat told him with a quiet confidence that was at once reassuring. "I will send you to Jerusalem. In that holy place you will become my eyes and ears." He spoke calmly and without inflection, as though it were already arranged. "I have need of a man there who can pass unseen, yet at the same time keep me informed of all that is said and done. In return, I will guarantee your safety. "

The traitor could hardly believe his luck. *Jerusalem!* It was beyond his wildest dreams. "Be assured my lord," he gushed gratefully, "I shall work tirelessly on your behalf. And if a single word is spoken, be it ever so casual, against you or this great family, I swear on every Holy Book you will be first to hear of it."

Bernat smiled munificently. "Then we are settled on the matter," he beamed. "Go to the outremer, and leave me to make plans for this so-called 'Robin who wears the hood'."

And after we have baited the trap and he has killed you, Bernat told himself, *my men will be waiting!*

TWENTY EIGHT

North East Vinland, the 'Great Eastern Woodlands Region'
The Feast of Saint Agatha of England
12th December 1182.

It had begun the way so many things in Vinland seemed to begin, with an uncommon calm and no warning whatsoever. Then all at once there was a whooshing sound, like the low whistle of a forest bird, and a fire arrow came winging out of the trees and struck Philip's kite-shaped shield with an unholy *thud*. Almost immediately arrows were hissing in the air all around them, and Harold of Leicester cried out as one hit him in the arm.

"They have us surrounded," Robin shouted, rapidly grabbing hold of Alyne and pulling him into the small defensive circle they were forming. "Hold fast and keep a low head until we have proper sight of them." Yet even as they hunched together and locked shields to form a protective wall, a second wave of fire arrows fell, this time descending on them from above in a blazing rain.

"By our gracious Lady, this is no courtesy," Gisbourne observed huffily, in what Robin presumed was a typically misguided attempt at humour. But before he could answer, a long solitary howl was raised somewhere in the adjacent woods. It was immediately answered by a sustained chorus of further howls, apparently infinite in number and seeming to emanate from every quarter in the surrounding vicinity. So terrifying was this second chorus that Brother Geoffrey momentarily wondered if the gates of hell had been thrown open and the underworld itself let loose on them.

Perhaps unsurprisingly, Gisbourne was the only one left untroubled by the sudden cacophony. And raising his head, he howled back in imitation, bravely mocking their unseen tormentors with customary gusto.

"Had I known there would be this much merry-making," he informed Robin cheerfully, "I would have travelled here long ago. What better way for a man to spend his final moments!"

Once again, Robin was unable to respond, because no sooner had the words left Gisbourne's lips, than the enemy were upon them. Converging suddenly from all sides, they poured in on the knights like a furious tide, whooping and hacking as they tore at the shield wall with their knives and hatchets.

Seeing their shaven heads and painted faces, Walter of Malmesbury exclaimed in horror, "we are assailed by demons!" And Robin saw several of the young knights around him buckle under the vicious hail of blows which now rained down on them.

Brother Geoffrey, attempting to rally them, cried out, "stand resolute my brothers. We go about God's work, and He will surely protect us." And for a few moments they did manage to hold off the onslaught, pushing back with their shields as the first wave continued to break against it in a sickening clatter of flint and bone.

But as in any struggle, numbers were quickly to prove decisive, and within seconds the defensive line had been breached. With the shield wall prised apart, a surge of Iroquois warriors had now flooded through, setting about them with war clubs and hatchets.

In as much as he was able to do anything, other than fight for his life, Robin saw at close quarter the indisputable proficiency of his enemy. Far from being 'like children', they were in fact consummate warriors, every bit as fearless and capable as Holger had described them back on the ship. And it wasn't just their obvious courage that was immediately apparent. Their agility was astonishing. Many appeared able to execute fighting movements quite unlike anything Robin had ever seen back in England. And the speed! It was all done at such pace a man hardly had time to draw breath. Moreover, every warrior wore an unwavering expression on his face, as though an oath had been taken beforehand to fight on until triumph or death.

In the face of such stoicism, an opponent had little choice other than to stand his ground and fight as best he could, all the time hoping the faith he placed in his own abilities wouldn't prove unfounded.

Yet despite being heavily outnumbered, the Europeans certainly began the fight with at least one advantage. Though slower and physically less agile, they were clearly much better equipped and armoured than their adversaries. The trouble was, this 'advantage' also rendered them sluggish, and with their enemy able to manoeuvre at such speed, it swiftly became an encumbrance. Even so, the initial few moments of battle were inconclusive, with the Iroquois prising apart the shield wall, only to be hacked down by the heavy swords and crossbow bolts of the European defenders.

Lesser foes might have faltered at this point, falling back in disarray, or simply relying on their archers. But the Iroquois continued to press forward, and as the Europeans began to cede ground, the encounter developed into a collection of much smaller, separate contests, each one matching individual against individual.

Gisbourne quickly established himself undisputed master of these mini duels. Having waited patiently for an opportunity to wield his blade in earnest, he now took to the fray with unbridled enthusiasm. His swordplay was swift and continuous, slashing down-swing and back-swing in fluent sweeps. Within seconds he had dispatched four warriors and was already lining up a fifth when a random blow dropped him to his knees. As he tried to struggle up again, more blows rained in on him from all sides, gashing through his helm and shoulder mail and quickly rendering him insentient.

With Gisbourne down, the surrounding fight proceeded without pause or hesitation. The howls and whoops of just moments before had now been replaced by heavy grunts and cries of anguish as the *clang* and *thud* of each deadly impact bore testimony to the skirmish's inevitable outcome.

No longer able to rely on anything other than sheer instinct, Robin and Philip stood back to back and hacked away at every Iroquois warrior who came near them. Encumbered by shields and armour, they more often than not missed their targets and flailed wildly in the air, much to the amusement of those warriors who, having finished their own private battles, now gathered to watch the fight's inauspicious conclusion. In a fit of pique, Robin discarded his sword, pulled around his bow and defiantly notched an arrow. *Let them find amusement in this*, he thought angrily.

Yet even as he heard them laughing, Robin knew that should he survive beyond the next few moments, this was the way he would choose to conduct all future engagements. Striking quickly and without warning, just as the Iroquois had done, using the forest as cover, and bringing to every mêlée both the stealth and reserves of stamina necessary to wear down a better-equipped opponent.

For the moment however, all he could do was stay at Philip's side, and pray. *Pray!* He thought suddenly of his mother. *Say the prayer*, he told himself. *Say the prayer she taught you.* He began to mumble the words aloud, even as he discharged the bow. "Hail Mary, full of grace. Our Lord is with you. Blessed are you among all women…" As to whether or not he finished, only the Holy Mother herself would ever know, because at that moment someone fetched him an almighty blow to the back of the head, and the last thing he saw before he lost consciousness was the horned face of the devil looking down at him.

So ended the era of Robert Fitzooth; only son of William and Mary, occasional poacher and sometime 'finder of trails', skilled bowman and so-called 'Earl of Huntingdon', on account of his mother and the Saxon line. When he regained consciousness a short while later he would find himself born into a new world, first as Iroquois warrior, then as 'hooded man', and finally as Sir Robert of Locksley, the forest prince and robber knight who would one day become known to the world simply as *Robin Hood.*

Robin Hood in America *concludes in 'Robin Hood in America: Book Two – Great deeds done beyond the seas'.*

18926798R00195

Printed in Great Britain
by Amazon